Sololand

Hassan Blasim

Translated from the Arabic by Jonathan Wright

To my dear friend Ahmed al-Nawas.

ALSO BY HASSAN BLASIM

The Madman of Freedom Square
The Iraqi Christ
God 99
Iraq + 100 (editor)

First published in Great Britain in 2025 by Comma Press.
www.commapress.co.uk

'Elias in the Land of ISIS' and 'The Law of Sololand' were published in Finnish under
the title *Kelloja ja vieraita* by Werner Söderström Ltd, Helsinki, Finland. Translated
from the Arabic manuscript. Published in the English language by arrangement with
Bonnier Rights, Helsinki, Finland. The original was first published in Arabic by
Al-Mutawassit. 'Bulbul' has not previously appeared in print. The Iraqi ammiya
original was first published on the internet. Published in the English language by
arrangement with the author. All rights reserved.

A CIP catalogue record of this book is available from the British Library.

ISBN-10: 1912697807
ISBN-13: 978-1912697809

This book has been selected to receive financial assistance from
English PEN's 'PEN Translates' programme.

The publisher gratefully acknowledges the support of Arts Council England.

Printed and bound in England by CPI Group (UK) Ltd., Croyden CRO4YY

Contents

Elias in the Land of ISIS

PROLOGUE

IN 2000, THE DOMINICAN friars in the Clock Church in central Mosul celebrated the 250th anniversary of their presence in Iraq. In 2014, the Islamic State group took control of Mosul and converted the church into one of their command centres. Mosul, with a population of about two million people, is the capital of Nineveh Governorate and the second largest city in Iraq after Baghdad. As Nineveh, the ruins of which now lie in the eastern suburbs, the city is first mentioned in about 1800 BCE, when the goddess Ishtar was worshipped in the area. Reports of her miracles helped make the city famous in many parts of the Old World. The Greek historian Ctesias, who was physician to the Achaemenid king Artaxerxes II, attributes the building of the city to Ninus, a legendary Assyrian leader. The people of Mosul are ethnically and religiously diverse. They include Kurds, Arabs, Turkomans, Shabaks, Christians, Muslims and Yezidis.

Having taken control of Mosul, the Islamic State group blew up many antiquities and museums and damaged the churches on the edges of the city. But the churches and mosques in the city centre were turned into command centres because the Iraqi army and its foreign allies refrained from bombing places of worship, in line with international conventions.

The Dominican church lies in what's called the Clock Quarter of Mosul. The area and the church both take their name from the church's distinctive clock tower, which is one of the landmarks of the city. The church is officially known by several names: the Latin Church, the Church of the Fathers, the Dominican Church and Our Lady of the Hour Church, but the name used by ordinary people is the Clock Church.

The fictional story that follows incorporates some real characters and events from history and from recent events, and I am indebted to *al-Ābā' al-Dūminīkān fi al-Mawsil 1750-2005* (The Dominican Fathers in Mosul 1750-2005) by Behnam Salim Hababa for much valuable information about the history of the church, for which the foundation stone was laid on April 9, 1866. Hababa says in his book:

'Work proceeded with great enthusiasm and exertion for seven years under the supervision of Father Lion, the French Dominican. Thanks to the skill of the builders in Mosul, the church turned out to be a model of beauty and intricate ornamentation, a splendid monument with two domes 11 metres high. The church is 35 metres long by 17 metres wide, with three aisles and a beautiful high altar in the apse. Behind the altar, there is a semicircular bench for the monks to sit on while praying. Beside it lies the vestry. Four smaller altars were built inside the church: on the right, a chapel dedicated to the Virgin Mary and one opposite dedicated to Saint Abdel Ahad, a third chapel to Saint Katherine and, opposite that, a chapel to Saint Mansour. Towards the eastern end of the nave they built a raised platform, known as a *bema*, for the choir. This high platform can hold about a hundred choristers and in the middle of it is a large organ, the first of its kind in the city of Mosul. The grand church rests on massive marble pillars with capitals decorated by skilled Mosul craftsmen by methods that were only emerging at the time. Visitors to the church are impressed by the artistry and skill, and it is widely regarded one of the most beautifully designed and decorated churches in Mosul. It stands on 26 pillars of Mosul marble, which is known for its strength, its subdued colouring and attractive veining. The round pillars are topped with square capitals decorated with depictions of Acanthus flowers, which are common features in Mesopotamian civilisation. Six of these capitals have been painted while the others retain the natural colour of the marble. Inside the church, there are 49 windows stained with dyes brought from France. The colours, designs and iconography of these windows form a harmonious and integral whole. The crypt is extensive, almost as large as the whole church and monastery. At first, it was used as a printing house and a library and for storing essentials, such as jars of communion wine. Another part of the crypt was a burial ground for Franciscans who died in Mosul during the period of the French fathers. The courtyard of the church measures 22 metres by 13 metres. In the mid–1950s the friars decided to set up a shrine dedicated to Our Lady of Miracles: they set aside a section of the wide colonnade in front of the convent gate and made it into a replica of the grotto of Lourdes. They installed a statue of the Virgin Mary beside a small altar on which candles were lit. At the end of the last century a large hall was built overlooking the street. The hall, known as the Clock Arts Hall, displayed works of art by Mosul artists. The clock tower over the church was raised in July 1882 after the Ottoman authorities issued a permit for it, in recognition of the medical and humanitarian services that the Dominicans had provided to the country, especially in 1879 and 1880, when famine and a typhoid epidemic swept through Mosul. Empress Eugénie, the wife of Napoleon III, rewarded the Dominicans by sending them a large chiming clock with four faces. Each circular face had a diameter of 75cm. To hold the clock a square tower 27 metres high was built. The massive metal clock mechanism was installed inside the hollow tower. Because of the clock's importance at the beginning, in the late 19th century, they assigned a special employee to wind up and maintain the clock. This position was such a source of pride that the clockman's mother boasted about it when she went to arrange for him to marry a girl from a prominent family. 'What does your son do for a living?' she was asked. 'He looks after the clock at Bayt al-Batri,' she answered. Bayt al-Batri was the name used for the Dominican monastery, meaning the house of the *padri*, or the Italian fathers. That was the name used in Mosul at the time and it is still used today.'

I. EUGÉNIE'S CLOCK

As soon as the sun went down, Elias slipped into the tower. He took a deep breath, then climbed the wooden stairs to the rusty metal mechanism. He opened the zip in his pants and, as usual, held his cock in his right hand and a cigarette in his left hand. This time, however, before he had time to ejaculate, he heard a commotion outside. A black crate had arrived. A light, intermittent rain had been spattering the Church of the Dominicans since early in the morning. When Elias ran to find out what was happening, he slipped and fell on his back. 'God, the shitty bastard!' he whispered, frantically getting back to his feet to look over the parapet. In the courtyard, there was a small truck and two Toyota pickups loaded with armed men. Elias rushed back into the tower and took a bite from the onion he hid in a plastic bag inside the clock. He made his hand into a ball in front of his mouth like a surgical mask and blew twice to make sure the onion smell had overwhelmed the smell of tobacco smoke.

A commander from the local battalion of Islamic State in Iraq and Syria came into the church square and gave orders that all the mujahideen should gather. The Information Department staff came out of the basement – ten young men. Their group was also known as the caliphate's Digital Army. From the nave of the church, Abu Qatada, the cook, came out, looking around for his young assistant, Elias. The commander asked the two church guards, known as the Couscous brothers, whether Commander Abu Khalid al-Mosuli was around. They told him he wasn't there. The brothers were very nervous: this was the first time they had met a commander from the Shoura Council. 'And where's Abu Omar al-Ansari?' asked the commander. Both the Couscous brothers called Ansari on the walkie-talkie simultaneously and the others laughed, including the commander. Elias slipped down the tower stairs as nimbly as a cat and joined the crowd. Abu Qatada looked at him disapprovingly. Ansari finally emerged from the corridors of the monastery, gave the commander the standard Islamic greeting and embraced him warmly. The militiamen took a crate wrapped in black cloth down from the truck. Two men worked together to push the crate, which moved on four wheels, into the nave of the church. The crate was about two metres high and two metres wide. Abu Qatada noticed the proportions of the crate and smiled to himself at the thought that it looked like a miniature version of the Kaaba in Mecca. With great effort, the crate was pushed into one of the monastery's rooms, then two large, well-armed men stood stock-still at the door as guards. Everyone listened to the commander, who brought orders from the Shoura Council. He said it was forbidden to approach the crate, to talk about it or ask any questions. Anyone who mentioned the fact that the crate was inside the church would be very severely punished.

The messenger from the caliph and his group then left and the church went back to its old rhythm. Elias followed Abu Qatada back inside to prepare dinner for the mujahideen and their guests. 'Elias, my boy,' Abu Qatada said, 'do you know what the sharia punishment is for smoking?'

'I don't know,' said Elias. 'All I know is that sometimes they flog smokers and sometimes they cut off their fingers, and they say that, in Syria, they threw someone off the roof of a building for smoking!'

Abu Qatada shook his head sadly and asked Elias to soak an extra amount of rice for the men guarding the crate.

In the nave of the church, which Abu Qatada had turned into his kitchen, there were sacks of potatoes, aubergines, courgettes, cucumbers, onions, rice, lentils and beans, boxes of tomatoes, bags of salt and crates of tinned goods stacked up on the wooden pews. The marble altar was used for cutting up meat and vegetables. Behind the altar, there was a semicircle of benches where the monks used to sit and pray, and above it now there were shelves loaded with all kinds of herbs and seasonings, like a giant spice rack. Around the altar there were large cooking pots, frying pans of various sizes, gas bottles and kitchen ranges.

When he'd made dinner, Elias said, 'I don't want to take the food to the Couscous brothers. They're idiots. They laugh at everything for no reason and they're always jabbering in French.'

'Never you mind those fools,' Abu Qatada said, smiling. 'I'll serve them myself.' The cook sprinkled some salt in the stew pot. 'Okay. let's divide the work up this way. We'll serve the Digital Army people together, because there are lots of them. I'll serve Ansari and the brothers, while you handle Sara, the pharmacist, and the guys guarding that crate,' he added.

'And the women prisoners and the guards on duty outside?' asked Elias.

'The women in the Arts Hall are going to cook for themselves, by order of Commander Mosuli. So thank God we won't have those poor things complaining about our cooking as well. As for the six oafs on guard duty outside, we'll take them their food together.'

Elias smiled and started lining up the trays and putting bowls and spoons on them, while Abu Qatada ladled out rice and okra stew.

The relationship between the cook and his assistant had changed since Elias discovered Abu Qatada's big secret. Though it had never been bad, even before the truth came out. Since Abu Qatada chose the fourteen-year-old boy as his assistant, he had treated him like a loving and devoted father. One could even say that after the secret came to light, Elias might as well have been the legitimate son of the ISIS cook. The 'father' was very protective of his 'son' and showered him with love and affection. Elias called Abu Qatada 'Dad', and every night before Elias went to sleep his 'father' would amuse him with stories about the clock and the Dominicans, in the hope it might alleviate the nightmares that the boy had after seeing so many horrors as a child.

After washing the dishes, the pots and the other kitchen equipment, Abu Qatada lit a candle close to their beds as usual. The commanders had given strict orders that no electric lights should be used at night, in order to protect the headquarters. The Digital Army people in the crypt of the church were the only ones exempt from this order. The father and son laid out their bedding under the plinth of the statue of the Virgin Mary, which the jihadis had destroyed. All that remained of the virgin were her feet. Elias curled up under his blanket, while Abu Qatada sat on his bed and wrote out his shopping list for the kitchen in a small notebook. Elias could see the enlarged shadow that Abu Qatada's head and bushy beard cast on the marble wall of the church.

'What happened after the Italian fathers left?' asked Elias.

'Keep your voice down, my son,' said Abu Qatada, as he continued to write out his list for the next day. Then he put the notebook aside, stretched out on the bed, and said in a low voice that was almost a whisper: 'First, what do you remember of last night's story?'

Speaking softly out of caution like the cook, Elias said, 'The pashas and ordinary people of all religions in Mosul loved the Dominican friars because they provided many services to people. They treated the sick and gave them medicine for free. Eventually, the Ottoman authorities gave them official permission to live in Mosul, and they stayed until ISIS entered the city. There was a Mosul businessman called Abdel Ahad who loved the friars and gave them plenty of help. His wife, who was called Istanbul, gave them a house and that was the origin of this church we're living in now. Then the Italians left.'

'Clever boy!' said Abu Qatada, 'very good memory. But tell me, for God's sake, why won't you learn the recipes I try to teach you? I've been over them so many times I'm exhausted. Believe me, my boy, cooking will prove very useful to you in the future, especially as you're not going to school.'

'Dad, why don't you learn the Islamic law stuff I've been trying to explain to you for months?' replied Elias. 'One day, the ISIS people will see through you and slit your throat.'

Abu Qatada stroked Elias's head and said, 'You're a devil.' Then the cook looked up and glanced around the church to check that no one could overhear them. 'You're right, Elias, my boy. They say the city of Mosul was struck by famines and plagues for many years during the Ottoman Caliphate. After the Italian Dominicans left, the French Dominicans came. There was one French priest called Hyacinthe Besson, who was also an artist. He became the first head of the French Dominican mission in Mosul. When a typhoid epidemic spread through the city, he became famous here for his medical skills. He made a major contribution to treating the victims of typhoid, which the local people at the time called 'the hot pain'. He continued to work with compassion and selfless dedication, because he was pained by the wretched state of the city's poor. But he too fell ill and his strength waned. He went to the monastery of Mar Yacoub near the town of Duhok to rest, but his condition deteriorated and he died and was buried there. Father Louis Lion replaced him as head of the mission in Mosul. Lion deserves most of the credit for building the new church on the remains of the old one built by the Italians. He used the money he had inherited from his father to finance the expansion of the church. While he was in Mosul, a cholera epidemic broke out and the Dominicans went into the backstreets of the city to treat sick people of all religions. They won the admiration of the people and the rulers, so everyone welcomed the construction of the new church and helped them move building materials. It was hard work moving heavy slabs of marble through the narrow lanes of the city.

'But you know, even today, because of their ignorance, people still attack doctors in hospitals when their relatives or loved ones die. Just imagine what medical services were like in those days, Elias my boy! Once, one of the friars gave a patient orange juice, and the patient died. The patient's family accused the friar of poisoning him, and they killed him. The friars would often walk long distances, sometimes for days, eating only bread and yoghurt, just to reach a patient, especially when they'd been summoned by the rulers or the pashas in the area around Mosul or in Kurdistan. In one sad incident, Father Vincent Ruffo was murdered on the banks of the Tigris. He had been called to treat the ruler, Fattah Beg, and the patient had died in his presence. The rulers' relatives attacked him and stabbed him to death. Yet often the friars were able to bring about significant achievements. People welcomed them and admired their medical skills. The Dominicans' first dispensary in Mosul was set up in the name of Baron Lejeune in 1874. The baron, a diplomat who was trying to open relations with the Shah of Persia on behalf of Napoleon III, had fallen ill on his mission and died on his return. His mother bequeathed a large sum to set up a clinic in the Orient in memory of her son.

'The days passed, as the song says, and news of the Dominicans' heroic humanitarian and medical services reached France. Empress Eugénie, the wife of Napoleon III, heard about them. Eugénie was not just a charming and attractive woman, she was also cultured and intelligent with an engaging personality. Eugénie was born in Granada, but she was educated in France. She spoke Spanish, French and English. She had known the Dominicans since her childhood when she spent vacations in Toulouse in southern France. Maybe you remember, Elias my boy, I've already told you the Dominicans were founded in Toulouse in 1215.

'One day, Empress Eugénie and her husband were riding in their carriage on the way to the opera. Three firebombs were thrown at the carriage in an attempt to assassinate the imperial couple. The bombs exploded in front of and under the carriage, killing some of the military escort. Security was tightened at the palace and the next day all visits were cancelled. But Eugénie insisted on meeting Father Charles Denise, who was waiting for her in the palace garden. The emperor went to parliament and made a speech: "I thank God, who gave the Empress and me his protection, although I am very sad that the conspiracy, which was intended to assassinate two people, ended up causing distress to so many people. These cowardly methods show how weak and despicable the perpetrators are. If they consulted history, they would find that such crimes do not serve the interests of the perpetrators. The people who killed Caesar or Henri IV gained no benefit. God may allow the just and the righteous to die but he does not allow evildoers and the unjust to triumph."

'Father Charles Denise admired Eugénie's wisdom and sophistication. In her turn, she appreciated his courage and wide knowledge of the East. Father Charles was an explorer, a scholar and a writer who spoke several Oriental languages, including Arabic, Turkish and Farsi. He had translated several books about Islam and was always open-minded, unlike other Western travellers who wrote about Islam with contempt. Eugénie told him about the Dominican friars in Mosul and the important charitable work they had done in the city. She decided she wanted to give them a clock for their church and that she wanted Father Charles to take on the task of moving the clock from France to Mosul, which would not be an easy undertaking at that time. Father Charles agreed, saying it would be a great honour and that he was happy the Empress had such confidence in him. He promised that the clock, her gift, would reach the Dominican fathers safely.

'Father Charles set off on his journey. The metal frame of the clock was massive and heavy. At first, it travelled by sea, which was the easy part, but the trouble began when they reached the desert. The clock was carried on the backs of two camels, and the task of leading the camels across the desert was entrusted to three bedouin brothers – Dahish, Dahsh and Dahshan. As soon as Father Charles met them he was struck how similar they looked. They told him they were triplets. That was rare, of course, and their family were so surprised at the birth that they gave all the triplets names connected with the idea of *dahsha*, surprise. Father Charles noticed that Dahsh didn't speak and was deferential towards the other two. He even showed signs of being a little simple-minded. As for Dahish and Dahshan, they always disagreed over the most trivial details. Dahshan was wise and well-informed and could read and write. A bedouin sheikh had taught them all to read the Quran, and Dahshan's curiosity led him to read other kinds of books, especially books by Western travellers and explorers. The triplets were well known as guides to people travelling across the desert. Dahish was content with what he had learned from the sheikh and was proud that he knew the Quran by heart. But Dahsh, after a miraculous escape from death, had forgotten all the letters and words he had learned.

'Night fell and the travellers pitched their tent in a small oasis, ate, drank and chatted. Father Charles explained to the bedouin how the mechanical clock worked. "Why do we need this monster to tell us the time?" asked Dahish. "To give our days some rhythm, so that we know when to pray, when to work and when to rest," he replied. Dahshan chuckled, baring his broken teeth. "The sky is our clock – the sun and the stars and God," he said. Father Charles smiled: "I know, and the sun is the clock that shows you when to pray – the dawn prayer at first light, the noon prayer when the sun's at its zenith and things are the same size as their shadows, the afternoon prayer when the sun is half way down, the sunset prayer at sunset, and the evening prayer between the end of dusk and midnight." "You know a lot about us too," said Dahish, "my grandfather used to say you European Christians want to know about us so that you can invade us and steal our resources." "Like the French ambassadors and explorers who went to Egypt," commented Dahshan. "They were spies who made maps and paved the way for Napoleon to invade." The Dominican was evasive, knowing there was plenty of truth in what the bedouin were saying. He merely said that not all explorers or travellers had bad intentions and many of them were only interested in knowledge and exploration. Father Charles then started telling them about how people in history had tried to understand time, about the importance of organising time and the kinds of clocks that various civilisations have used. Clocks that used sand, water, wax and steam, for example. "But what is time?" asked Dahish. "That's a difficult question and it's puzzled scholars and philosophers in the past!" answered Father Charles. "In the eleventh book of his Confessions, Saint Augustine reflected on the nature of time. 'What then is time?' he asked. 'If no one asks me, I know. If I try to explain it to one that asks, I know not.'" Father Charles watched Dahsh, who was sitting alone close to the two camels and whispering something to them. "What happened to him?" the Dominican asked. "Maybe he's lost his sense of the time you're talking about," said Dahshan. "I don't think he's aware of night following day or of the events taking place around him." Dahish spat and lit a cigarette. "In the past we weren't bedouin," he said. "We were farmers living in a village. But staying in one place always brings problems. To keep moving is the solution. Dahsh, come here!" Dahsh came over, sat down without speaking and started to draw circles in the sand with his finger. "If you ask Dahsh any question, he always replies with the same story," said Dahshan. "Whether you ask him about the weather or how he's feeling." Father Charles didn't understand exactly what the men were trying to say about their brother. "Are the camels all right?" he asked Dahsh directly. "You know better than me and it's still a long way to Mosul," he added. Dahsh looked up at the sky and the stars and went back to drawing circles in the sand. Then, without stopping to take a breath till his last word, he spoke:

"'After the last villagers died, I decided to leave. We had no idea how the only well in the village had been polluted. The weak animals and the old people died first, then the healthy ones. I put some supplies in a bag over my shoulder and left. I walked aimlessly, just to keep moving and escape disaster. As soon as I'd crossed the dead fields around the village, images of the people dying started to fill my head. Their tears, their pleas to the heavens and their pale faces saying farewell to life. 'Why and how did I survive?' I asked myself, as I walked through the barren hills. A dust storm blew up and I almost choked on it until I found a small cave. I was hesitant to go inside, since the cave looked like it might shelter wild animals and snakes. But I had no other choice. I went inside and lit a candle I was carrying in my bundle, along with three loaves of bread and some dates. I was thirsty and hungry but I was worried the sugar in the dates might make me even more thirsty. It wasn't easy to find water. I bit off a piece of bread, then fell asleep. I dreamed that I slept a long time and when I woke up I was still in the village, stretched out on my bed, with my mother sitting beside me, stroking my hair. 'You were dreaming, my dear son,' she said. 'What happened?' I asked. She said I'd started vomiting and writhing with stomach pains after drinking water from the well. People thought the only well in the village had been poisoned. After an old woman and her daughter died, almost everyone left, taking their animals with them. 'I couldn't leave you alone!' my mother said. 'But please forgive me for what I'm going to say. If you don't die soon I'll die of thirst myself,' she added. We cried together in silence and fear. I said, 'How can I speed up my death? I'm sure I couldn't stand up and leave with you.' Mother sighed and said, 'If only your father had left his hunting rifle.' I knew what she meant. She had thought of a way that would be less painful for both of us. I could ask her to go, but I was terrified of dying alone. I asked her to suffocate me with the pillow. Mother didn't dare budge an inch. I pulled the pillow out from under my head and put it over my face. Mother put her hands on the pillow. 'I can't! I can't!' she sobbed. I asked her to fetch a knife. I pointed at my chest and asked her to stab me deep. She was looking into my eyes, her hands trembling. I covered my face with the pillow again. My mother plunged the knife into my heart and darkness fell.

"'I opened my eyes and found myself sitting in the animal pen close to our sick cow. I was freezing, but I also had a burning sensation in my throat. What is this damned recurrent dream, I asked. Why don't I wake up to find that everything's finished? I was paralysed, unable to move, and my lips were parched. I was worried that if I closed my eyes I would wake up in another dream, maybe one that was worse. I stared into the cow's eyes for ages, oblivious of who I was. I was dead, and almost everyone in the village was dead. Yet someone was having this nightmare and they would be the last to die."

'Dahsh stopped, and his brothers laughed. Father Charles was amazed at the way the man had spoken. The bedouin summed up their brother's story in another, more coherent way: When the only well in the village was poisoned, all the livestock and animals died, along with many of the villagers. Thirsty and desperate, the survivors decided to leave. Dahsh was too ill for them to move him without camels, so they left him to his fate, alone in the village. No one knew how he survived the illness and the thirst, or how he walked across the desert by himself, or how he found the encampment where the villagers were staying. Dahsh rejoined his family but his mind had flown off somewhere else and there was only one story left in his head, which he repeated on every occasion.

'The clock's journey to Mosul would have ended peacefully if bandits hadn't ambushed the convoy on the outskirts of the city. There were six of them, armed with rifles and swords. They seized Father Charles's rifle and the daggers of the bedouin brothers. As they were leaving, they examined the frame of the clock with curiosity, laughing together as if they had seen some strange creature. They asked about the clock and Dahshan explained the story to them. Father Charles was tense, although he had expected to run into bandits and was therefore carrying a quantity of cash. He went up to the bandits and offered them the money, on condition that they left the clock alone. A massive man, who smelled of camel dung, came forward and said, "I'm the one who sets the conditions here." Then the bandit asked the bedouin brothers which tribe they were from. When Dahshan told him they were from the Anaza, the bandit's face lit up and he gave Dahshan a hug. Then he took his hand and pulled him aside for a private word. The two men chatted for more than twenty minutes, and then the bandit leader went up to Father Charles, took the cash and shouted at his men, who mounted their horses and rode away.

'Father Charles asked what Dahshan and the bandit had spoken about. Dahshan said the man was from a tribe that had once been in alliance with the brothers' tribe. "And when I told him that the clock helps to keep time, he asked me, 'What is this time? Is it valuable, like gold?' He kept asking me stupid questions like that, and I told him that time has no value. But he insisted on seeing the clock work so that he could see time. I told him that, on the way, a great sandstorm had blown up and that time fell out of the clock and we lost it." Father Charles laughed. "Was he asking seriously, or just joking?" he responded. "I don't know," said Dahshan, "He seems to be stupid. He asked me where we lost the time, and I described an oasis to him, out of my imagination."

'Father Charles laughed again, hugged Dahshan and thanked him for saving them...'

Abu Qatada paused a while and then continued. 'Elias my boy, it's getting late. I have to get to work. We'll continue the story tomorrow.' He blew out the candle and put it in his pocket. 'Good night, my son.' Elias stayed awake in the dark, listening to Abu Qatada's cautious footsteps heading to the pulpit. Then he heard the trapdoor opening and the cook going down into the crypt. Silence reigned in the church: Elias closed his eyes and sank into a deep sleep.

2. The Prince of Smugglers

Sara watched Elias as he picked up the empty plates and put them on a small tray. 'Okay, another question,' she said. 'What's the difference between a human walking and eating a banana, and a chimpanzee doing the same thing?'

Elias froze at the door with a smile on his face. He thought hard, but hardly dared to look at this beautiful, intelligent woman, who didn't wear a hijab in his presence. Sara was in her early thirties, with long, jet-black hair and rosy cheeks she had inherited from her Armenian grandmother, who had escaped the Turkish massacres in her time, come to Mosul and married an honourable Muslim man.

'Okay, I'll tell you,' said Sara, 'the human can walk and eat the banana at the same time, but the chimpanzee can't do that. It has to sit down to eat the banana.' Elias smiled at the oddness of this factoid, while Sara started explaining that when their spinal cords evolved humans could stand upright, which helped to free up their hands and make them more flexible, so it's easy for us humans to walk, peel a banana and eat it, whereas it's hard for a chimpanzee to do that. Sara asked if Elias had understood anything she'd been saying. 'Well… I don't know,' he mumbled. Before he left, Sara reminded him to tell the cook to go easy on the amount of oil he put in the food.

After Elias left, the Afghan guard locked the door of the room from the outside. But as he rounded the monastery colonnade on his way to the churchyard, the Couscous brothers blocked his way. 'Hey boy, why you no the food come!' said the one called Abdallah. Elias laughed at his unsuccessful attempt to speak standard Arabic, and answered him in the same language: 'What mean you, donkey?' he asked. Mohammed Couscous gripped Elias's neck with one hand and said, 'He's asking why you no longer bring us food yourself.'

'Great, well done! Finally someone who knows how to put a proper sentence together in Arabic,' Elias replied. Abu Omar al-Ansari noticed what was happening and hurried towards them. He kicked Abdallah and the walkie-talkie fell out of his hand. Then he gave Mohammed a sudden punch in the guts. Mohammed went down on his knees and threw up his breakfast – two eggs and a tomato. The commander gave them a lecture: 'All Islamic State is on high alert and you're behaving like idiots. How many times have I told you to stop getting into these childish arguments?' He told them to go away and warned them never to harass the assistant cook again. Before they left, Mohammed, the elder of the Couscous brothers, gave Elias a threatening look. Ansari whispered in Elias's ear and went down into the Digital Army's basement offices.

Ever since the Islamic State people had abducted Elias from his Yezidi family as a young boy, he had learned that revealing other people's secrets, however small they might be, could provide him with strength and protection at the same time. He came to understand the value of secrets when he went through training in ISIS camps at the age of twelve. Islamic law and the strict discipline that Islamic State enforced did not allow for even the most trivial mistake. So Elias's senses were on the alert to pick up any information as he warily watched others, at work or in his spare time. Elias was like a genie, the way he appeared and disappeared. After just a year working as assistant cook, he knew most of the people who lived and worked in the church, so it bothered him that he didn't know the secrets of the Couscous brothers. There was something unusual about them, but he hadn't managed to solve the puzzle. Almost all the mujahideen had their own women prisoners, who were kept under lock and key 24/7 in the Clock Arts Hall, with nothing to do but cry and listen to the Quran on Islamic State radio. There were special rooms in the monastery for the mujadiheen to be alone with their girls or women. The Couscous brothers had two of these women, but they rarely took them to the special rooms. Elias was almost certain there was something behind this. Now Abu Omar al-Ansari was the only person in the church to have discovered Elias's own secret, even before Abu Qatada picked up on it. But the discovery of Elias's secret worked in his favour in the end. One day, Ansari stopped Elias as he was passing by and asked him if he smoked. The boy was scared and said he'd never smoked in his life. Ansari smiled, took Elias's hand and smelled it. When Ansari insisted on knowing the truth, Elias finally broke down and showed him the place where he smoked. He took the commander to the clock tower where he hid cigarettes and onions in the metal frame of the winding mechanism. The commander didn't punish him: in fact he smoked a cigarette with him. After that, Ansari would slip off with Elias every now and then to have a smoke in the tower. Elias neither liked nor disliked Ansari. The man was grumpy and silent most of the time, and temperamental too. He was frightening when angry, like a violent storm. Ansari had many problems with Commander Mosuli, who was also based in the church. Most of the problems were over Sara, the pharmacist who was also Commander Mosuli's wife. During these smoking sessions in the clock tower, Elias gradually learned more about Ansari's life. Later, two months before the Iraqi army attacked Mosul, it would be Elias who wiped Ansari's blood off the library floor, then picked up the commander's head, put it in an empty flour bag, and, with the Couscous brothers' help, carried his body outside. The monastery library had been set aside for torturing and murdering leading figures in the Islamic State organisation. Once, they brought a senior official and his son to the library. They forced the son to slit his father's throat and then they threw the son off the church roof. The mujahideen in the church never knew the charges against the people the organisation brought there for execution. All they were given was some vague word, such as 'debauchery', 'high treason', or 'heresy'.

Commander Abu Omar al-Ansari was born and brought up in the town of al-Bukamal, a Syrian town on the Euphrates, close to where the river enters Iraq. His real name was Khaled

Saad. His mother was Iraqi and his father Syrian. Khaled was from one of the biggest clans in the town, a clan that clearly dominated the town's affairs. Most of the people in al-Bukamal worked in the smuggling business – mainly weapons, livestock, cigarettes and medicines. Khaled Saad specialised in weapons and cigarettes and was one of the biggest smugglers in town, with a vast network of contacts on both sides of the border. Two days after he married his cousin, Karima al-Jamal, the protests against the Syrian government broke out. At the time, he was 30 years old and popular among the local people thanks to his generosity towards those in need and his lack of tolerance for any injustice. He had four brothers who worked with him in the smuggling business, but he was the boss. No one dared to disagree with him, except for his wife Karima, who taught geography in the local primary school. He never denied her anything, and she meant the world to him.

When the protests spread like wildfire across most of the towns in Syria, some of the people in al-Bukamal came out in a demonstration against the Assad regime. The security forces opened fire and eight young men were killed. The biggest clans gathered to discuss the events. The security forces withdrew from the town and said they were willing to negotiate with the locals. It was clear from the start that Khaled's personality dominated the debates between the town leaders. He was calm and prudent, decisive and eloquent, and what he said combined wisdom, circumspection and an ability to arouse people's emotions. The tribal leaders asked the government to punish the men who had killed the demonstrators. The government refused and prepared to move its forces back into the town. Many of the people in the border town owned light weapons and they organised themselves under Khaled Saad to defend the town. The battle lasted all day long. Although the Syrian army had more firepower, the men of al-Bukamal put up a stiff fight. Khaled displayed great courage and the mind of an outstanding leader. The fighting ended at nightfall, when Khaled and his men withdrew from the town to the neighbouring villages. His wife insisted on leaving with him and stayed with him through all the battles he fought. The army took control of the town and restored order there. Khaled's group started to launch raids on the checkpoints around the town, and it soon became clear to Khaled that many of the government troops had no desire to fight, so many army patrols began to fall into the hands of his group, which acquired many heavy weapons, even tanks and other armoured vehicles in the process. Khaled eventually managed to break into al–Bukamal and drive out the government troops, with plenty of support from his tribe, and the townspeople of course. Khaled set himself up as military governor and allowed tribal leaders and others to run the civilian administration in the town. Khaled Saad's lightning victory over the army attracted the attention of the Free Syrian Army (FSA), which had been set up by deserters from the government army and had become the main opposition force. The FSA established contact with Khaled Saad and started coordinating activities with him. Then they sent military supplies to the town, along with food and medical supplies. Khaled and his group joined the FSA, which formally appointed him the town's revolutionary commander. The leadership of the FSA later chose Khaled Saad and others to travel abroad to speak on behalf of the Syrian revolution, negotiate and establish relations with governments that had an interest in Syria. Khaled took off his military uniform and put on a suit and tie. It was the first time Khaled had travelled by plane. His wife Karima had flown once before, when she took her mother to Athens to have a cancerous tumour removed. Khaled and his wife moved from hotel to hotel. They visited Turkey, Saudi Arabia, Qatar, Moscow, London and Paris. He met politicians and intelligence agents from Britain, the United States and France. He met Chinese businessmen and religious leaders from the Gulf, and made deals with Russian and Scandinavian arms traders.

The couple were very happy with this transformation of

their lives, which took them from a small border town dominated by clans to jet-setting between famous capital cities. Khaled took Karima to fancy restaurants, parties and embassy receptions. He took a liking to whisky, especially in the hotel bars where they were staying. Karima warned him not to drink too much, but he didn't care. One night, they had a heated argument when he was drunk and Karima refused to sleep with him. They were staying in an Istanbul hotel overlooking the Bosphorus. Khaled took a bottle of whisky, a gift from British intelligence, out of his suitcase and went out to stroll along the shore. He sat down on a bench and started to sing to himself the song *Taybeen* by Yas Khidr. Two young men came up to him and greeted him in Syrian Arabic. They recognised him from the televised press conferences that the Syrian opposition often held abroad. They told him they were refugees, homeless and penniless, sleeping in parks. He was happy to be with them that night and they started talking about events in Syria and the fate of the refugees. Their Syrian accents and the whisky stirred Khaled's emotions and suddenly he burst into tears right in front of them over what had happened to Syrians. He gave them all the money he had on him and went back to his hotel. He sat by the bed watching his beloved Karima as she slept. He held her warm hands and she opened her eyes and asked him to lie down beside him. He took off his shoes and curled up like a baby, and Karima hugged him. He apologised to her and told her he planned to go back to al-Bukamal. He said he felt he was betraying his country. Karima told him that, come daybreak, he would go back on the decisions he had taken while drunk. But Khaled was insistent, saying that however much he hated what he called the criminal dictatorial regime, that didn't mean they should sell the country to warmongers and spies for countries that sought only their own interests. 'It's our battle and we have to fight it on our own land and defend our people,' he said. Karima agreed with him and said she missed her family, the Euphrates and the air in al-Bukamal. She told him Mother

Teresa used to say, 'If you want to change the world, go home and look after your mother.' Khaled didn't know about Mother Teresa, so Karima brought him up to speed. Khaled had never finished school: he left when he was young and went into the livestock smuggling business. Because of his competence and intelligence, his business thrived.

The next day, Khaled wrote an email to the FSA leadership, asking to be exempted from diplomatic work and reminding them that his real mission was to stay in al-Bukamal and defend the town. The leaders agreed. Khaled went back to his town, where he began to govern like a minor despot.

News reached al-Bukamal that Islamist groups were trying to infiltrate the town because of its strategic location between Iraq and Syria. There were two groups planning to do this – Jabhat al-Nusra and al-Qaida. Khaled was living in a grand, two-storey house with a large walled garden. The walls were made of concrete and had barbed wire along the top. His four brothers, his wife and his elderly parents all lived together in the mansion. One day, someone parked a car bomb outside the house and detonated it with a remote-controlled device. One of Khaled's brothers was killed and his mother was slightly injured. Khaled tightened the security around the house and started looking for the bomber. Some fingers pointed at al-Qaida and others at al-Nusra. Days passed without success in the search. Then another incident took place. One night after midnight, two masked men broke into Khaled's house. They killed the guards at the main gate and came in through the kitchen window. Karima heard suspicious noises and woke her husband. Khaled killed the men with his pistol. This only added to his reputation for heroism and bravery among the locals. The men who had tried to assassinate him were from al-Bukamal. Khaled had many people brutally interrogated and launched a campaign of arrests, torturing the detainees in an attempt to find out who had tried to kill him. He didn't reach any firm conclusions. At the time, the Free Syrian Army was growing weaker and fragmenting as the Islamist and armed Kurdish groups grew stronger. Khaled felt uneasy and tried to strengthen the town's defences. But it could not hold out against the strength and ruthlessness of al-Nusra Front, which killed two more of Khaled's brothers and finally seized control of the town. Khaled left al-Bukamal again and took refuge in a nearby village, taking only his wife this time. Although Khaled had lost his militia, and his authority over the town, he knew the real secret of his strength in al-Bukamal – the loyalty of the local people and of his large clan. He was their boy, the symbolic hero of the town, and they would not readily abandon him. Khaled hated with a vengeance the brutal politics of the Islamist groups, which made no distinction between the oppressor and the oppressed. He didn't trust al-Nusra, al-Qaida or the Islamic State group, which was growing stronger and more influential, but his desire to avenge the murder of his brothers and his own expulsion was burning inside him. He eventually formed an alliance with Islamic State, explaining to them how, with his help, they could take control of al-Bukamal. There were major disagreements between the Islamist groups. A brutal civil war was raging in Syria and many other countries in the world were feeding the war, each in their own way and according to their own interests. Chaos and destruction were everywhere. With Khaled Saad's help, the Islamic State group attacked al-Bukamal and took control of the town. Islamic State was well aware of the tribal setup there and Khaled's status, so they appointed him commander of the town under a new name – Abu Omar al-Ansari. Khaled ruled the town once more, but this time under the Islamic State banner and with the title of *amir*, commander. The Islamic State leaders didn't trust him because he had been politically inconsistent and he had a network of relationships with all the political factions as well as with foreign intelligence services. So the organisation kept a close eye on all his movements. Khaled quickly realised that Islamic State was really in charge of his town and he was just a figurehead. This didn't bother him too much and he spent most of his time looking for the people who had killed his brothers. But then he came across evidence suggesting it was Islamic State that had tried to assassinate him and had killed his brothers. In their turn, the Islamic State intelligence people were well aware of his desperate attempts to uncover the truth. Karima suddenly fell ill and the doctor diagnosed cancer of the uterus. Khaled was shocked: his concerns and priorities changed and he postponed all his plans. Travelling abroad was no longer possible, because Khaled was now Abu Omar al-Ansari, a 'terrorist' wanted by several governments. His only option was to go to Mosul, the largest city under Islamic State control, where the hospitals were still operating with the same professional staff as before. Islamic State gave Commander Ansari a private house in Mosul and Karima began treatment in the hospital. Her condition rapidly deteriorated. She started to fade and eventually passed away. The Islamic State leaders thought this was an opportune moment to bring an end to Ansari's dominance in al-Bukamal, so by decree from the Caliph's office, Ansari was appointed to a new position in the Clock Church. Ansari went along with it because after Karima's death his hometown and everything else in the world no longer meant anything to him.

Abu Qatada and his assistant Elias mopped the kitchen floor, put some chickpeas and beans in water to soak, and went off to bed. That night, Abu Qatada finished the story of Empress Eugénie's clock. He told Elias that the tower where he went to smoke on the sly was built after Father Charles brought the clock to the church following an arduous six-month journey. When the clock was installed in the tower, some of the local people gathered angrily and demanded the tower be removed because the clock was overlooking their houses, and invading their privacy. The Dominicans finally convinced them that the purpose of the clock was to remind people of prayer times and no one would climb up into the tower. Anyway, the clock started ringing the hours and asserting its presence in the city. The bells were said to have been audible as far as Tel Kaif, ten miles away, because at the time there wasn't any traffic or factories or tall buildings. The cook then told his assistant the story of how the first Dominican nuns came to Mosul. There were six of them and the journey from France had taken them 53 days. The Dominican Sisters of Charity started teaching in the girls' school and opened a workshop for girls and an orphanage. Their convent was next to the monastery in the house of a Christian man called Antoon Daghdou. In the year of dearth, also known as the year of the pound, when a great famine struck Mosul and the price of a bushel of wheat rose to one Ottoman gold pound, people sold their possessions to buy food and the convent swelled with starving people. It is said that the Sisters of Charity went to the homes of rich people begging for bread for the poor. Three of the nuns died in a cholera outbreak. People called the nuns the 'kite people' because the headdress they wore looked like the wings of a bird. The Sisters of Charity played an important part in the expansion of education for girls in Mosul.

The cook stopped telling his story and told his assistant he felt ill, possibly with the flu. He said he needed some rest and wouldn't go down to the crypt to do his usual nocturnal work. Elias volunteered to work in his place. 'No need for that, my boy. There's only one box left and I'll move that when I feel better,' said Abu Qatada. He blew out the candle and darkness fell. A few moments later, the cook asked Elias what he had heard from the others about the black box. The boy said the stupid guards were still pretending that the contents of the box were a secret, but everyone knew there was a hostage inside. 'Imagine, even when we give them enough food for three people, those wild bears think we don't know what's going on,' he said. 'They argue all the time over who's going to empty the bags of the prisoner's shit into the toilet.' Abu Qatada put his lips close to Elias's ear and whispered, 'It's true. There's a hostage in the crate. He's a Spanish man called Antonio Manuel.'

'What?' asked Elias.

The cook put a hand over Elias's mouth and said, 'Shsh. Your voice! Remember what we cooked yesterday?'

Elias murmured in discontent: this wasn't the time for Abu Qatada to test his culinary memory. 'What are you talking about, Dad?' he said.

'Last night we cooked fish and served it with pickled beetroot, celery and onion.'

'Okay, right. But what's that got to do with what you were saying about the crate and the Spanish hostage?'

'When you brought the empty plates back, he'd written a message in Spanish on the plate. '*Thanks, your food was delicious. I'm Antonio Manuel*, it said. You know, I speak French and Italian, so I can understand some Spanish.'

'Written?'

'Yes, I think the hostage used a celery stick as a pen and some beetroot juice as ink.'

3. Poetry and Pharmacy

After the afternoon prayers, Abu Qatada picked up the teapot and Elias took a tray of teacups, and they went up on the church roof to enjoy the spring breeze, swap lessons in cooking and Islamic law, and take a short rest from filling the insatiable bellies of the mujahideen.

Cook: 'Let's do some revision. The varieties of Mosul kebabs.'

Elias: 'Okay, and I can test you on Islamic law?'

Cook: '*Kebagh* kebabs?'

Elias: 'The ingredients are cracked wheat, mutton and spices. You boil it in water and salt, and stuff it with currants and pistachios.'

Cook: 'Exactly!'

Elias: 'What's the penalty for blasphemy?'

Cook: 'Death.'

Elias: 'And the penalty for insulting the prophet?'

Cook: 'Death as well.'

Elias: 'And then?'

Cook: 'After death?'

Elias: 'The full answer is death, even if the person repents.'

Cook: 'Ah, right. But why is it death for blasphemy, while for insulting the prophet it's death even if the person repents?'

Elias: 'I don't know, Dad. You tell me why *kebagh* kebabs are made with cracked wheat, for example.'

Cook: 'Okay, I understand. Now calm down. And *kebba hamid*?'

Elias: 'It's made of rice and...'

Cook: 'Rice, you say.'

Elias: 'Hmm okay. Okay, I remember. It's made of rough-ground wheat, boiled in a lemony soup with lean meat, squash, onion, celery and peppers.'

Cook: 'Well done, my dear son. You're a clever lad.'

Elias: 'What's the penalty for sodomy?'

Cook: 'Death for both of them – the active one and the passive.'

Elias: 'And for extramarital sex?'

Cook: 'To be stoned to death for married people and a hundred lashes for unmarried people and exile for a whole year.'

Elias: 'You're clever too, it seems. They'll make you a judge in the sharia court at this rate.'

(They laugh and continue the lesson as they sip tea with cardamom.)

Cook: 'And *kebba qaysi*? How would you make that?'

Elais: 'It's a small type of *kebba* made with rice. The stuffing includes mutton and celery but without spices. It's cooked in a sweet sauce made with dried apricots. It's usually cooked for New Year's Eve parties.'

Cook: 'By the way, how's Sara the pharmacist?'

Elias: 'She wants you to cut down on the olive oil. What's the penalty for banditry?'

Cook: 'If they kill and steal money, they're to be crucified. If they kill, they have to be killed. If they just take money, they have their right hand and their left foot cut off. Does the commander beat Sara?'

Elias: 'No, I think he's afraid of her.'

Cook: 'He's afraid of her? *Kebba hamid*?'

Elias: 'I told you that already. It's made from rough-ground wheat boiled in a lemony soup with lean meat, squash, onion, celery and peppers.'

Cook: 'Does Ansari really have a relationship with Sara?'

Elias: 'What are the penalties for theft and drinking alcohol?'

Cook: 'For theft amputation of the hand, and for drinking eighty lashes.'

Elias: 'Sara doesn't like either Ansari or Mosuli. She hates Islamic State's ideas and all the men in the organisation.'

Elias noticed the Couscous brothers coming out of one of the church's side rooms and stopped talking. The brothers came towards them, greeted them and sat down. Mohammed asked for tea for him and his brother Abdallah. 'We've run out,' Elias replied. Abdallah asked in French if Abu Qatada could cook a chicken and vegetable tagine. Abu Qatada answered them in French: 'Abdallah, dear boy, as I've told you before, we're living in Iraq now. You need to get used to Iraqi food. You're always asking for Moroccan food, but you were born and lived in France.'

'Come on, sir, it's easy to make a tagine,' Mohammed insisted.

Abu Qatada got up and said, 'Let's go, Elias my son, we have to get dinner ready.'

'What's for dinner today?' asked Mohammed.

'Tagine ratatouille niçoise,' Abu Qatada answered sarcastically.

'What's ratatouille?' asked Elias as they headed down the stairs. Abu Qatada smiled and said it was a kind of French vegetable stew. 'And what's tagine?' asked Elias.

It was Abu Qatada who first called Mohammed and Abdullah the Couscous brothers. When they first came to the church they ordered Elias to ask Abu Qatada to cook them couscous. Elias thought they were making fun of him, deliberately repeating the word *kuss* ('cunt') to him. When he told Abu Qatada about it, the cook laughed and said that they didn't mean a woman's *kuss* and that couscous was a well-known North African staple, used in many dishes. Jokingly, Abu Qatada said you could have *kuss* with fish, *kuss* with onion, *kuss* with vegetables and *kuss* with sausages. Ever since then, Abu Qatada would say to Elias, 'Elias my boy, take this food to the Couscous brothers' or 'Fetch the empty plates from the Couscouses.' Then Elias, in turn, started to promote the nickname among the mujahideen, who adopted it with enthusiasm and started calling them the two *kusses*.

Abu Qatada put a leg of lamb on the altar and started to chop it up. 'Dad, can I take a bag of biscuits for Sara?' asked Elias.

'Okay, but don't be late. You have to peel the potatoes and chop the onions. Take some orange juice for her too,' Abu Qatada added. Elias left. Abu Qatada sighed and put down the knife. He looked around the church, mumbling something as if praying to himself as tears glistened in his eyes. When Elias reached Sara's quarters, he was surprised and flustered to find Mosuli, Sara's husband, standing in front of him. The commander wasn't usually there in the evening: he would usually be with his other wife or with one of his slave women. Elias put the biscuits and the orange juice on the table and was about to leave when the commander addressed him. 'Aren't you going to greet me the Islamic way, boy?' he asked. 'Sorry. Al-salam alaykum,' Elias replied, then left. Most people in the church treated Elias kindly because of his calm demeanour, his intelligence and the childish sadness that was etched on his face. He was fair-skinned, like most of the people in the north, and green-eyed. The freckles on his cheeks and his red hair made him especially handsome. Except to the Couscous brothers, who thought Elias was annoying and malicious. Just like that, like love or hate at first sight, the two sides never got on with each other.

Just as Abu Qatada was eager to teach Elias how to cook, Sara was interested in stimulating Elias's imagination with strange scientific information that she crammed into his head whenever he brought her some food. She often spoke to him about poetry and literature. 'Your imagination mustn't get rusty here in the dark cage of sharia,' she once told him. Sara's intentions were not wholly innocent when she tried to make friends with Elias. In her head she was working on a plan, and for her Elias was the key that might free her from her imprisonment.

Before Islamic State occupied Mosul, Sara had had 500 copies of her poetry collection printed at her own expense, with the title *Enheduanna*. She hadn't been surprised when most of the publishing houses refused to publish it. She knew the country had been suffering from the cancer of *haram* and *halal* for centuries. If a woman wrote poetry about her own body, that was a stain on the honour of a country where the men believed that their honour, their freedom, their very existence was dependent on the vaginas of women, as Sara put it in a local radio programme. After the interview, the presenter turned to his colleague, the producer, and muttered, 'Does she think we're living in the West, this feminist whore?' Sara was a fan of Enheduanna, the Akkadian princess whose name she adopted as the title. Sara thought Islam had buried the diverse and rich civilisation of Mesopotamia under its ossified laws and philosophy. That civilisation was now lost in the mists of forgotten histories. So Sara felt compelled on many occasions to explain to people who Enheduanna was. She spoke about the princess with enthusiasm, memorised her poems and daydreamed about them being close friends and wandering around the colonnades together in the palace of Sargon, Enheduanna's father, listening to her poems and her thoughts on life and death. Some historians and literary scholars have called Enheduanna the first writer in the world whose name has come down to us. Why wasn't this simple fact taught in schools, Sara asked herself angrily, and grumbled about the decline in education and culture in her country. Why don't we tell children that here, in their country, literature was born, along with agriculture, alcohol, law, the calendar and poetry? Why don't we recognise that poetry and writing started in the imagination of a woman? 'Just imagine. Enheduanna, who lived thousands of years ago, wrote about sex and love and politics in her time, and today women can't speak out clearly, because their voices are thought to be too seductive. Why do you think this happened?' Sara asked the radio presenter at the time. But the presenter and the producer then went and cut the interview down from an hour to twenty minutes, and eventually decided not to broadcast it at all.

When Islamic State was attacking Mosul and advancing towards it day by day, Sara was at home with her friend Widad. The poet was signing copies of *Enheduanna*, while her friend stuffed them into envelopes and wrote the names and addresses of the recipient on them. In the end, it seemed, all Sara could do was hand out copies of her book herself to her acquaintances and fellow pharmacists and a few friends who were writers or critics. Widad was in hysterics laughing at a joke Sara had made about Muqtada al-Sadr, a cleric followed by millions of Iraqis, whose family name happens to mean *breast*. 'Do you know why women have stopped wearing bras in the holy city of Najaf?'

'Why?'

'So that al-Sadr can have a rest.' Sara's husband came in, breathless, covered in sweat and radiating a sense of disaster. He turned on the television and they all listened in horror to the news. Islamic State had entered the city, with ease, and the army had fled, abandoning its heavy weapons to the invading forces.

The Islamic State forces took over the city and raised their flag, with its slogan *There is no god but God*, on the city's hospitals, schools, theatres and churches. Life was turned upside down. Sara thought the margin of freedom available was too narrow as it was *before* the city fell to Islamic State; suddenly the life she had been living till now seemed like paradise. Who would ever have imagined that Sara, that spirited and headstrong young woman, would wear a burka – that cloth cage, inspired by the dark tenets of sharia. She could no longer drive herself to the pharmacy each day. Her husband, who grew a beard and fell into a depression, had to drive her. A month later, Sara closed the pharmacy because she could no longer tolerate Islamic State people interfering in her work and constantly asking her for Viagra pills. Then they sent an armed patrol to her house and forced her to re-open it. Her father, a surgeon well-known in the city, had helped her to open the place after she graduated from university. Ever since her student days in the pharmacology faculty, Sara was known for her energy. Despite being busy with her university work, she regularly attended plays, literary events and art exhibitions. She enlivened literary and artistic circles with her passionate contributions to debates on patriarchal society, accusing the elites of cowardice and saying that by remaining silent for the sake of their narrow personal interests they were helping to perpetuate backwardness and ignorance.

Bitterly and with sadness, Sara submitted like many others to a way of life shaped by sharia. She continued to work at the pharmacy but otherwise stayed at home, reading and writing and wondering why disaster had struck. Eventually, in the aftermath of the earthquake that ISIS had triggered, a nightmare from the past came back to haunt her, in a way that she would never have expected. Early one morning, a group of Islamic State men raided her house. They searched the place and checked it was safe, then an Islamic State commander called Abu Bakr al-Mosuli came in. Sara recognised him immediately. She knew that look of hatred and inferiority in his eyes from when he used to harass her in her first year at university. Mosuli, whose real name was Bakr Abdel Qadir, had lived next door to Sara's family before she got married. Sara came from a family of academics who lived in the old part of the city centre. During the years of international sanctions against Iraq in the 1990s, the standard of living in the country declined, and many people migrated from the countryside to the cities, seeking work. This migration brought Bakr Abdel Qadir and his family of farmers. They sold their farm and livestock and bought a house on the same street as Sara's family. Bakr worked for the security services during Saddam Hussein's time, as Saddam relied on village people in most of his many security organisations. Bakr fancied Sara at the time and, whenever she passed by on her way to university, he would follow her to tell her how much he liked her. Sara rejected him and asked him to stop pursuing her. One evening, Bakr and his father came to Sara's house to ask her family for her hand in marriage. Sara and her family rejected him and, as far as Bakr was concerned, the reason was clear – the difference in class. In order to avenge the rejection, Bakr set up a trap for Sara's brother, who was an eye doctor. Her brother was arrested on a charge of belonging to the Muslim Brotherhood. Sara's father, the surgeon, was on good terms with the governor of Mosul and most of the leaders of the security agencies. Sara's brother spent only three days in the cells before the security agency released him, and the governor personally punished Bakr for his conduct by having him transferred to some remote location.

Now the situation had dramatically changed. Mosuli, on entering her house, demanded Sara's husband divorce her. Her husband resisted so they threatened to kill him. Sara pleaded with her husband to comply, so that they wouldn't kill him in front of her. Mosuli didn't let Sara take anything from her house, except for some copies of her poetry collection. She wasn't even allowed to take any clothes, because Mosuli said they were too ostentatious, unsuitable for a woman who was going to become the wife of an ISIS commander. Sara never found out what happened to her husband. He disappeared forever; the chances are he was murdered and buried in an unknown location.

Sara was trapped in Abu Bakr al-Mosuli's house. She could only go out if she had permission and was accompanied by the guards at the house. Telephones and television were forbidden in the house. There were two young slave girls to serve Sara – one to cook and the other to clean the house. The commander didn't dare force Sara to have sex. He tried to rape her one first time, but she resisted violently and scratched his face with her fingernails, so he left her. Mosuli called the slave girls and raped them in front of Sara. Sara picked up on Mosuli's weak spot right from the start: he still loved her but he hadn't overcome his sense of inferiority, even after he had the title of commander and had guards, slave girls, servants and power. He was still that simple country boy and that insecure security man, a slave to the orders he was given. Sara knew when to act soft with him and when to act hard. She sent him cryptic messages that she might be willing to submit to him as his wife if he met her needs, and he would calm down. She was playing for time. Then, one day, she tried to escape, during a visit to the dentist's, but Mosuli's guards caught her. He decided to take her with him to the church headquarters where he worked and on her first night there he raped her in one of the monastery rooms. Sara spent her days in her new prison writing and thinking. She asked Elias to buy her notebooks and pens whenever he and the cook went to market. She wanted notebooks with covers in different colours. Elias longed to find out what she was writing, but he didn't dare ask. The boy was in love with her and started to dream about her. When he was alone in the clock tower, he masturbated over his imaginary version of her naked body.

Commander Mosuli led the mujahideen in prayer in the churchyard and gave the Friday sermon, ending with a verse from the Quran: 'God has bought from the believers their lives and their possessions in exchange for the gift of Paradise; they fight in the way of God; they kill, and are killed. That is a promise given by God in the Torah, and the Gospel, and the

Quran; and who fulfils his covenant more faithfully than God? So rejoice in the bargain you have made with Him; that is a great victory.' After Friday prayers, the mujahideen had a period of rest. Some of them went to market, some had a siesta and others went off to have sex with their slave girls. Mosuli came into Abu Qatada's kitchen to see how preparations for Friday lunch were going. The senior ISIS leaders met in the church from time to time, and Mosuli himself was in charge of the reception. Abu Qatada and Elias were exhausted from preparing the food. Abu Qatada suggested putting some chairs and a table in the monastery hall, for the leaders to sit at. Mosuli smiled, put his hand on the cook's shoulder and said, 'What does the Quran say about our role model, the prophet Muhammad?' Abu Qatada was puzzled and started to stroke his long beard in embarrassment. Elias butted in immediately to save him. 'In the name of God, the Merciful, the Compassionate. In the prophet of God you have a good example of someone who hopes for God and the Last Day, and remembers God often.'

'God has spoken truly,' added the commander. He praised Elias and his ability to memorise Quranic verses. Then he turned to the cook: 'Abu Qatada, lay places for us on the floor in the monastery hall as usual. We follow our prophet, may God bless him and grant him peace, as he is our model. The prophet used to eat while kneeling, or sometimes he would sit on his left foot, with his right leg upright. Wahb bin Abdallah, one of the companions of the prophet, quotes the prophet as saying, "I don't eat while reclining."'

As soon as Mosuli left, Elias let out the laugh he had been holding back with difficulty.

'What are you laughing about, boy?'

'Your face turned red as a tomato,' Elias replied. 'How many times have I taught you that verse? But you don't remember!'

'Shut up, you devil! Go and fetch me some red peppers and curry powder.'

That evening, Abu Qatada and Elias were eating ice cream in the kitchen, finally having a rest after their work on the leaders' reception. 'Why did you never get married, Dad?' asked Elias.

'Who would accept me when I'm so fat?' the cook replied flippantly. 'It just wasn't destined to happen, my boy,' he continued. 'Or maybe I was too frightened of marriage. I imagined I might have children and die, and then they'd be orphans.'

Elias stood up, washed the sticky dribbles of ice cream off his hands, then went back, sat close to Abu Qatada and said, 'You mean like me. I'm also an orphan.' Abu Qatada patted Elias affectionately on the head, and Elias started crying, saying how much he missed his family.

'Inshallah you'll meet your mother and brothers again, my boy. It's just a passing cloud.' Then the cook changed the subject. 'Let's go to bed,' he said, 'I have a nice, new story tonight.' That night, Abu Qatada told the boy about the printing press that the Dominican Friars brought to Mosul in the winter of 1857. He tried to add some excitement to the story but Elias was bored and started to yawn. The cook was telling him so many facts and dates that Elias felt lost and dizzy. He said the lithographic printer was replaced with a more modern one a few years later, and that this was the first printing press in Mosul. He said that the wheels of the press were still turning when the First World War broke out, and that the Dominicans faced frequent harassment in Ottoman times. In 1917, the director of education in the province of Mosul came to the printing press with the provincial police chief and confiscated the machines and the type. When the Dominicans objected, the official said, 'We're confiscating the type and the ones we can't use we'll throw in the river.' When the war ended and the British occupied Mosul, they gave the printing press back to the Dominicans.

Elias started snoring and the cook stopped telling his story. At the call to dawn prayers, Abu Qatada woke up to prepare breakfast. He gave Elias an extra half hour of sleep, then woke him. The cook needed more bread. Elias stretched like a lazy cat and, without washing his face, took a bag and went to the bakery. Abu Qatada boiled the eggs and cut up some cucumbers, tomatoes and onions. Elias came back and told him the bakery was closed. The baker's son had been killed in a suicide bombing during the night. Abu Qataba took off his apron and said, 'Let's go to market together and come back quick. I also need to buy some headache pills.'

'Will there be a pharmacy open at this hour?' asked Elias.

'My dear boy,' replied the cook, 'our friend Hajji Khaled, the greengrocer's father, could even arrange some cancer medicine for us, if we needed it.' They made sure they'd turned off all the gas, then Elias drove the pick-up used for purchases by the ISIS people in the church. On the way, they were stopped at a checkpoint and one of the men there recognised Abu Qatada, who got out of the vehicle. The man, who was in his mid-thirties, embraced him and greeted him with unexpected enthusiasm. 'You don't remember me! I'm Abu al-Harith and you're the best cook in the world!' It finally transpired that the man had been with Abu Qatada in training camp. Abu Qatada asked him how he was and what he'd been up to. Abu al-Harith's face changed and he looked despondent. Sadly he explained that his daughter had almost died because she'd been poisoned by the tap water in Mosul. They had a chat about how hard it was to find clean water in Mosul, the high price of cooking gas and unemployment. Suddenly Abu al-Harith's face changed again, as if he had had an electric shock, and his tone of voice changed too. His face came over all pious and humble, and he said optimistically that God would help Islamic State and things would hopefully improve when Islamic State took over the whole of Iraq and purged the country of the Shi'a and the infidels.

Elias drove off again and when they stopped at a traffic light, he asked, 'Who was that?'

'Some jerk from Islamic State,' the cook replied. Then he

wound down his window and bought a packet of paper handkerchiefs from an old man with a bent back who could hardly walk.

Abu Qatada gave a sigh and muttered to himself: 'For the Virgin Mary's sake!'

4. The ISIS Cook

There was a time when Abu Qatada didn't spread out his bedding under the statue of Our Lady of the Hour, the Virgin Mary, and or tell Elias stories about the Dominicans. Back then, he made his bed close to the altar, and as soon as he was sure that Elias had fallen asleep, he would get up and walk warily to the middle of the church, where there was a spiral staircase leading to the pulpit. He opened the secret trapdoor under the staircase and disappeared. One night, Elias noticed that the cook had slipped off and decided to follow him. Fearfully, the boy climbed down through the trapdoor but after a few steps found his bare feet were under water. Deep in the crypt he could see the light of the candle Abu Qatada was carrying, but then the light disappeared and it was pitch dark. The crypt was dank and eerie and Elias felt there were rats moving around everywhere. Frightened, the boy retraced his steps and waited for the cook under the pulpit.

The cook had no choice but to confess. When he came out of the crypt, Abu Qatada was dripping with sweat. He drank two glasses of water, then picked up his bedding and spread it out close to Elias's bed. 'Listen, my boy. I'll tell you everything. But for God's sake keep it a secret,' he said. Abu Qatada sighed, wiped his brow and started to make his confession:

'My real name is Youssef Najib Khoshaba. I spent my childhood and adolescence here in this church. I was an orphan – my parents died in a car accident when I was five. Father Benjamin Touma, a friend of my father's, took me in and gave me a place to live in the monastery. I'm a Dominican and I studied and lived here in the church until the war between Iraq and Iran started. I became a soldier when I was 20. Leaving the monastery was painful at the time, because it was my home and my school, and the friars and nuns were my family. The old dictatorial regime liked to have Christians, and even you Yezidis, working as servants to senior army officers, and as far as we were concerned that saved us from the living hell that was the front lines. They say this was because Saddam trusted the religious minorities. I did my military service in an officers' mess in Kirkuk. I was just a waiter who served food and drinks. While working in the mess, I learned how to cook from an Assyrian chef called Hanna Daniel. The man was so well-known that even the minister of defence wouldn't miss a chance to taste his food whenever he visited the city. I survived that brutal war, which wiped out so many young men of my generation. But when it ended in 1988 I wasn't allowed to go back to Mosul. A senior officer forced me to work as chef in a famous restaurant he had opened in a fancy part of central Baghdad. But I used to go to church on days off and on religious holidays. After Saddam was overthrown and the Americans occupied the country, I thought of going back to Mosul. The officer who owned the restaurant had fled to Jordan. But I hesitated. I didn't want to leave the restaurant workers without jobs. I took over as restaurant manager and sent the profits to the officer every month. But things rapidly deteriorated after the American occupation. Civil war broke out between the Shi'ites and the Sunnis. Christians were being murdered and their churches were being blown up in Baghdad, Mosul and other cities. I was disappointed and depressed. I had a nephew who lived in Finland. We spoke on the phone one day and he encouraged me to leave Iraq. Everyone knows that life for Christians is growing harder, and as you know, Elias my boy, there are people we know all over Europe. The friars who taught me in the Clock Church, and who later fled to Italy, got me a Schengen visa, so I could travel to most of the countries in the European Union. I went to see my nephew in Finland

and he advised me to seek asylum there, since it's affluent and peaceful. Although the winter is very harsh there, I loved the Finnish countryside and how calm everyone is. Silence, solitude and a contemplative life is what I longed for most. Even so, I didn't like to stay there without working, so I found a job in an Iraqi restaurant east of Helsinki that served kebabs and tikka. The young men who ran the restaurant didn't know anything about cooking and, frankly, gave Iraqi cuisine a bad name. But I understood they had a pressing need to work. Anyway, then Islamic State took over Mosul. We were worried about our Dominican brothers in the Clock Church and the other Christians in the country. I got in touch with my contacts and heard that the friars in the monastery had abandoned the church and fled. At the time, Islamic State hadn't yet taken over the church as a command base and no one imagined they would establish themselves in so many cities and towns in Iraq and Syria and get anywhere near governing as the Islamic State. Most people thought they would fade away like al-Qaida and other extremist movements before them. I heard from an acquaintance that one of the friars had hidden the rare books and manuscripts that had been in the church library in the old crypt. The Dominicans were worried the Islamic State soldiers might find this treasure and destroy it. I was anxious about the situation too. I followed the news and made some calls to friends and acquaintances. In a moment of madness, I decided to go to Mosul and try to smuggle the books and manuscripts out of the church. In fact, my assumptions were mistaken, and the people I knew in Mosul, Christians and Muslims, made inaccurate assumptions as well. They didn't expect the situation in Mosul to deteriorate so rapidly. A childhood friend of mine, a Muslim living in the Clock Quarter, a man by the name of Jabir al-Ali, agreed I could come to his house and we'd arrange to smuggle out the books and manuscripts between us. Jabir assured me that the church was boarded up and we could move the manuscripts if I came to Mosul quickly. I bought a ticket and flew to Istanbul first. The Dominicans there helped me. Through their contacts, as a precautionary measure, I got forged identity papers with a Muslim name, Adnan Abdul Rahman. I flew from Istanbul to Erbil and then took a bus to Mosul. We were stopped at an Islamic State checkpoint. They took all the passengers off the bus and started questioning them. Naively, I told them straight out that I'd been a cook in the Iraqi army before the American invasion, and when they found out I'd cooked for senior officers, they detained me and interrogated me more thoroughly. Later I gathered that they wanted information about senior officers in the Iraqi army, especially as many of them had joined Islamic State to fight the government. One of the commanders from the Criminal Justice Department visited the prison where they were holding me. As you know, they're the people in charge of prisons, interrogations and issuing arrest warrants to the Islamic State police. They're the people who decide on prisoner releases, among other legal things. The commander had heard about me, and he came to see me in my cell. He told me that if I was a really good cook he'd set me free. He took me out to the prison yard and told the guards to fetch a sheep. He slaughtered it himself, put its head in my lap, and said, 'Show me your skills.' I went into the prison kitchen and set to work. After the commander and his aides had eaten the sheep's head, he had a cup of tea with me and swore he hadn't had such a good *pacha* since his mother had died, and she cooked the best sheep's head in the whole of the Houla Plain. The commander ordered them to free me and told me to join an Islamic State camp for training. I was gradually sinking deeper into the mess I had created. I went to the camp and had a hard time there. As you know, I'm almost 60, and as you can see I'm a large man, so I couldn't run when we did training. Gunfire terrifies me and I hate weapons. In the end they were happy to let me do all the cooking in the camp, and I stayed there until news came that Islamic State had turned the Clock Church into the headquarters for the Media Council group. I had an idea and went to one of the commanders in the training camp, Abu Khalid al-Shishani, who thought well of me and had a childish passion for the custard I used to make specially for him. I told him I'd grown up in the Clock Quarter and I'd very much like to live there again. I said I was tired, with piles and high blood pressure, and I didn't have the energy to cook for all the mujahideen in the camp. I begged him to ask if it might be possible for me to work in the Church headquarters. Shishani promised he would do what he could. And indeed the man did what he promised and two weeks later I was appointed cook in the Dominican church.

'As you can see, I set up the kitchen in the nave of the church and set to work on the job I love. I felt safe again as soon as I set foot in the church. I found the books were still safe in the old crypt and the Islamic State people hadn't discovered them. The Digital Army group was working only in the main basement. The crypt was barely known about even by the Dominicans. In 1997 some restoration work had been done in the church because the ground water level was rising. The foundations of the church and the monastery had cracks and some walls had almost collapsed. During the restoration work the friars found a piece of marble, the Mosul kind of marble known as *qirsh*. It was lying on top of the tomb of one of the Italian monks. The piece might have been part of the original altar in the old church. It was engraved with the Greek letters alpha and omega, the alpha coloured blood red and the omega dark blue. Of course, the letters symbolise God's or Christ's status as both the beginning and the end. The friars guessed there was a graveyard under the old church, which went back to the Italian period, that is to say the 18th century. A burial ground was indeed discovered, in the form of traditional catacombs. They could be reached by a narrow entrance and a sloping passageway that led to the bottom of the cemetery, more than thirty feet below street level. When I went down into the crypt to check up on the books and manuscripts hidden there, I discovered that the ground water was rising again, and there was another problem: the books in the crypt were directly beneath the library, which, as you know, the Islamic State soldiers have turned into an execution chamber. Blood was running between the wooden floor boards and dripping onto the books. So I had no choice but to move this valuable treasure to somewhere else in the crypt until an opportunity arose to smuggle the books and manuscripts out. But as you can see, it's now virtually impossible to escape from the grip of Islamic State in Mosul. I've accepted reality and I'm just waiting in the hope that God will come to the rescue.'

Elias kept the cook's secret and sympathised with him. In fact, the boy often acted as lookout when Abu Qatada went down into the crypt to move books to the safe place he had constructed on top of an Italian friar's tomb. Elias knew that Abu Qatada had learnt several languages in the monastery – French, Italian, English and Turkish – and that he was well-informed about the history of the church and of the Dominicans. He explained to Elias all the inscriptions, icons, symbols and archaeological features inside and outside the church. At night, Abu Qatada told the boy stories about the Dominican friars' many achievements in Mosul. They were very much involved in education and set up several schools and institutes. They taught boys and girls, built orphanages and ran workshops to teach manual trades. They taught books in Arabic and books about Islam, and in their printing press, the first of its kind in Mosul, they printed many books on history, language, sciences and religion, in several languages – Arabic, Syriac, French, Latin and Turkish. The Dominicans had to stop working when the First World War broke out, but they came back later and resumed their activities. Their institutes, schools, dispensaries and charitable associations continued to look after and teach Mosul children of all religions without exception, but in the 1950s the Iraqi state started to supervise education and healthcare. In 1902, the friars published the city's first magazine, *Iklil al-Ward* (The Garland of Roses), which came out in three languages – Arabic, Chaldean and French. When the church celebrated its 250th anniversary in the year 2000, important people came from all over Iraq, as well as from France, the United States, Iran, Italy, Egypt and Lebanon. That was when they opened the Clock Arts Hall, the place the Islamic State would turn into a prison for slave women. After hearing the cook's confession and his stories about the Dominicans, Elias started to see the church and the monastery in a different light. He felt that the place was full of ghosts from the past and the ghosts were watching them and listening to what they said. For the first time, Elias started to think about all the different sects, religions and ethnicities that make up Iraq. He started to ask the cook questions such as why people belonged to different religions, how they could live together in peace, what religious differences meant to people, and how many gods there were in the world.

One day, Mosuli and Ansari had a serious argument in the churchyard, and both drew their pistols. Mosuli had issued strict orders against anyone approaching his wife's room and had posted a guard of Afghan origin at the door, who was as meek as a lamb and hardly spoke Arabic. Elias was the only other person who could go in and see Sara, to bring her food and run errands for her. Apparently, Ansari had twice ordered the guard to open the door and gone in to chat with Sara. He claimed he merely wanted to check up on her, but Mosuli was furious when he heard about it. The mujahideen in the church intervened to settle the dispute and asked the two men to 'seek protection from accursed Satan'. Mosuli swore by the Quran that from now on, if any man approached his wife's room, he would have him beheaded. He told Ansari his days were numbered and accused him bl of atheism and treason. The mujahideen in the church dispersed and Abu Qatada went off to market with Elias. They bought lots of vegetables and other food because Ramadan was approaching. Abu Qatada asked Elias what he thought about buying another torch battery for Antonio Manuel, the hostage in the black crate. Elias knew that the cook was very cautious and tended to exaggerate things.

'Antonio's addicted to batteries because of you. He'll suffer if you don't supply him with his drug,' Elias said. Abu Qatada was taken aback and looked at the ground as he thought about Elias's remark.

'Then let's stop supplying him with batteries,' he finally said.

'But then maybe he'd go crazy,' Elias replied, which made the cook even more confused and anxious.

The man in the black crate, Antonio Manuel, was indeed addicted to light. After he thanked the cook for the food by writing on his plate in beetroot juice, they had continued to communicate by the same method. Abu Qatada later slipped a pen into a bowl of rice and asked the hostage to write in small letters as far as he could, but not more than one line at each meal so that the guards wouldn't notice the messages on the plates. Abu Qatada and Elias had gone online to work out what the Spanish messages meant, and it turned out that the hostage was a big catch for Islamic State. Antonio was a well-known journalist who had covered the war in Bosnia. His father was German and his mother Spanish. He had grown up in Spain and never learnt German, which he hated because it was the language of his father, who separated from his mother when he was young. His father then married a German woman, with whom he had three more children, and Antonio didn't have a good relationship with him. Abu Qatada guessed that the journalist's father was an important factor in holding him hostage, because he was a general posted to NATO headquarters. Antonio had been severely traumatised by what he saw in Bosnia while covering the massacres there. He went to a psychiatrist regularly and when the anti-government protests began in Syria he followed the news and eventually decided that the only way to deal with his fears and nightmares would be to immerse himself in work again, like many war reporters. After hearing about a famous singer who had become a symbol of the protests, he travelled to Syria. Antonio made friends with the singer and wrote about his activities, as part of his coverage of what had by then become a full-scale war. They became close friends. Some of the Syrian rebels who later found asylum in Europe said that the singer was forced to join Islamic State, like many other Syrians, because he had lost hope in the other squabbling factions and because Islamic State was itself a growing force. But they also said they were surprised that the singer had handed his Spanish friend over to Islamic State, since they had been such close friends. The Islamic State moved Antonio around from place to place, never staying in one place more than a month. At first, his situation was tolerable: they would let him out into the open air from time to time and he was usually held in a room or a whole house. But when they found out that his father was a general, they built the black crate for him and put him inside in the dark. Through the messages he sent on his plates, Antonio begged the cook to help him get some light. Abu Qatada didn't understand at first, so Antonio explained, saying that all he wanted was a small battery, some wire and a small lightbulb. Abu Qatada was horrified at the idea and turned down his request, but Antonio kept insisting until Elias intervened and convinced the cook that they could slip things to Antonio inside stuffed vegetables. Abu Qatada sent Antonio a message on his soup bowl, asking what would happen if the guards found out about the light. Antonio explained his plan in full in messages spread over three plates – one with okra, one with salad and the other with bulgur wheat. He said the crate had a wooden door and undoing the old locks on it made a loud noise, so there would be enough time to disconnect the wire from the lightbulb, so that the light would go off. After much thought and hesitation, the cook finally put a small battery inside a large stuffed onion, the wire in a stuffed tomato and the small lightbulb in some stuffed vine leaves. A while later Antonio asked for another battery because the old one had gone flat. The cook obliged reluctantly. But on the third occasion Abu Qatada decided to stop supplying him with batteries because it was too risky. Sooner or later they would be found out and they would all have their heads chopped off. Eventually Elias and Abu Qatada found another way to make life inside the dark crate easier for Antonio. On the internet, there was the text of an interview Antonio's wife had given to a Spanish newspaper, and there was a beautiful but sad photograph of his wife with their daughter. Elias printed out the picture, the cook covered it with a piece of plastic wrap and sent it to Antonio with a plate of beans. 'But how will he see the picture in the pitch dark?' Elias asked.

'Don't worry, love will find a way,' answered the cook. Antonio was delighted with the picture and said he was taking advantage of the moments when the door opened and the light came in to look at the faces of his wife and daughter. He sent another request for a new battery but Abu Qatada ignored it.

One cold, Mosul-winter night, Antonio fell ill. He had a terrible stomach ache and the guards were worried he might die, so they consulted Commander Ansari. Ansari made some calls and told the guards that a doctor couldn't come till the morning. Ansari then had an idea: he went to Sara his wife and asked her, as a pharmacist, to examine the hostage. At first the guards refused to let Sara go in to see Antonio, but Ansari reminded them that they would have their heads chopped off if the hostage died on them and promised them it would stay a secret between them. Sara went into the black crate and examined Antonio. She came out holding her nose because of the awful putrid smell that the man gave off. Sara reminded them that she wasn't a doctor, but said that the symptoms and the location of the pain suggested that the man had appendicitis and should be moved to hospital immediately. A small truck arrived at the church and took away the black crate. Antonio Manuel never came back to the church, and nor did his guards.

Nothing inside the Clock Church stayed secret for long

from the eyes and ears of Commander Abu Bakr al-Mosuli. The next day, his guards grabbed Ansari, tied him up and took him to the library. Mosuli slit his throat personally. Elias cleaned up the blood and put Ansari's head in an empty flour sack, and Mosuli sent it to the Caliph. It was clear that the Islamic State leaders had already agreed the time had come to get rid of Khaled Saad, the smuggler, turned military commander turned diplomat, the legend of the town of al–Bukamal.

5. The Couscous Brothers' 'Weddings'

Celebrations of the Couscous brothers' 'weddings' went on for two days. Two vehicles rigged up as car bombs were decorated with flowers and the Couscouses put on fragrance in readiness to become martyrs and meet the houris of paradise. The young, European men in the Digital Army started work on a propaganda video before they carried out the operation. Islamic State generally depended on its European members for media and propaganda activities because they knew about technical things such as the internet and cameras. These were the guys that ran al-Bayan Radio Station, which broadcast Islamic State programmes in several languages – Arabic, English, French, Turkish, Kurdish and Russian. They also helped to edit *Dabiq Magazine*, which Islamic State published in English, and *Dar al-Islam Magazine*, which came out in French and had had a profound effect on the Couscous brothers before they joined the organisation. The brothers were filmed for a whole day. Every now and then they took shots of them from various angles as the brothers said farewell to the mujahideen with hugs and smiles. Then they took some extended shots of them talking straight to camera, urging fellow Muslims in Europe and all over the world to join them in the gardens of eternity through martyrdom helping Muslims. In the last shot, the two Couscous brothers raise the index fingers of their right hands, a reference to belief in the oneness of God. The Digital Army group then tracked the two car bombs until they reached their target – a concentration of Iraqi government forces on the outskirts of Mosul. They filmed the moment of the explosion by drone. Most of the mujahideen in the Clock Church were surprised that the two brothers had been recruited as suicide bombers and that had suddenly they signed for intensive, suicide operations training by order of Commander Mosuli.

The Couscous brothers were not real brothers, just close friends. They hadn't been apart since travelling from Brussels to Iraq, and they were known as just 'the brothers' until Abu Qatada added the 'Couscous'. The cook didn't know much about their lives, other than some of the things Mohammed, the older one, had told a young Dutch man in the Media Council. Before Islamic State was set up, Mohammed had travelled to Yemen and spent six months with al-Qaeda, which gave him intensive training and preparation to be part of a sleeper cell in Europe. When he went back to Brussels he met his childhood friend Abdallah, who was working in the same place as him, in the red light district in among all the sex workers. Abdallah sold marijuana and stole mobile phones off tourists who were either drunk or distracted by the sight of naked women in the shop windows. Abdallah only knew a few words of Arabic and he was in his early twenties when he joined Islamic State. His father was from Morocco and his mother from Senegal. His mother had left them and disappeared when he was a young child. Abdallah noticed that a great change had come over his friend Mohammed since he'd been to Yemen. He'd stopped drinking, talked about God all the time, prayed regularly, spent time alone and smoked far less hashish. He also started urging Abdallah to return to the path of righteousness and give up the lifestyle of unbelievers in the West. Mohammed had a Moroccan background and was five years older than Abdallah. His father sold vegetables in a street market and his mother was paralysed on one side of her body. He had four sisters and a talented younger brother who played football at a local club. When Mohammed read the manifesto of the Islamic State Caliphate in *Dar al-Islam* magazine he went wild with enthusiasm. The ideas and operating methods of al-Qaeda struck him as old-fashioned, hesitant and more secretive than necessary. Al-Qaeda depended on creating chaos without proposing specific alternatives. Islamic State, on the other hand, had taken great steps forward and had a clear vision of a system of government that should replace existing governments.

Abdallah didn't understand much about Islam or jihadist ideas, but his friendship with and trust in Mohammed gave him courage and helped persuade him to travel to Islamic State territory with him. Abdallah also longed to escape the routine of his life, whatever the price. Sleeping all day, making a living in the red-light district at night, constant fear of the police or of trouble. Mohammed broke his mother's heart, and she died of a stroke two months after he arrived in Mosul with Abdallah. The 'brothers' weren't as well-educated as the other European mujahideen and they didn't have any special technical expertise. They had qualities similar to those of most of the Asian mujahideen – blind obedience and a willingness to carry out orders to kill, rape, or plunder without hesitation, without fear or any sense of guilt. These qualities were not always found in the local mujahideen, who might be reluctant to carry our certain assignments, out of a sense of attachment to a town or because their clan was linked to other clans through intermarriage and other ties over hundreds of years. The 'brothers' moved around all over Islamic State territory in Syria and Iraq and always worked as guards, because they were reliable and obedient. At first, they worked for the Financial Council, which supervised revenue collection, including the sale of oil and weapons. After that they moved to the Security Council, which oversaw the police in their territories and carried out executions. For only a month they were guards at the Intelligence Council, which was in charge of collecting information for use in preparing military operations. Eventually they settled with the Media Council and were chosen to guard the Clock Church.

A few days after the suicide of the Couscous brothers, Elias heard an interesting story about them from the Afghan who guarded Sara's rooms. It seems the Afghan had become suspicious about their behaviour and decided to follow them one day. They went up to the roof of the church and hid away in one of the alcoves. Speaking broken Arabic, the Afghan said: 'I swear by the Quran I saw Mohammed kiss Abdallah's ass.' Elias was surprised he had never noticed such a thing, even though he had been careful to monitor them all the time. Elias wanted to share this information with Abu Qatada, but the cook and his assistant were on bad terms at the time. Elias kept going over the story in his head: maybe Commander Mosuli had turned the Couscous brothers into suicide bombers in a hurry, instead of having them executed for homosexuality by throwing them off the church roof, the standard punishment. The Afghan, who was as meek as a sheep, must have told his superior what he had seen.

Elias was keeping his distance from Abu Qatada. He no longer spoke with him, unless it was about essential work matters. The reason was that the cook had finally made up his mind not to take part in Sara's plan. One day Elias was helping Sara clean her room and she was telling him about memory and forgetfulness. 'As you grow older, my dear Elias, you'll discover that fear and love are the emotions most present in the lives of humans and they have a strong influence over our other feelings. You have to learn to control your fears, not just by the power of love but by playing the game of memory and forgetfulness. In our folk proverbs and songs we praise what we call the blessing of forgetfulness, and this makes sense because, if it wasn't for the cleverness of memory and the mysterious magic of the way it works, we'd be stuck in the nightmares of our past life forever. If we ever escape from the nightmare of Islamic State, we'll all remember the events here in the church in a different way, because the memory, Elias, is not an exact record of what we lived through, like a documentary on videotape. Each of us remembers what happened through their own personal feelings and fears. Our memories will be affected by what we know, the kind of people we are, the ways we think, and by other subsequent events that we experience. In the end, each of us will produce a different film of the same events.'

Elias continued to sweep the room, stopping from time to time to listen and concentrate on what Sara was saying, which struck him as amusing and fascinating. Her words heightened his feelings of love for her and his childish fear of her beauty and intelligence. The poet continued: 'One school of thought says that memories wilt like flowers or are worn away and lose their shine with the passage of time. That would explain the idea that forgetfulness is a blessing, but there is another school of thought that says that memories are distorted by other memories. To put it simply, we forget because events and life experiences overlap in our memories and the more similar two experiences are, the more likely we are to remember them.' Sara felt that the subject had become too complicated and poetic and that she could no longer focus on it. So she paused and asked Elias to come and sit beside her.

Sara took Elias's hands between her own and kissed them. The boy was flustered and almost cried. Sara thought her relationship with Elias was strong enough for her to tell him what was going on in her head! She told him that the pharmacy she owned was still working, run by an Islamic State pharmacist who had been a colleague of hers in college. 'This is the land of wonders! I don't understand how people can live under such conditions without a rebellion or a real revolution. At one moment, they're willing to fight in Saddam Hussein's random wars, the next moment they're growing long beards and killing people in the name of God.' After that, Sara calmed down and started talking seriously about the plan she had devised, so as not to alarm Elias. She said she usually hid a spare key to the pharmacy under the door mat at the pharmacy, because she was very forgetful. Sara wanted Elias to slip into the pharmacy after closing time and bring her all the sleeping pills they had in store. Elias would then dissolve the pills in water and slip the mixture into the food in the cooking pots. The mujahideen would all fall asleep and then they could escape in the van they used to go shopping for the church. Sara said she knew the streets of Mosul well because she'd been driving since she was a student, and she was certain they could find a safe way out of Mosul towards Erbil. She promised Elias she would stay with him and look after him until they escaped the hell of Iraq and reached Europe. She said her family was rich enough to help them emigrate.

Elias spent days thinking about what Sara had said. He wanted to tell her that they could bring in Abu Qataba as a partner in the plan, but he was reluctant to reveal the cook's secret to her. Elias eventually told Abu Qatada the details of Sara's plan and said, 'Maybe it's a chance for all of us to escape, me and Sara and you and the books and manuscripts. Abu Qatada wasn't convinced. He said the plan was unrealistic, like the plot of an Indian film, and he wasn't prepared to take what he called such an irresponsible risk. 'Even if the guards and the mujahideen really do fall asleep, how would we get through all the checkpoints in the city? That would be impossible!' he said, and asked Elias to forget about the whole thing. Elias accused Abu Qatada of cowardice, and after that he was caught between Sara's promotion of the escape plan and Abu Qatada's rejection of the idea. Elias started to swing more to Sara's side and to feel confident about her plan. When he brought the subject up again with Abu Qatada, they had an argument. Elias threatened to expose Abu Qarada's activities to Islamic State if he didn't take part in the escape plan. But Abu Qatada continued to refuse. He said he would not get upset with 'his son' because of the threat, but he asked Elias to think about it rationally and realistically and not to indulge in any action film fantasies.

At about this time, Islamic State went on full alert because the Iraqi army had started to mass its forces on the outskirts of Mosul and there were reliable reports that the international alliance was ready to provide air cover for an Iraqi army attack on the city. Ansari was replaced by an American commander of Uzbek origin by the name of Abu Salah al-Uzbeki. A teenage girl killed herself in the Clock Arts Hall. She slit her wrists with a razor blade. Commander Uzbeki questioned all the fighters thoroughly to find out how the razor blade had found its way to the slave girls in the hall. His suspicions centred on Elias, since he was of Yezidi origin and might have colluded with the slave girls. But Elias denied it and said he had nothing to do with the incident. He said he no longer considered himself Yezidi and now he was a proper Muslim. Another back-up patrol was added to the usual patrol around the church. The slave women were moved out of the Arts Hall and into another building in the area, and the Arts Hall was then designated as a workspace for the editors of the magazines and newspapers that Islamic State published.

A few days later, Islamic State decided to transfer Mosuli to Anbar province in western Iraq. The commander asked Sara to get ready to move. Elias came to say goodbye and couldn't help being silent and sad. Sara gave him a hug and the boy's tears made her neck wet. 'Please don't leave me,' he told her. Sara realised that Elias's childish shyness prevented him from saying honestly what he felt about her. She told him that when she was a child her father taught her she could express herself in writing rather than by speaking, because our voices often let us down and it's easier to put things in writing. She opened a drawer where she kept the coloured notebooks she'd been writing in throughout her captivity in the ISIS church, and pulled out two pieces of paper and a pen. She told him she used to write to her father when she was too shy or frightened to say what she wanted to say, and now Elias could do the same with her. She said she went on doing this with her father even after she got married. 'Most girls, when they got their first period, would tell their mothers about it. But I wrote about it on a small piece of paper and stuck it in my father's trouser pocket, and then he in turn told my mother.' Elias wrote something, and Sara did too, and then they both hid their notes in the other's pocket. Elias only wrote a few words ('I love you, and I love the way you smell!'). Then he finally plucked up courage and asked her what she wrote about in her coloured notebooks. She told him that ever since she'd moved to the church, she'd stopped writing poetry and had started trying out other narrative forms: very short stories and prose texts. She said they were just drafts and asked Elias to chose a notebook at random as her gift to him. Elias chose the green notebook and she wrote a dedication in it: 'To Elias. Trust your imagination. It's your most loyal friend.'

After Sara left, Elias slipped impatiently into his hiding place in the church tower, sat on the frame of Eugénie's clock, lit a cigarette and started to read the green notebook.

Iblis Village

The group of young guys objected to the first proposal but they agreed to the second. For a long time, the people of Iblis Village had been thinking of applying to the provincial government to upgrade their village to a *nahya*, a district: the population had grown in recent years and it no longer made sense to treat it just as a village. All the villagers agreed on this. But what the young men didn't want was to change the name of the village, whereas their parents' generation thought the name had brought them only bad luck, mockery by their neighbours and jokes from strangers. No one knew how the village came to be named after Iblis, the leader of the devils. The young people thought the strange name made the village strong. Rare things are always valuable, and with time they grow even more so. The elders didn't share this view: they thought the time had come to get rid of the inauspicious name. When the young people started a hashtag, #proudofiblis, the village chief and the clerics were angry and decided to act swiftly. The provincial authorities finally agreed to change the name of the village, but the application for an upgrade to *nahya* status was tucked away in an office drawer somewhere. Municipal workers arrived, removed the old signs at the entrance to the village and installed new ones reading *Welcome to the Village of Bounty*. The new name made the young people even angrier because it didn't reflect the wretched state of their village, or indeed the state of the country or the world as a whole.

A week after the name change, a succession of mishaps befell the village. A flock of sheep was killed and the villagers blamed wolves, although they hadn't seen a wolf in the area for years. Then the grain stores burned down. Chickens disappeared and more than a few buffaloes went missing. Rumours spread that these things were happening because Iblis was angry. The village elders gathered to discuss it. The clerics suggested communal prayers asking God to protect them from the accursed devil. But Iblis continued his campaign of vengeance. The electricity pylons nearby were damaged and there were serious leaks in the main water cistern. There were several mysterious thefts, which the villagers were not accustomed to. Eventually the villagers reached a solution – to reinstate the village's old name, on the grounds that this was the best way to placate Iblis. But the provincial authorities categorically refused to change the name of the village again, saying that the old name was inappropriate in a new and promising millennium and changing the name had been the right decision. The villagers prayed that the sky would protect them from the anger of Iblis. In the end, nature gave a wonderful gift to the young people who had secretly arranged all these incidents in the village because they were angry that the name had been changed without them being consulted or listened to. Heavy snow fell on the village, a rare historical event. The villagers asked the oldest man in the village, a man 102 years ago, if his ancestors had ever told stories about snow falling in the region. The old man told them it was because Iblis was angry. The villagers hurriedly removed the signs, made a new one with the name Iblis and put it up at the entrance to the village.

The young people made the most of the idea of 'the curse of Iblis' from the start and started to drum it into the villagers' minds. They knew that the snowfall was just a sign of the climate change that was sweeping most parts of the world, but in some parts of the world you need myths to combat other myths. Logic, reason and scientific analysis are not enough. It's too late. Scientific progress has been much faster than the rhythm of the villagers of Iblis.

'So what myth can now convince the people of Iblis that climate change is real?' one of the young people posted in their Facebook group.

'Even Iblis couldn't do that,' one of the others replied.

'Hahaha,' commented a third.

6. Elias's Journey into the Land of ISIS

When Elias applied for asylum, he had just turned seventeen. He had spent two years as a clandestine migrant, from Turkey to Greece and Italy, and finally to Denmark. The man in the immigration department put Elias's watch on the table and told Elias that the watch seemed to be valuable. He said that, under a new Danish law, refugees with cash or valuables worth more than 1,500 euros could have their property confiscated. The watch had a picture of the Virgin Mary breast-feeding Jesus, with Roman numerals. Elias agreed with the interrogator that the watch was valuable, but not because of how much it cost, which he didn't know, but because it was a gift from someone dear to his heart. The interrogator said they would look into the question of the watch later and asked Elias to tell him why he was applying for asylum. Elias had heard from other refugees that Denmark had become very strict in recent years and most asylum requests were rejected. So he was flummoxed and didn't know exactly which important details he should focus on when he spoke about his journey into the land of ISIS. When he started telling the story, the interrogator interrupted him several times, especially when he brought up the subject of European members of Islamic State. At this point he urged Elias to give more details.

'My name is Elias Faqir Khidir and I'm from a Yezidi family,' Elias began. 'We used to live in a village close to the Sinjar Mountains. My father was crazy about birds of prey. He hunted falcons and sold them in the bird market in the Bab al-Toub area in the centre of Mosul. My mother was a registered midwife: she travelled to the nearby villages to deliver babies. When ISIS came into our village I was twelve years old and I had two sisters, one aged fifteen and the other twenty. An ISIS commander negotiated with the village elder about the possibility of the villagers converting from Yezidism to Islam. Most of the villagers refused. The ISIS people gathered the villagers in the primary school. They put the women and children in the classrooms. It was a strange sight for us children, to see our mothers and sisters sitting at our school desks and sobbing. They took males over sixteen years old outside and then we heard gunshots and women and children screaming. We found out later that the ISIS people had executed them and buried them in a mass grave. They separated the older children from the women but left those under six with their mothers. They put us older children in a bus and we set off on a long journey until we reached Raqqa. There, they put us in the training camp for young Muslims containing about 400 children from Iraq and Syria. We trained to use guns and grenades and to make bombs of various kinds. Some of the children were chosen to become suicide bombers. Many of the children from Raqqa were used as spies in the city, to inform on anyone who spoke ill of ISIS. They called us the Caliph's cubs. In the academic lessons, we learnt about jihad and sharia law, as well as mathematics, reading and writing, and English. In maths class we used bullets for counting, and in the reading class the letter *t* stood for *tank*, the letter *r* for *rifle*, *s* for *sword*, and so on. They put monitoring cameras in all the classrooms and we learnt how to kill unbelievers by practising on dummies.

'There were harsh penalties if children neglected their schoolwork or were reluctant to carry out orders. These included flogging, detention and the denial of food. But the person we feared most at the time was the explosives trainer, a Syrian from the city of Hama. The children nicknamed him Mr Hilli, after the popular Iraqi singer Saadi al-Hilli, whose name came up in Iraq mainly in jokes about men who like to fuck men. Once my friend Zanest came back from Hilli's room with his lips and his left eye swollen. He told me that Commander Hilli had forced him to suck his cock and after ejaculating into Zanest's mouth the teacher started to beat him up brutally. Hilli raped many of the boys and didn't stop doing it until a senior ISIS commander visited the camp and one of the boys dared to tell him that Hilli had raped him. The commander asked the group of boys if Hilli had done that to anyone else. After some hesitation, many of them put their hands up. The commander ordered Hilli executed in front of the children, then he gave us his head to play football with and sat watching the match. Our team won the match eight-four.

'Some of the boys went on a rapid training course and others on a slow course. On the rapid course, the boys had lessons in sharia for 20 days and military training for a month. They were then thrown into battle or used as suicide bombers with explosive belts. I spent two whole years in the training camp, learning how to use weapons and explosives and lots of other military stuff, but the thing I was best at was driving vehicles of various kinds. One day, one of the commanders in charge of the camp, a man by the name of Abu Ali al-Shami, summoned me and told me the teachers had praised my steady nerves and intelligence and my driving skills. Then he told me about eunuchs in the time of the Umayyad, Abbasid and Ottoman caliphs, when they cut off the testicles of slave boys so that they could serve the women in the caliphs' palaces. He said that Yazid Ibn Muawiya was the first caliph to use eunuchs to protect his women while he went to lead his armies in war. Shami promised he wouldn't castrate me, but then he said he would give me a job and if I made a single mistake he would cut off my balls personally. 'Are you Yezidi?' he asked me. Of course I knew how to answer that question: 'My family lived in the darkness of heresy and polytheism, but I have been guided to the true path and I'm a Muslim, thanks be to God.'

'I went to start the job Shami had given me, as servant to a commander of Iraqi origin called Abu Farouk al-Anbari, who lived in Raqqa. Abu Farouk was 52 and had a 19-year-old wife. He was insanely protective of her and wouldn't let her out of the house. She cried all the time and threatened to set fire to herself if Anbari didn't let her go out shopping. She loved to buy necklaces and rings. The shopping area was only a hundred yards from the commander's house. My job was to drive his young wife to the market and then bring her home. I did the job for six months, driving a 1990 Mercedes to market and back at the age of fourteen, until the commander was transferred to Mosul and took me with him. Many of Anbari's relatives joined him and became his guards and assistants, so he no longer needed my services. He sent me to work with the women's police set up by Islamic State. The policewomen were known as the Khansa Brigades, after an ancient female poet, and people nicknamed them 'the biters'. These women went around the markets and private houses to check that women were dressed in the Islamically approved way and were behaving according to the rules. The punishments they could impose on women who broke the rules included cutting out a small piece of flesh from a visible part of the woman's body. For this, they used an instrument that looked like a set of metal teeth and the 'biting' caused horrendous pain. My job was to drive the patrol car that took the 'biters' around the Mosul markets. One day, I saw the patrol grab a twelve-year-old girl who was buying some face powder for her elder sister, who was getting married later that day. I'll never forget the brutal beating she received and how the policewoman bit the girl with the teeth-machine until she fainted. In the women's police station there was a girl called Asma, who was about the same age as me. She worked on a computer, managing their records. Asma was the daughter of the station manager, Umm Hanan. I started a secret relationship with Asma. She was a daring, crazy girl, and we had many dangerous adventures together. We used to hide away in the bathroom at the centre and kiss. The day a policewoman took us by surprise, while we were wanking each other off on the roof of the station, I was almost executed. In no time, she had told Asma's mother. If her mother hadn't been worried about the scandal and possible punishment for her daughter, my life would have come to an end. But Umm Hanan just transferred me to work in the supply depot in the city centre.

'In my new job, I drove a small pick-up delivering food and other basic essentials to Islamic State offices. One day, I took some gas cylinders to the Islamic State people in the Clock Church. I took the cylinders into a kitchen run by a chef called Abu Qatada. The man asked me who I was and where I came from and what kind of education I had had. Two days later, Abu Qatada came to the supply centre and asked the manager if he could take me to work as his assistant in the church kitchen. I later discovered that Abu Qataba was famous for his culinary skills and no ISIS commander would turn down any request he made. I packed my bags and went to work in the church. Abu Qatada was a good and patient man, he treated me as his son and I felt safe only in his company. A while later I learnt the man's secret. Abu Qatada was a Christian and he had come to Mosul to smuggle out some valuable books and manuscripts that were hidden in the church. But things got complicated and he ended up working there, waiting till the Iraqi army came to liberate the city. The church was the headquarters of Islamic State's Media Council, and sometimes the heads of other departments met there to coordinate their activities. There are also some Yezidi women imprisoned in the Arts Hall next to the monastery. There were eight young women and two of them had babies. Whenever the chance arose I would chat with them in Kurdish and ask what had happened to their Yezidi relatives. There was a girl there from our village by the name of Jiyan and she told me what had happened to my mother and sisters and the other women. They had separated the young women from the older ones, who were taken to work as servants to the wives of commanders and other leaders. "They took us to a big house that had belonged to a displaced Christian family," Jiyan told me. "They had divided the young women into groups. There were twenty of us and they started selling us to the mujahideen. We thought that if someone bought us that was the worst thing that could happen to us. In fact, that was the least bad thing that could happen, because then you'd be at the mercy of only one person." Jiyan told me that a Tunisian member of Islamic State bought her sister and took her with him to Syria. When they had sold the rest of the girls, Jiyan was left in a house with twelve other girls, and large numbers of mujahideen would visit. On one occasion there were more than 50 mujahideen in the house, taking turns to rape Jiyan and the other women. She was later bought by a Chechen fighter who worked in the Media Council and he brought her with him to the church headquarters. The Chechen would tie Jiyan's hands together and rape her. She begged me to help her end her life. She asked me to bring her a knife or a razor blade. She was desperate and a complete wreck. She finally got hold of a razor blade, slit her wrists in the bathroom and died.

'In the church, I met the wife of one of the commanders, a pharmacist called Sara. She was confined to a room in the monastery. She proposed an escape plan to me. I would slip into her pharmacy secretly and take all the sleeping pills. I'd put them in the food, the mujahideen would all fall asleep and we would escape. When I told the cook about it, he wasn't convinced it was worth the risk. He thought the plan was childish and unsafe. I thought long and hard about her plan. The idea of escaping had been bugging me ever since I came out of the training camp, but I never dared do it. The commander took Sara with him to another city but before she went, she left me a piece of paper on which she had written the names of the sleeping pills and explained how to get into the pharmacy. Sara always said it was worth the risk, better than a slow death. When Ramadan came, I went to the pharmacy during the extra prayers they perform in the evening. The street was almost deserted. I easily found the spare key she had hidden under the mat. I looked for the pills by torchlight but it was hard to find them and it took me a long time.

'Abu Qatada and I were in the church in the early hours, having something to eat before the start of the Ramadan fast, when I put the sleeping pills down in front of him and begged him: 'Dad, for God's sake, let's escape. If we don't get killed by ISIS, the government's planes and artillery will kill us when they attack the city,' I said. Abu Qatada finally seemed to be warming to the idea, but he was a cautious man and planned everything carefully. We thought Ramadan might work to our advantage. The unusual routine of refraining from food and drink until sunset and then gorging at *iftar* time left most of the mujahideen listless and drowsy, even without sleeping pills. So being drowsy would seem normal and the fighters, full of food spiced with sedatives, would no doubt sleep like logs. We would carry the books and manuscripts to the pick–up we used for shopping and make our getaway. We discussed the food we would serve to those fasting. We were worried about the European members of the Digital Army, because some of them didn't like Iraqi food and they cooked for themselves. The Iraqis, the other Arabs and some of the fighters from Asian countries were no problem: they usually had lentil soup and drank lots of milk, especially in Ramadan. Abu Qatada suggested we feed them whatever would go down as comfort food, each according to his country. We counted the nationalities of white Europeans and found we had Germans, Swedes and Dutch ones. When it came to Europeans of African or Arab origin, it was easy because they understood and liked Iraqi food.

'I did a reconnaissance in the crypt where the Digital Army worked, cautiously making inquiries about what food from their countries the Europeans would like. We came to these conclusions: apfelstrudel for the German, stuffed with almonds, raisins, cinnamon and sugar, a beef and mushroom sandwich for the Swede, and for the Dutchman a side dish of minced meatballs in sauce.

'In Ramadan we set up a large dining table in the courtyard for the mujahideen to eat together. They said grace, ate and drank after the hunger and thirst of the daylight hours, then they fucked the slave women and prayed the evening prayers. That night, the table was laden with all kinds of dishes, laced with sleeping pills. When I put the meatballs in front of him, the Dutchman said, 'You know what, Elias? In Holland the unbelievers eat these meatballs as a mezze with beer!' Then the fighters around him started chatting about which of them used to drink and then gave it up, and about the wines in paradise, which don't make you drunk and don't give you a headache, about the houris beside the river of wine, and other such talk.

'The last one to fall asleep was the German. Abu Qatada and I hurried down into the crypt and carried thirteen boxes full of books and manuscripts to the pick-up. Most of the valuable manuscripts were in Syriac, Italian or French. Each of us took a Kalashnikov, I took four hand grenades, and off we went.

'First, I drove the truck down the narrow lanes of the poor parts of the city, avoiding the main roads. There was little traffic because of Ramadan, when people spend most of their time at home. Our spirits rose as soon as we reached a deserted dirt track between the villages around Mosul and the outskirts of Erbil. I started imagining with relish the moment when we would reach the first checkpoint manned by the Kurdish peshmerga, which would mean deliverance from the hell of ISIS. Abu Qatada told me it all seemed unreal, everything that was happening, the road and the dinner we had cooked, all seemed like just a nightmare. We stopped several times to check the route because we were worried we might lose our way in the maze of winding roads. Abu Qatada was telling me he would be willing to adopt me legally if I agreed and I could go to Finland to live with him there. But then I noticed that a car was following us. It was probably an ISIS patrol. When I put my foot down in an attempt to shake them off, they started shooting at us and sped up too. It was hard to manoeuvre the truck in the hilly terrain. Then a bullet hit Abu Qatada in the back. I panicked and was about to stop and surrender, but Abu Qatada asked me to keep driving. They fired two RPGs at us but missed. After the hills, we came to some flat land that seemed to be farmland and after that there were some woods. I drove into the woods and turned off the engine. I ran to the edge of the wood to check the situation. The ISIS patrol was still making its way between the hills. Then it came to the farmland and carried on towards a village, whose lights shone in the distance.

'I opened the pick-up door and helped Abu Qatada get out and lie on the ground. He was bleeding and I had no idea what to do. He was calm, as if surrendering to death. He said that time wasn't on our side and asked me to listen carefully and not to interrupt or object. He said he wasn't going to survive his injury and I'd do best to leave the truck where it was and continue on foot so as not to attract attention. Then he begged me to bury the books in the woods, and he gave me his wristwatch. He said there weren't many other watches of this kind – with the picture of the Virgin Mary breastfeeding Jesus. The cook had inherited it from his father, who was given it as a reward for his services to the Dominican church. Ever since Eugénie's clock arrived as a gift to the friars, giving timepieces had become a tradition among the Dominicans, as a token of esteem and appreciation. He said that when the Dominican friars saw me wearing the watch, they would trust me and trust my story. They would come one day and recover the books I was going to bury. In despair, I cried bitterly. 'Please don't die, Dad,' I said. 'Come on, hurry up and bury the books. There's a spade in the truck,' he replied.

'By the time I finished digging, dawn had broken. Abu Qatada was dead. I dragged his heavy body, buried it on top of the books and manuscripts and covered the top with soil.

'I don't know if the friars ever found the books and the body of their faithful son, Youssef Najib Khousana. I described the place to them in detail when I reached Erbil. By the time I arrived in Italy, the Iraqi army had already liberated Mosul. I looked out for news of the church on my mobile. There were many videos and pictures showing massive damage to the church. ISIS blew up the clock tower but it didn't collapse completely. Before leaving the church they looted many of the contents and stole Eugénie's clock. Some of the Yezidi women were freed after paying large sums of money to ISIS. I received news that my mother had died of a stroke, but the fate of my sister remained unknown.'

Elias paused and asked for a glass of water.

'Did you help Jiyan kill herself in the Arts Hall?' the interrogator asked.

'Yes, I did,' said Elias.

The interrogator pushed the watch across the table towards Elias and asked him to keep it.

Elias put on the Virgin Mary watch and wiped his eyes. Another tear fell.

The Law of Sololand

Don't hope for things elsewhere:
there's no ship for you, there's no road.
Now that you've wasted your life here, in this small corner,
you've destroyed it everywhere in the world.
    – Constantine Cavafy

MANY PEOPLE KNOW MY name today. Most media outlets and social media sites have talked about what I did, but they haven't spoken about me. Fuck them, and fuck what they say. You're the ones I'm interested in now – the new refugees and the old refugees, those who have residence rights and those who have had their requests for asylum rejected. Those who have been granted citizenship, like me, and those who are still waiting. Those who are on the road and those who are still at home planning to risk their lives in order to reach the promised paradise. Those in detention pending deportation and those in hiding without official papers.

I'm writing for those who haven't been born yet, refugees from future wars and future poverty and climate change. From my cold prison here, I write to you, just for you. You are the ones who will remain outsiders and outcasts. You are the ones who will be pursued till your last breath by the curse of having fled your homes. You are the ones who will be turned into slaves and scapegoats in the countries where you end up living. This is not a declaration of hatred or violence or a celebration of brutality. This is my story, a guide for those in despair. I'm writing for those whose peace of mind has been shattered by disasters and injustices and who are now laboratory mice for people who've had a serious superiority complex for centuries. I'm writing to settle accounts with those wearing masks in the fancy-dress ball called 'human rights'. I'm writing in order to desecrate the banners of racism that fly over the cities of this cruel, selfish, dark North.

Take me out of this mental hospital and put me on trial. Prove that I was in full possession of my mental faculties when I committed what they call my crime. Without the slightest doubt it was in fact *their* crime. A whole year has passed since I was put in prison, and I do not feel any remorse. On the contrary, I have grown angrier and more profoundly resentful. If the racist prisoners do not kill me and I am released in a few years, I will have only one cause – to explode the myth of this arrogant North.

In the country where I was born I studied insects. My main interest was in locusts. I didn't study them at university. It was just a passion that had stuck with me since childhood. I pursued my interest in locusts, or you might say my obsession with them, through private research. After I finished secondary school, I studied French at the Faculty of Languages. At that gory dinner, the story of which I intend to tell you, I reminded both the guests and the hosts of the French proverb that goes: "*Porte fermée, le diable s'en va*" (When the door's closed, the devil turns away). A year before fleeing my home country, I had a little book published about locusts. It wasn't a massive success, but some newspapers commended the lively way in which I presented the scientific facts. The book was the imaginary autobiography of a female locust. Speaking in the first person, the locust talks about her life, from her birth to when she's killed by poison sprayed from a plane on a locust-eradication mission, along with millions of her peers. Then civil war broke out in the country. I was abducted and tortured because on Twitter I'd made fun of the fanatical clerics who were throwing the firewood of ignorance into the furnace of hatred. I was blindfolded for more than two weeks, abused, beaten, intimidated and threatened. They finally released me and I decided to flee the country, where we had had our fill of violence and humiliation. I crossed the border on foot through the mountains, then I crossed the sea in a rubber dinghy. I finished the journey in a meat truck. After a long, nightmarish journey, I finally reached the North and, shortly after I arrived, one of the cities here won the title of Happiest City in the World. Two years later another nearby city won the same title and, two months before I went to prison, the very city I lived in won this gold medal for happiness. So these perpetually morose people win gold medals in the Northern Happiness Olympics, leaving all their competitors in the dust. These happy, healthy, affluent people are damned frightened that the sorcery and trickery of outsiders might taint their frozen paradise.

I was working in a fancy restaurant that specialised in fish dishes for tourists in the centre of the capital. My life would hardly qualify as even ordinary or routine – washing the dishes in the restaurant, and then home, which meant hours spent online. I went to sleep late but woke up early. After I arrived here as a refugee, my passion for locusts began to wane. My fellow refugees would try to fill the emptiness they felt in exile by cooking traditional dishes from back home and listening to romantic music from their youth. I would drown myself in YouTube videos. It should come as no surprise to find that most refugees, after a few months in exile, become skilled cooks. Meat, vegetables, spices and oils, in all their variety, act like drugs to calm nerves strained by exile, but there is always something missing that would make the food taste perfect, something you can't find in the markets in your new country. It's a trademark, a brand that is part of a lost shared identity. I would eat at the fish restaurant and have just a small sandwich for dinner. Sometimes I would long for a locust! My admiration for these beautiful but destructive insects remained a mystery to me. I didn't mix much with the other refugees. I was a loner in the full sense of the word. On rare occasions, I'd go out in the evening with some of my workmates. Even these rare excursions would make me feel embarrassed. My shyness and my constant sense of boredom drove me to withdraw from social encounters. I would make up an excuse and leave the others to enjoy their night out. My loneliness would climb on top of me and I would have to carry it home on my back. One day, I was thinking about myself and my loneliness, and wondering which of us was in charge. I could easily have been the horse, with loneliness riding me. It did indeed tame me to a large extent: I became docile and obedient. I even liked the loneliness as it stroked my hair in my stable, that is in my bed before I went to sleep, dozing off like a tired, frightened child.

I had a short relationship with a woman five years older than me who was a social worker and now lives with a refugee who recently arrived in the North. In two months, I'll be 35 years old.

Maija, my ex-girlfriend, never stopped talking about migrants and refugees, especially the men among them. Of course I understand, because of the nature of her work and the direct, daily contact she had with their problems, which were often repetitively similar. Many times I had to listen patiently to her monologues, with her analyses and opinions and her implicit mockery of the culture of some place or other! If my opinion was very different from the one she expressed, Maija would soon set up the cross and hammer in the nails: I was another male chauvinist Eastern mind that needed to listen and learn Northern wisdom about justice, equality and respect for women. One night, when she was crazy drunk, Maija revealed to me that her last Northern partner had broken her hand in one of their squabbles. She didn't give many details and she never wanted to discuss the subject again. Maija's hobbies were embarking on short-term relationships with refugees, binge drinking at least twice a month, an obsession with sarcastic analysis of the politics of the North and the men of the East, and shedding tears over her own life and the lives of refugees.

A year after we split up, I wanted to satisfy my sexual

impulses, so I tried some dating sites. It wasn't a useful or pleasant experience. Over a whole year of trying, my self-confidence declined and twice I was subjected to implicit racist abuse. Once I managed to go out with a woman. I went to her apartment with her. There was a young man asleep in the bed when we arrived. He was pale and he looked like someone had sucked the blood out of his veins with a giant syringe. He offered me some ketamine. Then I gathered that the woman wanted to fuck me with the other guy. I withdrew discreetly and deleted the dating app from my phone.

On those lonely days I was still going through the nymph phase! The life cycle of locusts goes through three basic phases: the egg, the nymph and then the complete insect. Like my locusts, I went through the three stages in my attempt to understand my relationship with my new country and its inhabitants. As I write this page, it's been eleven years since I came to the North. I obtained nationality easily, four years after arriving. I've been working all the time, paying taxes, and I've learnt the language well. From an early age, I've been troubled by things I don't understand, especially human relationships. The mysteries of insects, plants, animals, rocks, the universe and the oceans are understandable to some extent. All these forms of life speak to us in a completely different language, and it takes many years of effort, patience and research to decipher some of their codes. But not understanding someone of your own species, someone who speaks your own language, is what damaged my relationships with others and messed with my mind! You can spend five years with some insect and learn lots about it. But you can spend the same amount of time with a person and discover that you haven't learnt much about them or from them. It's true that the nymph stage is the second stage in the life cycle of locusts, but it's the first stage in which they really see the outside world. Unlike my locusts, it was my inner world I really wanted to see. I didn't know much about psychology. At university, I had read some basic texts which bored me. But in recent years, I've gone back to studying the inner workings of the human mind. It hasn't been easy. Being a balanced person in this life is hard work. It takes experience and practice. That's what I told myself. As soon as the typical egg stage had passed, I started jumping all over the place, trying to pull together the parts of me that had been torn apart by violence and fear. I started by getting mentally accustomed to my status as an outsider discovering a new country. A locust can jump twenty times the length of its own body. Imagine if you could do that as a human! The nymphs are like adult locusts, apart from the fact that they have no wings or reproductive organs. At this stage, they rely on jumping and use their legs like catapults. For a time, I was shifting from one idea or feeling to another, until eventually I decided to focus my psychological enquiries on the problem of relations between immigrants and their host communities. My motivation was my oversensitivity and maybe the fact that I was bored and annoyed about the things written by journalists and on social media about refugees, integration, xenophobia, hatred, cultural diversity and racism. Superficial stereotypes spread like a dangerous, deadly virus. The host community felt threatened but they didn't know much about the nature of this virus. That remained the area of expertise of a small number of specialists who appeared on television with tedious regularity. Social media was like a jungle full of parrots. Everyone was singing the same lyrics, even if each parrot had its own colour and its own melody. I started to take a serious interest in what was said about refugees and the North. I collected lots of books about exile, identity, violence, racism and the history of the North, novels written by migrants and exiles, autobiographies and everything related to stories about outsiders. Adam and Eve were the first exiles in this journey that we humans are on. Our ancestors' desire to taste the fruit of the tree of knowledge was enough for them to be expelled from Paradise and end up wandering the Earth as homeless refugees. There have been massive human migrations throughout history, from Africa to Asia and into Europe. The European migrations to the Americas. Refugees and exiles because of wars, political persecution and mass extermination. Migrants because of hunger and epidemics such as bubonic plague, smallpox and tuberculosis. Few peoples in history seem to have been spared this ordeal. I felt enthusiastic and excited, and sometimes sad, desperate and angry, as I set sail into this vast ocean: human migration. Gradually, certain aspects of an eternal tragicomic story started coming to light. The leaves that covered my ignorance fell away one by one, and I was increasingly afraid that I might end up standing there, alone, exposed, naked in the face of many cruel truths about human beings, which have barely changed through history.

I carried on working in the restaurant, and I finally found something that saved me from wasting my time on social media or watching YouTube videos. The old enthusiasm I had had when gathering material for my book on locusts revived. My mental faculties were back at work: there was the pleasure of research, of organising one's thoughts, honing one's imagination, taking off the thick coat of fear and the rough hat of hesitation, and putting them aside in the wardrobe of my mind. Knowledge beckoned like the sun at dawn, and my imagination took on the world playfully. But this time, instead of flying around with swarms of locusts, I was trying to probe the depths of human beings.

The nymph stage can be subdivided into five sub-stages, known as instars, which lead up to full maturity. At each transition they shed their exoskeleton, gradually growing wings. In order to survive, the nymphs continue to eat soft leaves after coming out of their eggs, and it takes five or six weeks for the nymphs to mature into fully grown locusts.

I began writing down some thoughts, some quotes and observations day by day. Isabel Allende describes refugees, deportees and exiles as 'a tragic contingent'. Stefan Zweig, on the other hand, thought that only the misfortune of exile can provide a deep and overarching understanding of the way the world really is. Calvino thought the perfect way to live was as a foreigner. I love this remark of Rumi's: 'When people fall asleep their senses leave exile and go back home.'

I wasn't asleep. But I was dreaming about how to discover things again. At the time, I felt that the whole world was my home and that all the creatures in it were my partners. Which poor nymph was I?

★

Yes, that's right. It was me who finished off cleaning up the house after dinner. I washed the dishes, wiped up the blood, swept the floor, tidied up Katrina's bedroom and even cleaned the bathroom. I put the dead bodies in the living room. I asked Katrina to finish her food and tell me about her life. Then, naked, she took me to the sauna and I closed the door.

Now I'm a fully-grown locust, able to fly freely and energetically. No illusions, no hesitant, fearful leaps through the forests of life. If peace approaches the real world at the pace of a tortoise, violence is a crushing hurricane that sweeps away all conventions, fears, delusions and false appearances. After violence, only the bare skeleton of the truth remains. Is it violence alone that brings about real change in our world? Only those whose imaginations have wings can answer this question.

The story that many people want to hear from me personally began on a Saturday morning in autumn. It had to be that way, because no other time matches the beauty of autumn in the North. I feel excited at the mere approach of this season, which produces a mysterious, delicious feeling inside me, a mixture of beautiful sadness and contemplative pleasure. I had breakfast and went on a bike ride through the woods near my flat. I was listening to Philip Glass. The music gave a dreamy cinematic flavour to the carpet of fallen leaves – orange, red and yellow. I connected with the colours and the music and started to breathe deeply, trying to inhale as much beauty as possible and make it touch every cell in my body. And then my phone rang, ruining my breathing exercises. It was Raman, my workmate at the restaurant. He was a relatively recent refugee, but he had permanent residence and was married to a Northern woman who worked in a bar near where they lived. He was tense and wanted to meet me to ask for some advice. I told him I'd ride over on my bike and meet him downtown. 'I'll be with you in about twenty minutes,' I said. I like Raman: he knows how to learn from our troubles as refugees and turn them into comedy. He's a romantic soldier in the battle of life, as he used to describe himself. On my way to meet him I was lost in my thoughts. I was thinking about the differences and the deceptive borders between places, people and times. The sight of the trees in their blazing colours made me think about wonderful, beautiful things that will take you in their arms as long as you have even a little inner peace. In the present, you can probably feel the value of the things around you. But the past brings only trouble. I was thinking about the way people are here in the North and about the Law of Jante. What kind of law do you think we would need back home, if we were to ever break the cycle of violence and destruction? For a long time, Jante's law has been a secret ingredient in the happiness of these Northern countries, so envied by other countries. The law was drafted by the Danish-Norwegian writer Aksel Sandemose in his novel *En flyktning krysser sitt spor* (A Fugitive Crosses His Tracks), written in 1933. The book contains a critique of all the social phenomena prevalent at that time. A few years later, the commandments he mentions in the book became almost the law. Even those who hadn't read the book or heard of it followed his guidelines, which became the almost universal Northern code of social conduct. His ten commandments were as follows:

1. You're not to think *you* are anything special.
2. You're not to think *you* are as good as *we* are.
3. You're not to think *you* are smarter than *we* are.
4. You're not to imagine yourself better than *we* are.

5. You're not to think *you* know more than *we* do.
6. You're not to think *you* are more important than *we* are.
7. You're not to think *you* are good at anything.
8. You're not to laugh at *us*.
9. You're not to think anyone cares about *you*.
10. You're not to think *you* can teach *us* anything.

When I first examined the Commandments of Jante, they very much helped to cast light on the magical qualities of modesty, calmness and simplicity that the people of the North exhibit. They are not pretentious or excessive in their behaviour or their emotions. They don't boast about their possessions or about themselves. The Law of Jante emphasised social solidarity and minimised individualism. To put it simply, you're no better nor more clever than other people. You ought to feel that the jobs of all the people around you, however different they are from yours, have value and complement each other. I gathered that until the 1970s the Jante concepts were widespread and very much a presence in public life. But most young people today never tire of mocking the commandments, which they see as an obstacle to individual creativity, as something that underestimates the importance of self-confidence and discourages the competitive spirit and the urge to excel. Some young people in the North have even dug a mock grave for the Law of Jante, buried it and set up a tombstone. The spirit of capitalism, American-Dream style ('Me first!'), is the slogan that now beguiles many people all over the world. I felt disappointed and bitter that capitalism was sweeping aside the North's modesty, patience and reluctance to boast about trivial matters. The fact that people here in the North were quiet and didn't speak much didn't mean to me that they were unsociable or depressive. On the contrary, silence is the highest form of intelligence and self-expression. To be modest and simple reduces the stress of a hectic daily life. It's not rude or antisocial to put some distance between yourself and others. No, it's an advanced form of courtesy.

To put it simply, like many people, I was seduced by the myth of the happy North, with its humility, equality and justice. But behind this mask of happiness and humility there were many unspoken truths. These happy, civilised people, who inherited their Lutheran masks of humility from their dour forefathers, these people who unconsciously continued the peasant tradition of miserliness, are much crueller than they appear on the surface in the images they like to project, however much it costs them to conceal the tangle of phobias that grip their inner consciousness. These are people whose hearts and minds have been cloistered by the harsh climate and by their geographical location. Even their practical policies have been cruel and disturbing throughout history. The Nazis advance and they go into alliance with them. They lose and they make an alliance with the other side. The happy people in the North now apply their own law towards outsiders, especially against immigrants and refugees. These are the commandments of the North that you must not break, my dear refugee:

1. You're not to think that you can become one of us.
2. You're not to think that we will ever feel safe in your presence.
3. You're not to think that, if you speak our language and love our values, you will be welcomed unconditionally.
4. You're not to imagine that you can add anything new to our pristine culture.
5. You're not to make any mistakes, or you will be given double the punishment.
6. You can never be superior to our white Northern race.
7. You won't be able to trick us with your diabolical culture.
8. You will remain weaker than us whatever you do.
9. We will never forgive you for violating the borders of our country
10. You're not to think that we're interested in your past, your present or your future.

★

Raman was sitting in a corner of the bar, almost in the dark. He said he would order me a beer. I reminded him I was still striving to cut down on alcohol. I fetched myself a cup of tea and asked him what the problem was. 'It's the damned speed,' he said.

'The speed?' I asked, 'What are you talking about, what speed? Ah, I understand. You must have been driving too fast and the police caught you and you're going to complain because you read that report published a while back. I remember it by heart. The statistics show that immigrants are penalised more harshly than Northerners when they're caught driving under the influence of alcohol. More than half the immigrants go to jail, against only 30 percent of Northerners who commit the same offence and have the same levels of alcohol in their blood. Enough of that nonsense. I think we're both aware of this annoying fact, but it's not the end of the world.'

Ramon looked at me seriously. 'Have you finished?' he said.

I smiled stupidly at him and said, 'Yes, okay, sorry. So tell me about it.'

'It's not the car or the damn alcohol. It's my wife and the speed at which I walk,' he said, swigging down the rest of the beer in his glass. 'Listen,' he added, 'you know we live downtown and we don't usually use the car for shopping or to go anywhere. Okay. It's just that I move at the pace of a hare and my wife is as slow as a tortoise. Of course, I've tried to walk slower but she's still as slow as an old tortoise. Why won't she walk just a little faster? I know what you'll say, because you think I run rather than walk. You've complained about it yourself, and so have others. But I'm not fucking you, I don't split the bills with you, you don't share the damn daily routine, other than washing the damn plates of fish that the bloody bloated tourists gobble down in the damn restaurant.'

Raman made me laugh, the way he cursed everyone and everything in sight. I told him he was making too much of it and it was a simple problem that could easily be solved. He wasn't convinced. He said I didn't understand the facts of the case and I had to help him with some serious thinking. He said the walking speed problem led to arguments about other things. His wife thought he did everything too fast. He ate too fast, he ejaculated too soon, he went to sleep too quickly, he left the house too fast, he spoke too fast, he hated people and fell in love too fast. 'Do you think I'm that fast?' he asked.

I looked him straight in the eye. 'Raman, don't get upset with me,' I said. 'You do wash the dishes in the restaurant very fast, and often that causes me trouble with the owner. He values you more than me and thinks I'm lazy.'

'Nonsense,' he said, and hurried to the bar. He rushed back carrying a beer and a whisky. I tried to play down the problem, reminding him that Martta, his wife, was a good person and had been very helpful to him at the start of his life as a refugee. He agreed with me, especially on how generous she'd been helping him, and started to ramble on about his first days as a refugee and how Martta had acted as his mother, sister, friend, lover and wife. Then, with tears glistening in his eyes, he said, 'Martta has been a gift from heaven in this damn exile.' I told him I would break my alcohol ban and sip a glass of wine with him. That became three glasses when the conversation took us to the latest wave of refugees that had arrived in the North. Raman was upset by the behaviour of some of these refugees, after two young men had raped an underage girl. He said this would tarnish our image even more than it was already tarnished by politics, fate and the debris of history. Then he spoke about how hard life was for immigrants in small towns, especially in that remote town where the rape had taken place. The refugees up there had to fend off both the harsh winter and the anger of locals, especially the neo-Nazis and racists. In that town, he added, there had also been a serious shortage of translators who understood the languages of the people in the nearby refugee camp.

'What's the town called?' I asked.

'Sololand.'

Raman walked with me to the entrance to the Metro tunnel. After three glasses of wine, I didn't have the energy to go home by bike. I said goodbye to Raman and he rushed off. 'Not so fast, man! Run too fast and you might have an accident!' I shouted after him in jest. He stuck his middle finger in the air without looking back at me. Raman was a simple guy, a great guy and courteous. His good nature was almost indescribable, though he had a somewhat childish naivety. The only person to visit me in prison later would be Raman. He would be devastated the next time I saw him because his problems with Martta had grown worse and they had separated.

That evening, I searched the internet for refugees in the town of Sololand, and for news of the rape. There was a television report I found on YouTube, with the usual interviews with psychologists, sociologists and other academics, most of whom had never been to the countries the refugees came from and didn't speak their languages. There were also some interviews with refugees and local people. Most of the refugees were still at the romantic 'egg' stage – very enthusiastic in their ideas and feelings about their new home. But they were also divided. Some of them blamed other refugees for their shameful behaviour, while others were angry about their general mistreatment by the local community and the authorities, saying it was unfair that they should all be branded as potential rapists and criminals. 'Why are we all on trial because of a crime by two sick people?' asked a young refugee called Sami. 'All I want to do is develop my skills as a video game designer, start a new life here and help other people,' he added. This Sami would later play a major role in the events that I will never live down, whatever I do. Were it not for my thoughtlessness and stupidity, I wouldn't have gone to the 'integration dinner' and Sami wouldn't have ended up with two bullets in his chest.

After a week reflecting on the course of my life, I decided to go to the refugee housing complex in Sololand. There were several reasons why. To begin with, I felt equally sympathetic towards both the refugees and the terrified locals. I was also bored with my monotonous job in the fish restaurant after eight years without a real holiday. But the most important motive was the fact that during my 'nymph' stage I had developed some ideas, such as doing research on exile and on relationships between 'guest' and 'host' communities through history. I told myself that with the experience I had gained from life and from reading, I could help to interpret and build bridges between the refugees and the local people. Besides, I didn't know much about the new refugees' stories, and delving into their lives and relationships with their new home would help me develop the kernel of the book that had finally started to take shape in my mind. As a kind of foundation stone, I had settled on a preliminary title for the book: *Tough Love*. I planned to write about the complicated and troubled relationship between refugees and their new homes, and compare that with the relationship between a person and everything around them: the people they love, nature, time and death. I didn't realise that I was still a nymph, jumping here and there, and not a full-grown locust. On top of all that, my material circumstances made it possible for me to think about giving up my job and embarking on an adventure with the refugees in Sololand. I had a considerable sum of money in the bank and I didn't have many expenses. I had stopped drinking to excess a year earlier, mainly because alcohol triggered severe bouts lof depression. On special occasions, I would drink a little red wine and nothing more. I wasn't obsessed with buying new things. I would buy clothes from second-hand clothes shops every two or three years, except for socks and underwear, which I bought new. I didn't have many friends with whom I could squander my money. I had most of my main meals in the fish restaurant. I didn't travel outside the capital much. The last long trip I had made was a quick visit to an old friend in a neighbouring Northern country, and it was a cheap trip by ferry. Most of my spending was on rolling tobacco, which I smoked in moderation, never to excess.

I told the restaurant owner that I wanted to leave my job. He agreed at once without hesitation, which took me by surprise. Maybe he didn't like me after all. I said goodbye to my friend Raman, who didn't think I should give up my job and suggested I offer to help at the refugee camp in the capital instead of travelling to the far north. I told him that the refugees in the capital, where there was already a diversity of nationalities and cultures, were much better off than those in this small town suddenly invaded by strangers for the first time. I had two housing issues I needed to solve before I could leave. I knew it would be hard to find housing in a remote little town that thought it had just been taken over by barbarians, especially as my name implied I was one of those barbarians. Even so, I gave it a shot and applied to a local housing company online, knowing it would be a long wait. The other problem was my flat in the capital. It wouldn't be easy to find another place there later. My friend Raman came to my help. He suggested I sublet the flat to three new refugees that he knew personally, on the condition that they would vacate it a month before I came back. They would cover part of my rent, so I would be helping refugees in another way and I'd still have the place to return to.

As soon as I pulled into Sololand in the far north, a massive snowstorm blew up. I drove to the Loki Hotel in the town centre. The lobby was deserted. I waited ten minutes before the receptionist appeared. The man seemed surprised to see me there, and I was taken aback at how unusually tall he was. 'Yes?' he said. I told him I had booked a room on the internet and handed him my passport. He took it and leafed through it like an immigration officer at an airport. He looked at his computer screen and asked which country I was from. 'From here. I'm a Northerner,' I said.

'Yes, yes, I can see that, you have a Northern passport,' he said, 'but I mean your original country.' Instead of saying *What the fuck!*, I gave him an angry look. 'Okay, your place of birth is written in the passport, okay. You've booked for a month, yes, okay. We're not used to such long bookings here. Have you found work in the town?'

'No, I'm a tourist,' I said sarcastically.

He gave me the key. 'Your room is number 23. Breakfast is from six till eleven. You don't need a password for the WiFi.' I asked him if there was a restaurant in the hotel. Still typing on the computer, he said, 'There's a small restaurant nearby. In the bar we only serve drinks. The restaurant is past the petrol station. It's called "Sol" but it only serves local dishes.' So this tall man was guessing I wouldn't like the food there and suggesting I'd best go downtown to eat.

I had a hot bath and arranged my clothes in the wardrobe. It was past two o'clock in the afternoon. I sat on the edge of the bed watching the snowstorm through the window as it lashed the back of a tall, dreary building that hid my view of the town. Maybe it was a government department or a company's offices. I put on some clean clothes and went to the restaurant the receptionist recommended. A woman in her fifties welcomed me with a motherly smile. The only other customer was an elderly man sipping coffee. I checked out the food menu: salmon soup, meatballs with mashed potato and a dish I'd never tried before – strips of reindeer steak. I ordered that and a glass of water.

'Good choice,' the woman said, and went to the kitchen. I sat at the table and watched the old man, who was smiling at the storm outside as if it brought back beautiful memories. The cook brought my plate herself, and for a moment I thought she was the woman with the motherly smile. They looked very similar. Maybe they were sisters. But the cook didn't have the same smile. Her smile was bland, like someone reacting to a joke they didn't understand. She explained the dish to me: 'Reindeer meat fried in oil, seasoned with salt and pepper. It's cooked in beer until the meat is tender, with wild berries, sugar and pickled cucumbers. I hope you don't mind eating meat with beer?'

'Don't worry, I know what you mean,' I said. 'I don't have a god who advises me what I should eat or drink. I'm an atheist by nature.' The cook praised my accent speaking Northern and said I was the first refugee to come to the restaurant. I wanted to explain that I was no longer a refugee, but a citizen, but she went on talking: 'The refugees naturally prefer the kebab restaurant downtown. And they're right. Our tastes are linked to our memory and our mothers.'

I would have liked to hear her say more about mothers, but she went back to her kitchen, while the other woman listened to a local radio station talking about the snowstorm, which would grip the town for the next two days.

I went back to my hotel room, got undressed, and lay down naked on the bed. I took out my laptop and listened to a detailed news bulletin on the government television station of my home country, which has been bleeding for five decades. There was an analyst who belonged to the Islamic party in power, repeating the same old propaganda: the country's glorious future, regional difficulties, intervention by neighbouring states, denials of the clerics' racism. He said certain saboteurs and terrorists had no right to invoke the name of God. I felt tired, and slightly anxious about my headstrong decision to come to Sololand. Had I been too hasty? Was it my depression and loneliness that had driven me to come here? After a twelve-hour drive, masturbating might help me have a siesta. For some reason staying in a hotel always makes me horny. Maybe it was those recurring scenes in films that stuck in my mind; a beautiful woman lying in the bath with a glass of champagne and then the hero comes in naked and slips between the thighs of the heroine. On Google, I searched for sites that offered porn in my mother language.

There weren't many of them, but they did exist. Sex scenes in my mother language made me more aroused and I came quickly, sparing me too much exposure to such useless and noxious material. I often thought of finding a wife from my country, but I knew from other people's experiences that most such marriages failed. For your family and friends to choose a wife for you, and send her to you like a parcel, is very much a lottery. You might lose, you might win, but you couldn't count on it. Indeed, the chances of failure are much higher. As for finding someone through social media, that would be worse than having one's family choose. You'd need to be a psychologist or an experienced interrogator to tell the difference between the charlatans whose only interest is to escape a world of hellish violence and see you as a lifeline and those who really do have a burning desire to have an amorous adventure with someone far way that they've never met.

It was seven in the evening when I woke up. I got dressed and went out to have a cigarette. The receptionist was also smoking in the doorway. He asked me if I'd liked the Sol and said the owner was a relative of his. I told him the fish soup was good, though I had in fact eaten the reindeer. In my mind, I was devising a plan to undermine what I imagined to be his preconceptions. I had assumed in advance what he had in mind, especially when he asked what I thought of the restaurant. After all these years in the North I have considerable experience with small-minded people, especially men. I wondered what naïve idea was at work in his mind: 'You're a foreigner and you can never enjoy our food, our jokes, our music or our heritage. You only enjoy the cunts of women here, because they are very easy!' I wanted to demolish his assumptions, and even humiliate him, so I spoke to him about the best way to make fish soup, and about all the types of fish that are native to the countries of the North in general, and the lakes they come from and the right way to cook them. Of course, I didn't tell him I was an expert because of my job in the fish restaurant, and I added another lie to torment his imagination with more stereotypes, by telling him that my Northern girlfriend very much liked the way I prepared fish and that she said I could turn a fish into a piece of erotic art. The man sensed that I was exaggerating. The truth was Maija, my ex-girlfriend, preferred Eastern cuisine. We even had arguments because she stopped cooking, on the grounds that my Eastern dishes were so delicious and Northern cuisine didn't have the same sharp, fierce flavour as spicy Eastern dishes. Then, after a while, Maija started giving me advice on what I was cooking. She criticised the amount of oil I used, and my response was: 'The East is tasty because there's plenty of oil. Why don't you cook us a healthy, cold Northern meal?' Then it was the receptionist's turn to undermine my assumptions about what kind of person *he* was. He said his sister was married to an immigrant engineer. He also spoke about the engineer's cooking skills. He went on and on about his brother-in-law's qualities – his generosity, his kindness and humility. He had studied electronics at a Northern university and was now working for a large communications company, making good money. The receptionist said he had never met such an honest but modest man as this engineer. The only thing wrong with him was that he refused to go into the sauna naked with his family or friends, or even just with his wife. 'You Easterners make far too much of nakedness and bodies,' he said, but without hostility. He stubbed out his cigarette. 'Welcome to Sololand,' he added. 'Be a little careful these days, especially with the stupid fanatics. You must have heard about the rape incident and how angry people were.'

I spent my first night listening to music and browsing the internet. I had recently been trying to understand Northern heavy metal music. The heavy beat and the raucous singing were harsh and difficult for my eardrums to take, even though I grew up in a country that had seen raging wars since my childhood. My father was killed in the war with our neighbours, when we were still children. Our uncles took care of us and refused to let my mother work to support us. They gave us a basic monthly allowance and made our lives hell by interfering in every detail of our personal lives. My elder brother started working in the street market, leaving school when he was fifteen. He didn't earn enough to support the family. He was two years older than me and my sister was a year younger. By the time I went to university, we had finally broken free of the humiliating dependence on our uncles. My brother opened his own shop selling groceries and I found work in an icecream factory, where I went after school. My sister graduated from a college that taught management and economics, but then got married and stayed at home. She had four children within five years. My life in the country, like that of many, was fraught with worries, disappointments and fear of the unknown, and we were constantly forced to listen to the heavy metal music of strident warfare.

My online research into Sololand didn't produce much. There was nothing distinctive about the town, except for the dense forests, the lakes surrounding it on all sides and some farms that bred reindeer. I started looking for information about the refugee centre, in case there was a charity or some other organisation that helped them. I didn't know exactly how or where I would start offering my own services. Of course, I was thinking that I'd start by helping with interpretation. Through hearing about the worries and problems of the refugees I might be able to provide some solutions, advice or guidance. If I wasn't useful at least I could collect some material for my notional book. Eventually I found a Facebook page called 'Refugees Welcome in Sololand', with just 34 followers. The page looked old or inactive. The comments section was closed and the few posts had barely two or three reactions. There were photos of a large group of refugees playing football with three young men from the local community, and of a refugee pushing an old woman in a wheelchair. He seemed to be looking after the woman, who lived alone, and that's why he had caught the attention of the town's local newspaper. There was a link to an article, in a newspaper in a neighbouring Northern country, about the economic benefits of refugees, given the constantly declining population. Another link led to an angry anti-racist song by a well-known rapper.

I wrote a clear, precise message to the page administrators, introducing myself and saying I wanted to help the refugees and the town. Then I switched off the light and went to sleep. A nightmare struck! I woke up early, went to the bathroom and drank some water from the tap. I looked at my face, going over the details of the nightmare. I was in the Faculty of Languages with my girlfriend Mona in my university days. We were speaking French and laughing. Then I found myself in prison with a blindfold on and someone was raping Mona beside me. Someone else was asking me to speak French as I listened to my girlfriend being raped. Then a man turned up, someone all the jailers seemed to fear and respect. He asked me to recite a poem by Henri Michaux. I was amazed that the man knew I admired Michaux's poems. Of course, the nightmare had nothing to do with any real incident involving Mona, who had left me, left university and left the country after her family married her off to a rich man who lived in New York. I went back to bed, checked Facebook and Instagram on my phone, then dozed off again.

In the morning, I found an answer to my message on the Refugees Welcome in Sololand page, from someone called Marko Bohm. It was a pleasant message of welcome, with Marko saying he hoped we could meet up as soon as possible. I went down to the hotel restaurant for breakfast and found the room crowded with Japanese tourists. From the buffet I took some orange juice, bread, cheese, a boiled egg, fruit salad and coffee. I sat at a table and smiled as I watched the Japanese cheerfully move back and forth between the buffet and the tables. They made the room feel crowded, but they weren't noisy. They walked quickly and spoke to each other in such low voices that they were hardly audible, like a large family of ants. A waiter came around collecting used plates and glasses and I asked him if there was any particular tourist attraction in Sololand.

'Yes,' he said, 'but it's not on land. It's in the sky. There are some hills on the edge of town that are great for seeing the Northern lights.'

'Okay, thanks, now I understand,' I said. I picked up my coffee and went outside to smoke a cigarette. I wrote a response to Marko on my phone, thanking him and saying I was free all day and we could meet at any time that suited him. He replied immediately and sent me the address of a café close to the hotel.

Marko was in his late twenties, thin with glasses that made him look like one of those cool academic types who turn out to be murderers in TV dramas. His body language suggested mystery and intelligence. A conversation with him took longer than normal because he wasn't in a hurry to reply, but not in an annoying way. He didn't say 'mmm' or look you in the face while thinking how to answer. Instead he chose a spot somewhere around him to stare at, and when he replied he looked you straight in the eyes with a timid half-smile, and he often began his utterances with expressions that disclaimed any certainty, such as 'I'm not sure...' or 'I suppose...' or 'Maybe...' Marko was born in Sololand and had studied photography in the capital. He had a master's degree from Germany and when we met he was working at the town's local newspaper. He had been living in the capital before refugees started arriving in his hometown, and had gone back to his childhood home to live with his mother. He thought it would be hard work getting the local people to accept foreigners and refugees. He gave me a summary of the situation in the town and of the rape case.

The rapists had communicated with their teenage victim in English through Instagram and had raped her in the forest. The two young men claimed it was the girl who wanted to have sex and said she had even suggested some positions for having group sex. Some of the local men had formed a neo-

Nazi group called Fighters of the North and had started patrolling the streets, supposedly to protect the women of Sololand. Marko told me there hadn't been any serious incidents yet with the neo-Nazis, just one case where a man who was not a member of the group attacked a refugee in a bar and broke his nose. Marko said it was very important to have me in town, especially when it came to interpreting, and because I understood both cultures. There were only two professional interpreters in town and they were always busy with the immigration department, the court and the police. Then Marko spoke about the trouble he had had understanding the refugees. Few of them spoke English and some of them knew only a few words of Northern. I understood what he was saying and explained that the country we came from was in a bad way and the education system was rudimentary. For some reason, I also spoke at length about the terrible state of the health system. I asked him about his Facebook page and he confessed it was almost inactive. He had set it up with his girlfriend Lava, who worked as a director in the town theatre. They had received many insulting and sarcastic comments, and some racists had threatened them. Marko had told the police, but he was no longer very interested in Facebook because he thought that social media generally exacerbated the problem of hatred and didn't help spread awareness of the refugees' struggles.

Marko hadn't given up trying to reduce the local community's anger and shock at the presence of these unwelcome guests. He told me he was working on a simple, social initiative: one of the townspeople would invite one or more refugees to their home, and the refugees would make dinner for the host. By eating and drinking together, they would get to know each other. The food could be a bridge for communion and dialogue. Marko had tried to promote the suggestion through the newspaper where he worked, but his colleagues had dismissed the idea and made fun of it. He said the editor was a thorough racist with Nazi tendencies that he concealed from other people. Marko and his girlfriend then started promoting the idea through friends and acquaintances. They had arranged two dinners before I arrived on the scene. One of the dinners was a quiet, awkward, almost silent affair with a family that had a teenage daughter and a teenage son. The embarrassment of the refugees and the hosts, and the fact that that they didn't have a common language, meant that the dinner ended coldly, with confusion and polite smiles. But the second occasion was more than successful. A man who works in a sawmill invited four refugees to his house. The man had heard much about their cuisine and was very sympathetic towards them. He later wrote to Marko, saying he was embarrassed and sad about Sololand's racism towards these poor victims and thanking Marko for his lovely initiative in arranging the dinner parties. The man offered to cook for his refugee guests himself the next time.

I said I was ready to work with Marko on the dinner party initiative. He thanked me and advised me to introduce myself first to the refugees, in order to gain their trust, and promised to leave my phone number at the social services office in the refugee centre. He said he was sure they would need my services. Marko was watching the waitress and smiling at her from time to time. He saw that I noticed his glances at her. 'She's my niece,' he said with a smile, 'a wonderful painter and a lovely person. Her name is Laura, let me introduce you to her.'

★

My dear refugees,

Before I give my speech about this North, let me speak first about us, us refugees, who face insults and nightmares from every direction. We are the ones who spend our lives torn between two ordeals: the ordeal of going home and the ordeal of staying where we are.

I know that most of you will understand me. In fact, many of you will agree with me wholeheartedly. When you see yourself reflected in my words, some of you might jump for joy and shout: 'Fuck this for a life, this is the North, and these are the misfortunes of being a refugee!' I know some of you will be angry and take sides with the racists when they ask that poisonous question of theirs: 'Why don't you go home, given that you don't like the people in your new country?' This silly, misleading question really does embody Man's selfishness and fragility in this land of exile. But first let me tell you, in all honesty, that you and I and all refugees are sick.

My fellow refugees! I know that the virus of homesickness will creep into your head as soon as you say goodbye to your home. And I know that this virus is one of the oldest and strangest viruses in the life of Man, and so far no vaccine has been found against it, nor any effective treatment. Whether or not you can resist this disease depends wholly on your personality. There is no course of action, no road map for your exile. You have to go through all the stages of the crisis, so that finally you can live with the pain of loss. With the first step you take along the migration route, you'll feel the symptoms of the disease, but you cannot easily grasp what is happening to you. You'll go through several stages of shedding your skin as you try to deal with the severe shock of being in exile. Those who defend their new home and its people vigorously do in fact suffer from a hidden illusion: they see their new country in idealistic terms and believe that everything about it is close to perfect. Paradise is here, and Hell was there. They play down the shock of losing family and friends. They're enthusiastic about living in their new countries. They try to work even harder than necessary, denying their own feelings of fear and guilt. They are hostile to other refugees who complain about their new lives. But eventually they recoil, and their illusory peace of mind is shattered. Feelings of disappointment and shame overwhelm them and they sink into a void. Their delusions fall apart the moment they run into the first racist wall that separates them from the peace of mind they dream of restoring. Some of you will hide away in bubbles with friends from your homelands and refuse to explore your new country. At the start of this new life, you will feel paralysed and empty. Obsessively you will look for someone with whom you feel warm and safe again. And when you find that person, you will shatter them, or they themselves will make you feel even more off balance, and destroy the last remnants of your desire to forge new relationships on the rubble of your old relationships. Your feelings towards those you are attached to will be diminished. You will dream of having someone who is also vulnerable, to be your refuge and your saviour, to be your mother and brother, your house and family and friends. You will treat your new friends in the house of refuge, male and female, with extra kindness and with a sombre intimacy. You will cling to them obsessively. You are orphans who need more love and sympathy, You want a warm shoulder to cry on. You, dear refugees, go through the egg stage at first. Some of you experience that stage romantically, and others with severe depression. Remember that the only other experience as traumatic as migration under duress is the death of a life partner or a mother's loss of a child in an unexpected accident. In fact, moving to a new country under duress may be much more traumatic, because it's not a death, just a long process of dying.

In many ancient civilisations, exile was the cruellest possible punishment; dictators would expel their opponents from their territory knowing this. Exile is like a blunted guillotine blade that doesn't kill you with the first blow. It leaves a deep, serious wound and leaves you to bleed out slowly. Your wound is complex: it will have many side-effects on your personality. You will be scarred with feelings of anger and hatred. You will lose patience easily, and you will often be insistent and demanding. You will blame others for failing to meet your needs or desires. You will vent all your anger on the host country and everyone around you, although you know that it's up to you alone to make an effort to deal with the consequences of the disaster that has befallen you. Even your name, so familiar to you, will begin to sound strange. You'll feel that every day you're liable to be interrogated in a police station. 'What's your name?' This obvious question will sound like an annoying alarm clock that never stops ringing as long as you're in exile. Your name, which is just a few ordinary letters, will turn into a cross you have to bear, along with the other crosses: the colour of your skin, your features, your birthplace… so many others. Thanks to the hostility, ignorance and selfishness of the people in your new country, exile will lead you to judge harshly the home you have abandoned. That home let you down, so you abandoned it, but now it's abandoning you and you feel like you're the one that let it down. Those who stayed in your old home will see you as reckless, a traitor, a coward, selfish, seeking only your own salvation. Your friends and loved ones will die in WhatsApp and Facebook messages. Your mother died of a stroke yesterday and till the last moment she was torn apart in sadness at your departure. A childhood friend was killed in a traffic accident. Your nephew is poisoned by bad food he ate in a cheap restaurant. Your cousin is imprisoned for opposing the regime and comes out of jail paralysed. Your elder brother is going through a serious financial crisis and you have to help him. Why don't you send presents? Why don't you call more often? Have you forgotten your family? Exile has stripped you of everything. You'll turn into a spectator/suspect: suspected by everyone in your new country while you look on from afar at those who stayed behind. You're paralysed, shattered, you feel threatened: crying and moaning don't do any good.

Now you're rising again! You plunge into life. The egg stage, with its idealism and its pains, is over. You move into the nymph stage. You hop around, seeking your daily bread – emotional and physical. You struggle, accept your fate bitterly. You work at some trade that doesn't reflect the effort you put into studying or the sacrifices your family made so that you could go to university. Here you are, an engineer, washing dishes in a restaurant. And what are you going to do with your law degree? Serve kebabs to drunken, racist customers after midnight? And you, my dear, your business studies course will be a burden on you, not a tool with which to make your way in life. You have to learn a new trade, new skills. You have to forget what you learnt and what you tried to be. You have to shed your skin and slip on a new one. You have to put up with it even if it doesn't fit you. You'll have children who won't speak your mother tongue. You won't tell them stories or sing them your childhood songs. You won't understand the cartoons they watch or most of their pastimes. You'll struggle to know them at all, and they'll seem more complicated the older they grow. You won't understand their jokes, but you'll laugh at them politely. Yet they won't laugh politely if you tell them a joke they don't understand. You'll spend your life telling your hosts what you like about their country and what you hate. Imagine living in a cell with a loudspeaker that constantly asks the same questions day and night: 'What's your name? Where are you from? Do you like the winter? What do you think of our cities? Why did you leave your country? What do you think of us Northerners?' You'll discover that all these questions are just spurious variations of a single question that nags your hosts: 'Why did you come here?'

My dear refugees, at least you will begin to notice the strange symptoms of this disease called exile. In your backward countries you barely had anything to do with psychology, because psychiatrists were only for mad people. Your ignorance about your own volatile mental health will make the disease doubly severe and will give you another cancerous tumour, one that is called an inferiority complex. Your Northern hosts will play down your diseases and will try to deny their own equally serious disease: their superiority complex. Because they're at home, and their schizophrenic approach to hospitality cannot be likened to a disease. That would be ingratitude. Because they are the homeowners, and they are right whatever they do. They are the masters and you are the slaves. You know that we call the house-owner the master of the house, yes, dear refugee, he is the god of the North, the master of the house whose orders you have to obey, whose laws you have to observe, whose forgiveness you have to seek for your mistakes and for whose blessings and gifts you pray. You have to thank him day and night, without complaining about the way he behaves, because he has good reason for everything he does, even if you do not understand the reason, for he alone is omniscient, generous, experienced, civilised, democratic, intelligent and capable of everything. You refugees, whose names, skin colours and clothes smell wrong, for the rest of your lives you have to atone for the sin of coming to the land of the North without invitation. Who allowed you to travel such long distances, to cross deserts, mountains and oceans, to desecrate the land of the North, the legendary and eternal land of our forefathers?

If you complain to your hosts, for example, even timidly, about the hostile expressions of racism that you're subjected to, the happy Northerners will play down their disease. They will admit it is ugly, but they will tell you that it's just a trivial, limited condition, and they will lay the blame on the lesser educated among them, those who live in the countryside, or in small towns that are not used to the idea of mixing with foreigners. They will lead you to believe that it is a poison found only in the minds of a minority in their society, and that it does not represent the famous values of the North – the values of equality, justice and human rights. Those who deny the gravity of this racial supremacy come in different varieties. They have varying degrees of racism within them, just as you refugees carry varying degrees of the exile disease in you. Some people deny the racism out of ignorance, some out of arrogance, and others in blind defence of the idea of the North as a happy place. You won't understand their desperate attempts to downplay the problem of racism and bigotry. Instead, you should imagine a scene from a fantasy film: one of these Northerners wakes up one day and finds their skin has turned black and their faces look Eastern. Only then would they know what we're talking about when we talk about racism. That could be the theme of the film.

How often have you been surrounded by frightened, suspicious, angry looks, at work or in public places? How often have the eyes around you reminded you of the kind of CCTV cameras that the police use? How often have you felt that you're assumed to be criminal? How often have they refused to rent you a flat because of your name or the colour of your skin? How often have they avoided sitting close to you on the bus or the Metro? How often has some drunk suddenly shouted in your face, without warning and for no reason? How often have they made fun of your language, your culture and your identity? How often, as you wait in line to withdraw money from a cash machine, has someone offered to let you go first because they see you as a frightening presence when you stand behind them, and God alone knows what your intentions might be? How often has a clerk in a government office humiliated you or treated you rudely or with hatred? How often have the police given you double the usual fine for some trivial offence? How often have they refused to let you into a nightclub? How often have you sat down at the same table as a stranger and then they've walked off angrily without looking at you?

Once, I took my phone out of my pocket and an old receipt fell out by mistake. A woman came after me to tell me angrily: 'This is the North, not your rubbish country'. Then she headed to the rubbish bin and threw the receipt away, without even asking if I needed it.

How often have you been with a Northern woman and other people have tried to attack you and make fun of you? How often have you heard the expression: 'Go back to your own country, you terrorist'? How many times at an airport have you been searched with unusual thoroughness? How many times have they followed you to the plane, checking your passport for the tenth time? How many times has your job application been rejected on some feeble pretext? How often has your North-born child come back from school with racist ideas picked up from the teacher or the other children? How often have you been harassed with racial slurs? How often have they physically attacked you?

All this and much more. These happy people say the disease is under control, confined within narrow limits. They'll tell you these hostile attitudes are dying out. Remember, dear refugees, that white racism is a belief as entrenched as any other belief and the roots lie deep in their unconscious. If you're ignorant – because of wars and a poor education – and you're always asking yourself why the best health and education system in the world produces this misery and racism, then the answer is that these white people apply the law of 'deliberate ignorance'. They have been doing so for centuries, ever since they decided that their roots go back to Greek culture. Since the 19th century they have been insisting vehemently that Greekness is their identity of origin. As if it fell from the sky, without any influences from other cultures. They are the descendants of a uniquely pure, dazzling white lineage. Ever since they began obsessively opening up skulls, examining bones and writing dozens, nay hundreds, of books of enthnography, solely to prove they are superior and more entitled to rule the world. In the beginning, they carried the cross and invaded the world, in order to exorcise the devils in other people. Then the values of their cross and their religion merged with a Faustian passion for genealogy and ethnology. Their religion says we all come from the same origin, from Adam, but that does not at all suit their supremacist theories. How could we come from the same origin and be on the same level as the rest of humanity? You might think that these questions arose in the past. Remember, dear refugee, that even in this day and age some geneticists still theorise from time to time about racial superiority. These white people have a chronic disease and their racism is a schizophrenic religion: sometimes they perform its rites in secret and are embarrassed about it, while at other times they practise it openly, quite shamelessly. It is a disease that is powerfully entrenched in the social, economic and virtual environments, through history, art, literature, sociology and political sciences.

From the Romans, who massacred Jews and deprived them of citizenship in the reign of Caligula, to Hitler and his gas chambers, from Charles Darwin to James Watson, there is a long, barbaric and shameful history of desperate attempts to assert that white people are superior and should rule the world. After Darwin and *The Origin of Species*, eugenics was all the rage. There were campaigns of enforced abortions and sterilisations, genocides and apartheid. In the happy North, until the 1970s, a well-known institute continued to promote the idea of sterilising homosexuals, disabled people and immigrants. Institutes and universities financed research and theories liberally. You must have heard of James Watson, one of the discoverers of DNA, who suggested in 2000 that there is a connection between skin colour and sex. He claimed that black-skinned people have stronger sexual impulses than others and that Africans are genetically inferior. These white people have been shouting for years from scientific and academic platforms that miscegenation amounts to the suicide of the white race. In some places, interracial marriages were restricted and racial segregation became established policy. And here they are, dear refugee, the people of the happy North, with their advanced technology and in the midst of the information age, raising the banner of white centrality yet again. Behold the digital age vigorously reviving white nationalism. Behold traditional and social media feeding mass hysteria against other people. The new media have revived the racist tide. Hallelujah, superior race.

Dear refugees, congratulations! The people who have a superiority complex have taken a step forward. Today they are enforcing a new law: the law that behavioural differences based on ethnicity are unacceptable, while differences based on culture are acceptable.

Dear refugees, you are the slaves of the age.

*

Marko was right. The refugee complex in Sololand urgently needed someone who understood the language of the refugees. From day one, I threw myself into my work as an interpreter. The refugee centre was packed with young people, but there were only two families among them. The refugees spent most of their time on their mobile phones, trying to carry on the lives they had abandoned in their home countries. By day, they went into town to shop and came back loaded with vegetables, rice and meat, and with many tales of comical incidents caused by language differences. The town wasn't ready to receive the refugees, so the local authorities had given them housing in a residential complex on the outskirts, surrounded on all sides by trees and frozen lakes. The refugees described their quarters as a prison in a refrigerator. They weren't allowed to go out of town without permission from the authorities. Each refugee was given a monthly allowance to cover food and drink. Those who frequented the bars and looked for entertainment mostly borrowed money from others. It was the Red Cross that supervised the complex. There was also a social services office with four members of staff, plus two massive, sullen guards who patrolled the complex all the time. From the start, the guards weren't comfortable with my presence in the complex as a volunteer. What the refugees most needed me to do was translate the letters they received from the immigration department, the police, the health centre and their banks. I would also translate some of their simple requests, for example when they needed furniture, bed sheets, blankets and cleaning supplies. The centre provided some of these things and others came from voluntary contributions by the townspeople. The young people in the complex pooled their money to buy a PlayStation and a large TV screen to play FIFA, the virtual games between world-famous clubs being the most entertaining way of breaking the monotony and dreariness of the long winter nights.

The first problem I had to deal with was a simple matter that arose from the two sides misunderstanding each other's languages. Murad, a man in his mid-twenties, had bad teeth through his own negligence. He lost his temper with a man who worked in the social services centre because they wouldn't arrange for him to see a dentist immediately. The man explained the health system to him in English several times, but the only English Murad understood was a few greetings and a few swear words he had picked up from films. Murad shouted, 'Fuck you and fuck your system' at him and stormed out of the office. The man was very upset by Murad's behaviour and his stubbornness. Gently, I told Murad that he had to apologise to the man before I would interpret for him. The man explained to him again that it wasn't easy to get an immediate appointment with a dentist, even for the local people. That only happens in emergencies, he said. Murad wasn't in any pain and had no symptoms that required him to see a dentist immediately. The man made it clear to Murad that there was no reason for Murad to get angry with him, since he wasn't responsible for setting the rules.

Later, Murad told me he regretted coming to the North. I tried to cheer him up, reminding him that all of us refugees and immigrants had difficulties at first, but they began to adapt the more they understood what life was like in the North, and the more they saw the difficulties as just inevitable daily chores. I reminded him of a puzzling fact: we had come from the most chaotic and corrupt country in the world to the most rigidly systematic country. Here in the North following the rules and the laws was like a religion. Murad had worked as a barber before fleeing his country. He had supported his large family and was engaged to be married. He told me he had never had any problems, political or otherwise, with the sectarian religious militias. The only problem was that his work as a barber didn't produce enough income. How could he marry his fiancée, rent a house and support his wife and a family of six brothers and sisters, plus an elderly mother? His father had been killed in the recent sectarian civil war. The criminals had mutilated his father's body and thrown it onto a rubbish dump.

I began to meet the refugees one by one in the residential complex. To some extent, I was prepared for the ideas and emotions typical of the 'egg' stage, when people have random feelings about their expectations of a bright future in their new country, and they're angry and permanently disgruntled and disappointed when they come across counterexamples to the idealised image of the happy North that some of them had. But even so, many surprises came up in my work as an interpreter. For a long time, I had believed that human beings were like boxes of secrets, and this established fact had not troubled me so much as it made me inquisitive. Most of the refugees would not believe I had left the capital and my job in a restaurant in order to do volunteer work and help them. So they needed to invent a conspiracy theory that cast doubt on my sincerity – the kind of theory that flourishes in the countries of the East. After I'd been interpreting for a week, I met a young man called Jamal, who believed that half the refugees in the camp didn't deserve asylum and had come only for adventure and to make money. He told me that many of the refugees thought I was a spy for the local authorities or the police. I could see his point, and I shared with him some of the generational conflicts between refugees. Every ten or twenty years, our country bred a new generation of refugees, but instead of these different generations coming together to understand the reasons for the disasters that befell their country and seeking ways to bring about change, achieve peace and find safe ways to go home, they argued with each other, insulted each other and accused each other of treachery. Each preceding generation of refugees believed it was more worthy of asylum and international protection than the new one, and that it was better at integrating in the country of refuge and preserving the name of the culture they had left behind to wallow in the mire of war. There was always a feeling that the new refugees were tarnishing the image of the older ones, who had suffered greatly and worked patiently to be accepted by the host community.

I laughed and had plenty of fun in the first two weeks of my work as an interpreter. The cynicism of the refugees, when they compared life at home with life in the North, was astute and bitter. There's nothing so beautiful as hearing a joke in your mother tongue, something I had greatly missed in recent years. Sometimes I felt a delicious numbness in my forehead, if I merely heard someone whistling the tune of a song from my teenage years. The faces of the refugees, the smell of their food and the sound of their voices, energised me and made me feel protected, as if inside a cocoon woven out of friendliness and contentment. Of course, there was constant grumbling about the strict rules and bureaucracy, yet most of the refugees agreed that the Northerners' respect for the system and for the country's laws was the reason for their country's affluence. There was a young man called Salim who was nicknamed 'the miserly policeman' and was the butt of many jokes. Most of the people in the flats shared the costs of buying food and other essentials, but Salim thought his flatmates were very extravagant, so he kept his food separate. His flatmates said he only ate rice and what they called 'air sauce', by which they meant a potato sauce that he prepared, without any meat or beans or other vegetables. His flatmates annoyed him by filching his tea and sugar and other things. They accused him of never buying shampoo or toothpaste, instead using their supplies in the bathroom. They made jokes about his secret box, a cardboard box that originally held bananas, saying it contained stuff he had stolen from restaurants and other places: spoons, knives, a small salt cellar, glasses, toilet paper, and many other things. Salim complained of harassment to the social services office and asked for his own flat, but the answer was that such a privilege wasn't currently available.

While his flatmates shrieked excitedly over goals and missed chances in their FIFA games, Salim withdrew to the kitchen to learn Northern from a massive dictionary he had borrowed from the public library. By his own account, Salim had been a policeman back home until he uncovered some major corruption in the station where he worked, and someone had tried to kill him. The irony is that when he fled to a neighbouring country, policeman Salim worked as a fixer for migrant traffickers.

There were two niggling problems that I tried to help solve in the refugee complex. Predictably enough, one related to pregnancy and the other to alcohol. Marko, who was liked and respected by most of the refugees, knew about the first problem but not the second. In fact, the refugees nicknamed Marko 'the monk' because he was quiet, wise, good-natured and generous with his help. The pregnancy problem was serious. There was a young man called Mustafa, who was handsome and often went to the gym in the town centre. According to the others, his muscles and his athletic physique made him feel superior, especially when it came to making friends with the girls in the town. He had another advantage: he spoke good English, he was knowledgeable about Western music, and he was proficient at using social media. But his muscles didn't help him much when three men attacked him in the street one night and he was taken to the emergency ward at the hospital. Mustafa had met a girl and she had helped him get into a club that didn't let in refugees unless they had residence permits. After a while, the girl became pregnant by Mustafa. But apparently the girl also had a boyfriend who was in prison for dealing drugs, and the boyfriend sent the three men to beat Mustafa up. They threatened to kill him if he didn't leave the girl alone and get out of town. Mustafa didn't tell the police because he was afraid and embarrassed. The girl was demanding he take responsibility for the baby, while her boyfriend was a serious threat to his life. It seemed to me at the time that most of the problems, whether caused by the refugees or the people of the town, began with alcohol, drugs or sex. Apparently, there's nothing new under the sun. Then they were exacerbated by the unspoken racism that runs in the veins of the system and because both sides, the 'hosts' and the 'guests', were willing to blow misunderstandings out of proportion.

The other problem concerned a man in his late thirties called Qais al-Zuhairi. Zuhairi apparently came home very drunk one night and exchanged some words with the guards, which led to an argument. Zuhairi didn't say exactly what the problem was, just that he had drunk too much whisky but that he wasn't aggressive. All he could remember was that he woke up lying on the floor in a small room. It seems he had vomited so hard that blood come up from his stomach. The guards had held him in the room all night. The next day Zuhairi went to the doctor and he was in a bad state so they kept him in hospital. Zuhairi thought he could take his drink. He rarely vomited and that was usually the end of the matter. But this time he felt dizzy and had a severe pain in his guts. He thought that the guards had abused their authority and handled him with excessive force, and that they should have taken him to hospital that night instead of locking him up in a cold, bare room all night. I told him he should submit a complaint to the social services office or even the police if he thought he had been a victim of racial discrimination. I went to chat with the guards about what had happened to Zuhairi. They were clearly annoyed and one of them said I was interfering in things that didn't concern me. They asked me not to come to the residential complex because officially I didn't work there as an interpreter.

I suggested to Marko that we start an awareness campaign on the legal rights of refugees. Marko agreed and said that one of the most common problems was that refugees and immigrants didn't report hate crimes and incidents of racial discrimination. He told me this was why there was a dire shortage of accurate statistics on hate crimes. In the latest surveys on the subject, he found that 80% of cases of racial discrimination were not reported. Someone had done a survey on the reasons, and the results showed that most foreigners didn't trust the police because they didn't think the police took such reports seriously.

In my work as an interpreter, there were many funny incidents, and some that were saddening. One day, I went to the health centre with a mother and her daughter to interpret for them. When we reached the doctor's examination room the woman clammed up because she was so embarrassed. The doctor didn't understand the problem, and then I gathered from her daughter that she would prefer to be examined by a woman doctor and have a woman interpreter. The doctor understood and referred her to a woman doctor. But there was still the problem of finding a woman interpreter. We came to a solution. The girl suggested that she explain the problem to me without her mother being present, and then I in turn would explain to the doctor. The mother waited outside the room, while the daughter and I explained the mother's case to the doctor. Then the mother came in and I left, while the daughter stayed in the room. Then the mother came out and I went in to interpret what the daughter said her mother had said. After some back and forth we established that the mother had an itching in her vagina, so the doctor sent her to the laboratory for some tests. Before I left, one of the nurses turned to me and said, 'You should explain to them that women in the North don't live in the Middle Ages.'

'There's no need to be annoyed,' I replied. 'With a little patience and understanding, things can improve.'

After the case of translating the problem of 'the thing between the legs', as the embarrassed daughter put it, I went to the café where Laura worked. On the way, I saw a foot patrol being conducted by the Fighters of the North. They were all wearing black leather jackets, decorated with a picture of what looked like a monster of some kind. A police car approached them and the officer in the car exchanged some words with the patrol, smiling broadly. The police car then moved on. The café had no customers and Laura was setting some tables and dancing to a song. She greeted me and asked how I was. 'So far so good,' I replied, and ordered a coffee with milk and a glass of water. I asked her about the emblem on the racists' jackets and she said these vicious idiots had adopted Odin, a god of war in Norse mythology, as their mascot. They were just stupid, with nothing to do but hate foreigners, gay people and women. If they couldn't find anyone to hate, they would start biting each other like wild animals, she said. Three young men came into the café and Laura went off to take their orders. One of them looked at me with contempt. They sat down in the corner and each of them opened his laptop. Then they started discussing something or other. Laura turned down the music but she went on swaying and dancing to herself. I watched her dance moves from time to time as I wrote some notes about my work as an interpreter, about the refugees' troubles and various anecdotes from the stories they had told me. Laura was the opposite of stereotypical Northerners, who sometimes strike me, in some magical way, as statues that have accidentally come to life. Laura was cheerful, she had a clear voice and the lively way she moved suggested she had grown up on the seashore under a warm sun. The darkness hadn't worn away her spontaneity and the harsh cold hadn't dampened her spirits. The way she looked at you was deep and entrancing.

Marko called me and reminded me that his girlfriend Lava's play was on. I had been so preoccupied with my interpretation work that I had forgotten all about it. I asked Marko if he had any new volunteers for the 'dinner with refugees' initiative. 'Yes,' he said, 'I do have a host. She's called Katrina and we'll talk about the details when we meet.'

I wrote down some notes on Sami's case. He was the person I sympathised with most in the refugee complex and I hoped I could help. Sami was nineteen, he spoke little, rarely complained and made few demands. He was only interested in asking about the education system in the North. An American drone had killed his parents and younger sister when he was thirteen. The family was on its way home from the wedding of a relative when a house was suddenly bombed. His sister and his father were killed instantly, but he watched his mother die slowly. Her guts spilled out onto the pavement and no one was willing to help Sami or his mother. The drone fired another missile: the Americans usually struck twice. There had been a meeting of resistance leaders in that house when the family happened to be passing. Sami ended up in his uncle's house, an orphan with an amputated hand and shrapnel fragments buried in his back. His aunt wasn't very receptive to the idea of adopting the boy. To stop the disagreement coming to a head, Sami's uncle took him to an orphanage. After all the country was in the midst of civil war. So Sami grew up in an orphanage, where the services and management were poor. But then he ran away and hung out with street kids. When he was fifteen, he was imprisoned in a youth detention centre for stealing a motorbike. When he came out of jail he decided to flee the country. He reached the North after a long and arduous journey, like many refugees. Sami loved video games. He told me his dream was to get his residence papers so that he could study video game design, especially as the North was strong in technology and game design. As we were walking in the forest one time, he said he wished he knew the names of all the trees, plants and rocks. I told him the names of some trees that I recognised. A week late I bought him a detailed book on forest plants and we began to meet from time to time for me to translate excerpts from the book.

I liked the intelligent dialogue in Lava's play and the restrained, simple acting. The presenter of a chat show on a local radio station was the only character on stage. Listeners appeared on a screen in the middle of the stage, calling in to the show, which was broadcasting live. The listeners chose public issues on which they wanted to state their opinion: climate change, political parties, the economy, refugees, unemployment and other subjects. Not much happened and the conversations between the presenter and the callers were the substance of the show. The presenter was playful and treated serious subjects lightheartedly and intelligently. We saw one of the callers sitting on the toilet with a bottle of beer in his hand, accusing politicians across the world of wrecking the planet. We heard a child crying in the background in the caller's house. A woman driving her car talked on speakerphone about women and the hijab. The presenter tried to warn the woman about some racist words that couldn't be used on his programme. The presenter noticed that she was driving and asked where she was going, She said she was going to visit her mother, who was dying in hospital and whom she hadn't seen for two years. Tears glistened in the woman's eyes and she wiped them away. Then she said that the hijab is an insult to the feelings of women and to humanity in general. I was interested in the character of an old man of Jewish origin, who was sitting in his garden peeling an orange and talking to the presenter about the history of Jewish refugees in the town of Sololand. He was clearly speaking in generalities and wanted to remind the audience that people are selfish. Persistently, he urged people to be sympathetic towards the new refugees in the countries of the North. He said Jewish refugees had moved to Sololand in the 1930s in a very poor state, and the government gave them no assistance. It was Jewish organisations that tried to help them with the hardships of life. After 1941 their conditions grew worse. They were sent into isolation in the countryside, and some of them were used to carry out hard labour. In a written account of the experience, one of the Jewish refugees said they were forced to work until their fingers bled. Later, they were put into special camps, where they faced intense hostility and accusations of treason from the locals and the police, who interrogated them repeatedly. Some of them were handed over to the Gestapo, and some were executed. Others disappeared.

It was obvious that Lava, who wrote and directed the play, was speaking about the delicate relationship between people's personal interests and the interests of the wider world. In many cases, our ideas are delusions or assumptions that we filter through our emotions to make random judgments. Maybe the actors were addressing a familiar idea, just to remind us: that blaming our problems on others is the easiest way to hide our ignorance and our personal failings. At least that was my personal reading of the play. As the play continued, the calls from listeners illustrated more of the ironies of human life. It emerged that the presenter himself had personal problems of his own, as much as anyone in real life or in films. He was drinking heavily and his girlfriend had cheated on him with one of his colleagues. His peace of mind was shattered and deep down he had started to feel bitter about life. The play ended with a comic scene that suddenly turned into tragedy. The presenter was very drunk and a caller was talking about the refugees' culture, which he called 'rape culture'. The caller sounded confident about everything he was saying. The presenter asked him if he was widely travelled and had learned about other people's cultures, customs and traditions. The man said he had never left the town he was born in. The presenter asked him what books he had read on the subject. The caller replied that he had seen a documentary on an American TV channel about rape in Eastern communities and the film included evidence that their Satanic religion taught them all kinds of evil things. The presenter suddenly had a stroke and fell off his chair. At this point, the producer and one of his assistants come in and try to help the presenter. In the meantime we can see the caller on screen, continuing his attack on the Eastern culture of hatred. It went dark, the actors disappeared but the caller remained on screen, continuing to talk from what appeared to be a forest, with an electric saw in his hand. Then he noticed that the call had been cut off. He turned off his phone and started cutting up a tree: the sound of the saw grew louder in the darkness of the theatre.

The audience clapped and streamed out into the theatre bar.

I sat with Marko, Laura and the actors. Lava was happy that the opening night had gone so well. They opened a bottle of champagne and started to celebrate. I drank a glass with them, in order to avert the obvious curiosity: 'You don't drink for religious reasons?' If your skin is white, then for sure you don't drink for health reasons or simply because you don't like alcohol. It's like the colour and background of people who commit crimes. Unless they are white, anyone who kills innocent people is a terrorist, whereas white criminals are just mentally ill, driven to carry out massacres by complicated family situations. Laura noticed my discomfort. In fact, I had received a barrage of smiles from most of the crowd that had started drinking in the bar. When you're faced with so many smiles, it gets hard to tell what message each smile is sending: friendliness, welcome, contemptuous pity or covert hostility? As we were standing to urinate in the toilets, a man in a formal suit asked me if I had understood any of the play. I assumed he wasn't asking about the overt or hidden meaning of the play, but simply about my proficiency in the Northern language. I told him I was from the capital, spoke the language well and was a Northern citizen. 'Of course, you're a Northern citizen!' he said with a laugh. I washed my hands and left him standing, struggling to force the first drop of urine out of his cock. Clearly it was hard for him to urinate. I went back to the bar and everyone was smiling at me again, as if someone's pet had suddenly walked into the wrong room. I went outside for a smoke and Laura followed me. 'Is everything okay?' she asked.

'Oh yes, yes,' I said. Then I tried to explain away my discomfort by telling her that I wasn't very sociable. I made a remark about the town of Sololand and how it didn't seem to be accustomed to foreigners. I told her about the torrent of stupid smiles I had received.

'It's true our town is small and unfamiliar with strangers,' said Laura, 'but I think that most of the audience were trying to be nice to you. As you know, refugees and immigrants don't come to the theatre or other artistic events.'

'That's true. Maybe I'm exaggerating because I'm a shy person, or maybe most of us, us refugees, have a persecution complex, I don't know. But I don't think it's because I'm angry or afraid. Maybe. What I do know is that I'm grateful I live here in the North, and in order to improve their relationships people need to work harder and try new ways of thinking. But I like to think about relationships calmly. In fact, even in the capital there are public places where people are surprised and sometimes disapproving when a non-white person comes in. There are looks and smiles and comments sometimes that send the message: "What's this guy doing in our museum, or our theatre, fancy restaurant or art exhibition? The place we're meant to meet them is on the Metro, in restaurants and in the news."'

Laura said she understood, things would change with time and she thought that humankind in general was a failed experiment on planet Earth, because people were, by nature, destructive and out of tune with the environment because of their selfishness and because they knew all too well that they were just ephemeral nobodies. I liked the way she spoke, so I smiled.

'So what does your smile means?' she asked. I tried to clarify but she interrupted me: 'I'm joking! Listen, there's a great DJ at the club tonight. Let's go there and ditch this pretentious theatre crowd whose smiles upset you.' On our way to the club, we saw a parked police car with three refugees nearby. I asked Laura if she could help me find somewhere to live in the town, because the hotel was expensive. 'Of course, for sure,' said Laura, 'after the club we'll go to your new home. As long as I'm with you, you can relax, you over-anxious and over-sensitive interpreter of ours!' Then she grabbed the cigarette from between my lips and said, 'By the way, I'm gay.' She started blowing smoke like someone who didn't really know how to smoke.

★

I opened my eyes and Laura's face was asleep in front of me. I examined her face and she opened her eyes. 'Good morning,' she said. Her mouth had a strong, annoying smell. I didn't say anything. 'Cat got your tongue?' she said with a smile.

'The smell of my breath, after all the alcohol and the cigarettes I smoked, is probably even more horrendous than the smell of yours,' I said.

'Fuck you,' she replied, pulling the sheet off the bed and heading to the bathroom. She slept in black panties and a green t-shirt with a picture of an owl on it. I sat on the edge of the bed and looked around. It was a large studio apartment, clean, tidy and very opulent. Laura came out of the bathroom wrapped in a towel. 'Look away,' she said as she started dressing. 'Do you like your new home?' she asked.

'What do you mean?' I asked.

Laura opened the fridge and poured two glasses of fizzy water. I had a terrible headache.

'What I mean is you need a place to stay, and this will be your home. I know it's modest.'

'Please, don't make fun of me. Modest? I'm sorry but it looks like it belongs to a millionaire, not a young artist who works in a café in Sololand.'

'Really?' said Laura. Then she starting picking up some paintings and putting them away in a cupboard. It was clear she didn't want me to see them. 'This was my father's studio. He died of lung cancer two years ago. My father was a famous painter and he made a lot of money with his paintings. What do you say I order a pizza?'

'Thanks, great!' I replied as I went into the bathroom.

We tucked into the pizza and washed it down with lots of Coca Cola. 'Your father must have been a genius,' I said.

Laura gave a short, theatrical laugh. 'You think rich artists are geniuses? You clearly don't know the truth about the art market. The paintings on the wall are by my father,' she replied. They were abstract paintings, with strong colours and criss-cross lines, the kind of paintings that make you think that anyone could have painted them and we ordinary people don't understand why they are so valuable. Laura launched into a long explanation: 'My father was a major asshole and a drunk and he smoked like a chimney. He never came to terms with the idea that his daughter was lesbian, though he pretended he was a free-thinking artist and didn't care. When he was an unknown artist, he didn't like the idea of an artist selling his paintings, so when he took part in an art exhibition he put exorbitant prices on his paintings, so that no one would even think of buying one. Who would buy an abstract painting by an unknown artist at some astronomical price? But apparently there are always stupid people in the world and their mission is to turn worthless things into things of value. That's the art market! His fantastical prices caught the attention of some rich people, because people started making jokes about the prices whenever they were sold, and some rich people would buy them as an act of defiance. My father raised his prices out of perversity, but they persisted in buying his paintings whatever the price. It was like a game, with my father saying "You can't buy my art" and the rich people reminding him that their money could buy anything. This game spread in the press and the other media, bringing even more attention to his work, from rich people and even from people who weren't interested in art in the first place. The story began to spread around the world and my father became a star. He couldn't resist the whirlwind of fame. He gave in and his paintings started to be bought and sold at unimaginable prices and his wealth kept growing. That's the story, dear interpreter. Of course, you'll ask why the daughter of a wealthy artist would work as a waitress in a café. Firstly, I own the café and I opened it in memory of my brother, who drowned as a teenager. In the café, we sell the pastries Sololand is famous for. You have to try one!' Laura gave me a key to the studio and stressed that I had to sort the rubbish for recycling. Everything had to be in its proper place: paper, leftover food, plastics, cardboard, tin cans, glass, batteries and empty medicine containers.

I packed my bags, moved out of the hotel and went to live in the studio. Laura told me we could agree on the rent later. For the first time, I felt settled and relieved that I had found a place to live. I became more actively interested in the refugees' concerns and stepped up my efforts to make them aware of their legal rights. I discovered that most of them hadn't applied for assistance from the lawyer's office that offered free services to refugees. As soon as I alerted them to their rights, they started hanging around at the social services office, demanding to meet a lawyer. The staff in the office were taken by surprise when the refugees went on the offensive, asserting their rights. One of the refugees betrayed me to the staff, claiming I had incited them to turn against the social services office and the complex management, and that I had asked the refugees to complain to the media about mismanagement and racism. The social services office closed ranks with the guards, who then asked me not to visit the residential complex uninvited. They would call me when they needed my services.

I later discovered who had informed on me. We were gathered one day in the flat of Salim, the 'miserly policeman'. There were guests from other flats. We were talking about things in general and the conversation turned to the subject of women's freedom, status and power here in the North, compared to the shameful situation of women in the East. Some of them had ideas that stank of male chauvinism. Some of the refugees thought our women didn't need to be as liberated as Northern women. The idea annoyed me and I spoke on the subject at length, attacking the clannish and patriarchal mentality in our homeland. I asked why there was so much fear of freedom for women. 'I don't understand the problem with women joining us in cafés, for example, and playing dominos with us,' I said. 'What's the problem if they have relationships in the open – a boyfriend or just a friend outside the institution of marriage?'

A refugee called Majid, who had been a baker at home, strongly objected: 'You think women need to play dominoes in cafés? We have to give them a decent life in our country first.'

'But what does "a decent life" mean?' I replied, 'and why should you decide what women need? Why don't you ask your sister, for example, if she'd like to go to the café like you, and see what she says?'

Majid seemed to be annoyed that I had used his sister as an example. He stood up angrily and, in a trembling, aggressive voice, said, 'Don't bring my sister into this, understand? We're a conservative society and we have our own customs and traditions, and we don't have to jump through hoops just because we're refugees here in the North.' Then he stormed out and slammed the door behind him. A chaotic discussion ensued in the flat. The refugees fired questions at each other, and fired answers back. Yes, women in our country need to be liberated for the sake of peace. The North is based on moral degeneracy. Why are we linking ethics with women? What are ethics in the first place? We want to worship women's bodies while giving all the rights to men. Is religion the problem?

Marko came to visit me in the studio as soon as he heard I'd been banned from the refugee complex. He was sorry about what had happened and said he had a friend in the Immigration Department and would speak to him. I told him I was still in touch with the refugees by phone and I was meeting them in the town centre. They brought me their letters and their problems and I translated for them, gave them advice and suggestions. Marko told me he wouldn't be able to attend the dinner to be hosted by our new volunteer, Katrina, because he had to go to the capital for his brother's wedding. He said he would depend on me, adding that I would manage better than he would because I knew the language and culture of both sides. Katrina worked as an anaesthetist in the local hospital, but she was off sick at the moment. She lived in an isolated house in the forest, thirty minutes away by car. I said I was willing to take part in the dinner. I asked Marko about some details: how many guests should we choose, and how should they be chosen, for example? He said Katrina had told him the number of guests wasn't a problem, and we agreed I would choose three refugees. I told him I'd try to ensure some diversity in the views of the refugees, to show the host the simple fact that refugees are not a homogeneous group with the same ideas, interests and ideological inclinations. Marko agreed and suggested we take care to clean up after the dinner. I could contact him at any time if I needed any help, he added. I asked whether it would be awkward or inconvenient to have a group of strange men in the home of a single woman living alone in the forest. Marko said he had hinted at this to Katrina and she said he might invite a woman friend to join us for the evening.

The night before the dinner, I prepared two kinds of kebba, one with bulgur wheat and one with rice. I thought of inviting Laura to it but I dropped the idea when I started imagining having sex with her. I didn't know if she had any experience with men. My fantasies about wanting to have sex with Laura drove me to take a peek at the paintings she had hidden in the cupboard. Most of them were of men with exaggeratedly childish faces They seemed rather harsh and frightening. The one I liked best showed a man asleep on a bed, with the face of a child and the body of a man in his forties. Lying on the floor nearby was a young woman who looked like a cartoon character, staring at the ceiling with a devilish smile.

★

Omar, Sami, Karwan and I met to discuss what kind of food we would cook for Katrina our host. I was very interested in having Sami attend. He didn't really want to come to the dinner but he eventually agreed after I insisted: I wanted to give him a break from the isolation of the complex. Omar suggested we cook rice with three types of vegetables in sauces: aubergine, okra and green beans, the best known features of our local cuisine. Karwan objected, saying that most Northerners drank alcohol with their food and the rice and sauce would be too heavy on the stomach, so he suggested dolma, stuffed vegetables of some kind, instead. Omar made fun of that idea: 'So stuffed vine leaves are a light dish with alcohol?' he said.

'Have you ever drunk a bottle of beer in your life?' asked Karwan.

'God forbid. I would never make God angry,' replied Omar.

'And the dolma should be stuffed vine leaves,' added Karwan.

Omar objected again: 'I know they like stuffed vine leaves where you come from, but chard is essential if it's be to real dolma.'

Eventually Sami piped up, weakly and shyly: 'It's hard to find chard or vine leaves in the Sololand shops. You can only get them in some ethnic shops in the capital.'

In the end I suggested we make *dolma* with cabbage leaves. 'I'll also cook fish. The meal will lose its identity, but never mind,' I added. 'If she doesn't like our wonderful Eastern cuisine, she might at least like the great way we cook Northern fish,' I concluded lightheartedly. I called Katrina and told her we'd arrive around six o'clock. She said she would get the sauna ready and she'd be waiting for us. We filled the trunk of my car with the food and drink and I drove the refugees to the refugee centre. They were going to have showers, change their clothes and I would come by in two hours. I went back to the studio, had a shave and wrapped up my present for Katrina.

I had chosen Omar and Karwan for the *Hosting Guests* initiative because they best represented the two opposite types among the refugees. Karwan was uncommitted religiously, in fact he was hostile to religion, which, as he put it. paralysed and hampered talent in our society. Omar, in his early thirties, was religious but not fanatical. He was inclined towards Sufism and he was a skilled calligrapher. Omar thought the problem wasn't with religion, but with the behaviour of some religious people. Karwan tried to portray himself as open-minded, tolerant, liberated and adventurous. Some said he had been a lieutenant in the army, but Karwan denied that. He suggested the refugees forget their murky pasts and adapt to the rules and values of the society they were now part of, so that they could move on with their lives successfully. His constant slogan was a popular proverb of ours: 'Stranger, be polite.' Omar's slogan was 'My God is my refuge, my home and the one I love.' Once he said, 'Of course we have to thank and respect the community that has taken us in, but that doesn't mean we have to adopt its values or its culture or religion.' In this context. he quoted the famous Quranic verse that advocates religious tolerance: 'You have your religion and I have mine.' As for Sami, it was my sympathy for him and my desire to be a friend and brother to him that led me to invite him. I thought he needed to open some new windows in his life, not look back at the nightmares of the past.

After turning off the main road, I drove carefully along narrow, unpaved tracks through lines of pine trees. The forest was buried under snow, but the sky was clear. I was anxious about Karwan: he seemed to be slightly tipsy and he had drowned himself in some powerful aftershave, something that most Northerners wouldn't understand, since they have allergies to just about everything. Sami was silent throughout the journey and from time to time he took out his phone to take a picture through the car window. Omar broke the barrier of silence by asking me how I would characterise Northern society. It took me a while to think of an answer. Then I said, 'Listen, Omar my friend, personally I don't like generalisations or speaking about a whole society. It's beyond my powers. Suppose I asked you how you'd characterise society in our country, for example.'

'They're the best people in the world. They get angry easily and they forgive easily,' Omar replied, full of confidence and pride, and we all laughed. What Omar said is a common idea about society back home, but it's just a superficial generalisation.

'Okay, my friends,' I continued, 'a few years ago a research centre in the North did a survey, asking large groups of young people to describe their own society. They had a list of possible characteristics, such as envious, rigid, hard-working, nature-loving, cool, honest, xenophobic.'

'Xenophobic? Maybe a few of them!' interrupted Karwan.

'Are you okay? You look a little drunk,' I asked him.

He laughed dismissively, and said, 'Don't worry, I've been drinking since I was a teenager.'

'I'm not sure if we should be reassured by that or worried,' I replied. Sami opened the window and some cold refreshing air blew into the car. I took a deep breath and continued, 'In fact, stereotypical ideas can be deadly. We all know that Northerners, and Westerners in general, revere individuality. But we often criticise them for being burdened by stereotypes about strangers. I would say that, in spite of their deep faith in individualism, they treat refugees and immigrants as though they're a monolithic group with a single set of values, ethics and patterns of behaviour, and not as individuals. It's true that stereotypes make us feel safe within the confines of the herd, but they arise from laziness, ignorance and facile thinking. It's like canned ideas ready-made for lazy minds. And the contents of those cans are often old and rotten. Stereotypes ignore the fact that you are human beings capable of independent thought. They kill off the creativity inside you and stifle your imagination. Personally, I do my best to be balanced in my relationships with others and the world.' Then I told them I wanted to write a book about refugees and their new homes, with the title *Tough Love*. Karwan said the title made it sound like a romantic film. 'You're right,' I said, as I parked the car outside Katrina's house.

It was a two-storey wooden house urgently in need of repair. It looked a little shabby, with the paint peeling off. Some wooden planks had been dislodged from the roof and there was a small hut nearby for chopping and storing firewood. There was an old Saab outside, covered in so much snow that it looked like a piece of *halwa*. Katrina came out to meet us. She was in her mid-forties, with thin red hair. Her face showed signs of a beauty faded by time and one had the impression that her life had not been easy or comfortable. My first thought was that she had made a strange choice of attire for such an occasion. She had squeezed herself into a very tight, sexy dress made of a single piece of leather. The dress seemed to restrict her movements and showed off her legs rather provocatively. Her large breasts protruded and the dress barely covered the nipples. The dress looked even stranger than it might have because it clashed with the appearance of the house on the inside, which suggested that several drunks lived there and that nobody had thought of cleaning or tidying the house for a long time. There were empty bottles of beer and wine and the remains of meals everywhere.

We sat in a large living room that opened onto the kitchen. I gave Katrina the present and thanked her for the invitation. I introduced myself and asked my friends to introduce themselves too, and I started translating for them. Katrina didn't open the present, just put it aside. She said she was allergic to mobile phones, so it would be better if we turned them off. 'Of course,' I said, and looked at the others. Katrina went into a room nearby and fetched a small wooden box to collect our mobile phones, then took the box back to the room. 'First time I've heard of someone being allergic to mobile phones,' Omar whispered. Karwan replied, 'You're living in the age of the dinosaurs, Omar. Haven't you heard of allergies to WiFi, mobile phones and computers? They call it electronic allergy.'

'Would you like some juice?' Katrina asked. 'I know your religion doesn't permit you to drink alcohol, but is it okay if I drink?'

We all smiled. We hadn't expected such a stereotypical start to the dinner. Karwan said we all drank alcohol, except for Omar, who was worried his god might get angry. 'No, I don't drink either,' said Sami. 'But not because it's banned. I just don't like the taste.' Katrina showed no curiosity about what we were going to cook or about us as people. She was clearly uncomfortable and anxious, and she was looking at the wall clock every now and then. Maybe she was waiting for her friend to arrive to join us for dinner. We put our stuff down in the kitchen and I told Katrina it would take at least two hours to prepare and cook the food. I told her as a joke that in the East we cook for hours and hours and then gobble up everything in five minutes. She didn't react and her face looked tense. She said she needed more firewood for the sauna. Omar went out to chop up some wood, while Sami and I set about preparing the food and Karwan sat near Katrina at the dining table. They started drinking and tried to communicate with signs and a few English words. Again, I warned Karwan about the irresponsible way he was drinking. He started with whisky, and then vodka like Katrina. From time to time, he helped himself to the bottle of wine that I was drinking from slowly. Karwan covered the table with plates of mezzes – pistachios, jajik, chickpeas, tabbouleh, pomegranate, hummus, popcorn and green beans. He asked me to translate what Katrina was saying. I told him she was asking if all these plates were his dinner and if he was vegetarian. Karwan laughed and explained to Katrina the importance of mezzes, especially with strong alcohol.

Then he asked her what she thought of the refugees in the town. 'Closing the borders is the answer,' was her cold reply. I told her there was a French proverb that went 'When the door's closed, the devil turns away', and I tried to use the ambiguity inherent in the proverb to air some of my ideas on solidarity with other people and how to deal with strangers, but she wasn't interested in what I was saying. She just interrupted me, said 'I'll check the sauna', and went off.

When we'd been in the host's house for an hour, the sauna was ready. I suggested to Katrina that she use the sauna first, and then us. Omar said he didn't want to use the sauna and an argument broke out again between him and Karwan: over religion, values, the new society. Karwan was drunk and spoke to Omar in an impolite, sneering manner. 'You lot are going to have fun in the afterlife. Let us have our fun in this life,' he said.

'Who's stopping you having fun?' asked Omar. 'You speak about personal freedom,' he added, 'and you criticise religion, sometimes with good cause and sometimes without. But you don't respect my personal freedom not to drink, and not to join you in the sauna. Is drinking alcohol and having saunas a measure of how civilised or uncivilised one is?'

Katrina wanted us to go to the sauna first. Omar stayed in the kitchen to put the final touches to the dolma in the pot and the fish in the oven. Sami and I kept our underclothes on, while Karwan stripped completely naked and smiled like a devil. He started explaining to us the proper procedure for using the sauna: 'First, have a shower and drink two glasses of water before going in, then warm up your body in the sauna for about ten minutes, then have another shower and drink refreshing liquids before going in again.'

Sami and I laughed. 'Refreshing liquids doesn't mean that whisky you're drinking,' I said. The sauna had two doors, one connecting it to the house and the other opening on to the backyard, which we were using for drinking, smoking and cooling off after the heat in the sauna.

We were surprised when Katrina came in naked. 'If you don't mind,' she said and sat down on the wooden bench between me and Karwan. I thought of asking Sami and Karwan to leave, to give the lady of the house some privacy, but I was too embarrassed to say anything. I stood up and wished them a pleasant sauna. Sami followed me and Katrina said, 'Don't you trust yourselves?'

'Sorry, what do you mean?' I asked.

'Being with a woman in the sauna,' she said. 'Here, being naked has nothing to do with sexual arousal or animal instincts.' I was annoyed at the way she spoke and I left without comment. Karwan stayed in her company and started cackling like an idiot. We heard him describing us as retarded as we got dressed. We went to join Omar, who said, 'A quarter of an hour and the food will be ready.' Sami and I started to lay the table.

Everything happened at lightning speed, like a nightmare. Like someone who rushes into a forest and suddenly falls in a hole and breaks his ribs. Like a boy chasing a butterfly in a field until a mine left over from an ancient war explodes under his feet. Like lovers singing in their car together until a truck loaded with iron bars crushes their song and their car.

First we heard Katrina and Karwan shouting from inside the sauna. Katrina came into the living room wrapped in a white towel and started screaming: 'Animals… harassers!' Karwan came after her, wrapping a purple towel around his waist and in a hysterical state. He was talking so fast we couldn't make out exactly what he wanted to say. He came up to me and started shaking me violently by the shoulders and asking me to translate for him. He was shouting, 'It was that whore who was harassing me! And then she started shouting in my face and saying I was trying to rape her, the lying bitch!' What with Karwan in hysterics and Katrina screaming too, we didn't have a chance to find out what exactly had happened. I thought Karwan was drunk and maybe he really had groped her. Katrina went to her bedroom and we tried to calm Karwan down, but he was so drunk and so angry that it had the opposite effect. His towel fell down and he spun round naked like an angry bull, speaking non-stop, sometimes addressing us and sometimes the room where Katrina was. 'You don't know who I am, you scum! You idiots, you retards! This bitch thinks I groped her rotten cunt. Do you know what I left behind when I came here? Have you seen how beautiful my wife was? Do you know how prominent I was in my city? You're nobodies, nothing. You low-down lying whore. I was a respected senior officer. You? Who are you? And this horrible bitch.' When Karwan tried to follow Katrina into her bedroom, Omar threw him to the floor. Sami tried to persuade Karwan to drink some water in the hope he might sober up. I went into Katrina's room to speak with her. She was on her mobile phone, sobbing and weeping in a strangely dramatic way. 'I love you. Why are you late? They're raping me! They're raping me,' she said. I tried to speak to her but she shouted in my face: 'Don't come near me, you pig.'

I heard the sound of a car pulling up outside. The front door burst open and a massive man with long hair and a thick beard came into the living room carrying a hunting rifle. The man opened fire and Omar fell. Then he shot at Karwan. I ran towards the bathroom and Sami rushed upstairs to the second floor. I locked the bathroom door from the inside. My arms and legs shaking, I listened to the man's footsteps as he ran up the wooden staircase. Then I heard two shots. Katrina was still screaming hysterically: 'What are you doing? You're crazy. What are you doing? Stop, stop. We didn't agree to this. You're crazy.' Then I heard the man shouting back at her, calling her a whore. Moments later he started kicking at the bathroom door.

★

Dear mice,

Please don't feel insulted. It's not meant to be insulting or contemptuous. It's just a description of the reality of your lives as refugees in the laboratories of this happy, democratic, civilised North. If you didn't happen to be born under the blazing sun and your skin didn't turn as brown as barley bread, you would be happy now, blessed with the benefits of having a clean, pure white complexion. You would receive generous hospitality and enjoy all the pleasures of being a guest granted everything that is special, beautiful and wonderful. If you had names that didn't give away your origins, your hosts would have done everything possible to win your approval, by sharing their houses, their culture, their paintings and their music. Your hosts would even feel embarrassed if they were remiss towards you or if their customs at home seemed naïve. But you are not guests with privileges. You are merely fugitives from the prisons in which you used to live. You are potential criminals that need to prove their innocence, so that the system can give you a certificate of pardon. Remember that any hospitality towards you is obligatory once you have crossed their sacred borders. But they can't stand the international laws that require protection of the persecuted, though they helped draft those same laws in the first place, if only to express their commitment to humanitarian values. In fact, they can't stand most of the humanitarian laws they boast about night and day. You are scary, troublesome guests, and hospitality means you must submit to the law when in the houses of your hosts. It doesn't mean tolerance of any mistake or fault. We, your hosts, are not obliged to behave appropriately or try to win your favour. You are barbarians seeking refuge, not distinguished guests towards whom hospitality requires us to behave well. It's you who have to try doubly hard to satisfy us so that we will accept you, and the least you can do is make us feel that taking you in is worth it, and receive our hospitality with gratitude, by working hard at cleaning the streets, serving food in our restaurants, cleaning windows in the offices of our smart companies and wiping the asses of our elderly, and allow our hospitality towards you to provide good material for our comedy programmes. Fugitives, prove to us that you haven't brought with you the prison values, mental illness, filth, brutality and savagery of your police-state countries. You can prove this by simply living and dying on the margins, and never raising your voices.

Laboratory mice are raised and kept in laboratories for purposes of scientific and medical research, Throughout history, the mice have made great sacrifices and have provided significant services to humanity in the testing of medicines and the study of diseases. Of course, you know why mice were chosen. There are some similarities between the organs of mice and those of humans. Statistics show mice are involved in 95% of laboratory experiments on animals. There are several other reasons why mice are important in experimentation. They are small and simple to keep and maintain, they adapt to new environments, they reproduce rapidly and they are relatively docile so researchers can easily control them.

Dear refugees, your brains are worth studying because they have some similarities with the brains of those white laboratory mice. You are human beings, but of a lower rank. You are an irreplaceable opportunity for study and analysis. You also reproduce rapidly and, because you are weak and have little culture, it's fairly easy to look after you. You are docile, because you don't have many options. If you don't like the white laboratory, go back to the hell you came from. All your characteristics as human mice are very useful to the laboratory owners, so that they can develop ideas in the form of medicines for the problems of the host community. Do you follow the media, where analysts, politicians, academics and sociologists sit down to talk about your current and future effects on the country? Remember that, when they talk about you, they are really talking about themselves. They don't do research on you in order to develop the slogans of humanitarianism or for the sake of your suspicious dark eyes. You are just laboratory mice, helping to develop a remedy for the shortfall in births and to develop a 'cultural diversity' antidote for a society that has rejected this questionable antidote for centuries. How will this antidote be made, and what are its side-effects? You provide valuable hallucinogenic drugs for the artists, writers and academics who, here in the North, are bored of talking about nature, loneliness, depression and individualism. You're exciting new material for plays and art videos and films that are full of sarcasm and contempt. This affluent and fully-sated society needs your tragic stories to make mirrors to contemplate their own image in – mirrors that radiate narcissism and selfishness, mirrors framed in gilt that never rusts (the superiority complex). As for the politicians, those clowns, their only job is to turn your skin and bones into a game of musical chairs. Right left, left right. Tell me, for God's sake, is there anything more base, more vile and cowardly in any culture in the world than to attack guests in your own home? Isn't it depraved to abuse weak people, treat them with physical and psychological cruelty, and show no sympathy for their plight? Have you heard what a Northern philosopher who spent his life in isolation in the forest, living off the fish he caught, said about contempt for human solidarity: 'What should one do when a ship carrying a hundred people capsizes, and the only lifeboat has room for only ten people? If the lifeboat is full, the enemies of life are those who try to save more passengers, because they will end up sinking the lifeboat. But those who love and respect life will grab an axe and chop off the hands of those clinging to the sides of the lifeboat.'

The smell of burnt dolma and charred fish filled the house. With the rifle in my hand, I walked around Katrina, who was sitting naked at the head of the table, spattered with blood and trembling. She again begged me to let her get dressed because the cold was distressing her. I told her that if she opened her filthy mouth again I'd blow her head off. 'Only speak when I ask you to,' I added. I filled a plate with dolma and charred fish and put it in front of her. I took a bottle of white wine out of the fridge, sat at the table and started to take swigs straight from the bottle. I told her to start eating and started explaining the food to her: we should have made the dolma from vine leaves or chard but they weren't available in shitty Sololand, so we used cabbage leaves instead. It's a popular dish in our country, and preparing it takes time and patience. Every town in the country has devised its own cuisine, putting its own special touches on it. The ingredients for dolma are: black aubergines, bell peppers of various colours, tomatoes, onions, enough rice for the stuffing, parsley, mint, salt, black pepper, spices, tomato paste. The onion is mixed with spices, then the parsley, rice, tomatoes, oil and mint are added to the mixture. The aubergines are hollowed out and the peppers are deseeded, the tomatoes are also hollowed out. The vegetables are seasoned on the inside with salt and pepper and turned upside down for about half an hour. The aubergines, peppers and tomatoes are washed and then filled with the stuffing mixture. Whatever is left over from the stuffing mixture goes in the pot until it reaches halfway up the sides, oil is added and it's cooked on a high heat until it boils. Then the heat is reduced and it's cooked until ready.

I noticed that she hadn't eaten any of the charred fish, so I shouted in her face, telling her to finish off the food in front of her. I stood up and fetched her present. 'You haven't even opened your present, you useless woman,' I said as I pulled off the wrapping paper. I asked her to look at the wooden plaque and told her it was a piece of cedarwood from the woods around the refugee complex. Sami had brought the tree trunk from the forest himself and Karwan had taken it to the carpentry workshop for them to cut and sand the wood. It was Omar who carved the quotation from Rumi and I had helped to translate it. The plaque read: 'Yesterday I was clever, and I wanted to change the world. Today I am wise, so I will change myself.'

I asked her if she liked Rumi's idea. Trembling from fear and the cold, she said, 'I don't know. Please...'

'What do you know other than hatred, you racist? Say something,' I asked her. She stammered as she answered: 'I d-d-don't know. P-p-please let me get d-d-dressed. And let me c-c-call the p-p-police.'

I rolled a cigarette and started smoking. When she confessed details of the dirty plan she and her Nazi boyfriend had dreamt up, I felt an overwhelming urge to find out everything about her life. I wanted to dig deep into her mind:

in fact, in those moments I wanted to *be* her: a white anaesthetist, sitting naked in front of a strange Eastern man with a rifle. I asked her to tell me about her life and her childhood. She just repeated what she'd said before: 'Please, let me get dressed. I'll do what you want.' I hit the table hard with my fist and yanked the table cloth, sending the dishes and the flower vase flying. She asked me if she could have a glass of wine. I met her request, and she emptied the glass down her throat and started to talk:

'My father was a doctor with the World Health Organization and my mother was an accountant in an electronics company. I have a sister with schizophrenia. That began when she was nineteen years old. A company in a neighbouring, hostile country was looking for young models from the North. My sister was pretty and everyone who met her was impressed by her beauty and poise. She wanted to become an actress. So she travelled to the neighbouring country to join the agency, despite my mother's strong opposition to the idea. My father travelled a lot and was wrapped up in his work. He ran a WHO team in the South. It later transpired that model agency was a scam for luring young women into prostitution. They held my sister and some other women from various countries in an apartment and put drugs in their drinks. They would take them to meet rich men staying in fancy hotels, who posed as directors of international fashion houses. My sister finally managed to escape and came back to Sololand, but she was never the same again. Her psychological condition deteriorated and her doctor later diagnosed her with schizophrenia. Meanwhile, I was the girl who never caught anyone's attention, obedient to her mother and scared of everything. Everyone thought I was jealous of my sister. While I was a student, my father caught some kind of stomach disease in his work in the South, his condition deteriorated rapidly and he died. My sister recovered, to some extent, and went to work in the capital, selling women's clothes in a famous store. I married twice and separated. From my second marriage, I have a daughter who lives in the West, but we have a bad relationship and are rarely in contact.'

I had a feeling her mouth was dry, so I fetched her some water.

'When I was fifteen, something happened that I've never told anyone about before,' she said, then clammed up for 30 seconds. Then she continued: 'There was a man who bred horses in Sololand and sometimes I liked to go up to the fence around his farm to watch them. He noticed me and invited me into the farm. He took me to the stables and started talking about his horses in detail, and then he raped me.'

'What happened? I want the details,' I said, rather spitefully.

'Please,' she said. Then, with tears in her eyes, she added, 'After taking my virginity, he took me from behind. That's all. Please, I beg you, enough, please.'

I told her I had to put the final touches on the dinner initiative. I cut off a piece of extension cord, tied her hands together and started cleaning and tidying the house. I brought Sami down from the second floor: he had two bullet wounds in his chest. I dragged him by the feet and sat him on the sofa. Then I put Omar and Karwan's bodies in a sitting position next to Sami. I don't know why I did that. I dragged the body of Katrina's boyfriend out of the bathroom and laid it out near the sofa under the feet of the other three. I vacuum-cleaned the floor in the bedroom, the sitting room and the kitchen. I washed the dishes and the pots and pans and mopped the floor. I cleaned the bathroom and picked up all the dirty clothes, put them in the washing machine and turned it on. I opened the window to air the place and set some of the furniture straight. Then I took out the rubbish and collected all the empty beer cans and wine bottles in a big plastic bag. Cleaning the house took me more than two hours.

All the while I was cleaning, I thought about my life: the past, the North, my naivety! Had I been running away from my nightmares and memories, and from facing up to the psychological shocks I'd suffered, by trying to immerse myself in the lives of others on the pretext of extending a helping hand? My mind was racing and I started to feel a horrible headache. I fetched my phone and reactivated it. I sat opposite Katrina and started to browse through Facebook. I wrote a post: 'I want to go home, please!' I undid the cord around Katrina's wrists and took her on a tour of the house. She was shocked when she saw how clean it was. I'd swear she had never seen it like that. It was as clean and tidy as a five-star hotel. I yanked off the towel she had wrapped around herself, and took her naked to the sauna.

'This is your sauna, where you started your dirty piece of acting,' I said.

'Please, don't do that, please.'

'What do you think I'm going to do?' I asked. 'Rape you, then kill you?'

The morning light had appeared by the time I drove through the forest. I played a documentary video about locusts on my phone, and started weeping bitterly. Then I stopped the car by the side of the road and called one of my childhood friends, someone I hadn't been in touch with since I left the country. He was surprised to be called and was taken aback at first, but we were soon chatting away as if we had never been apart. We talked about our village and our childhood memories. At that time, we used to have competitions to see who could find the strangest kind of insect or scorpion or snake in the village. My friend reminded me I was always thinking about a game in which animals and humans changed size in bizarre ways. He reminded me of a short passage I had written on the subject, and said it was strange at the time and that he still remembered it:

One desolate night in our vanishing life, a mouse of the common melancholic variety decided to bring an end to a life of fear and humiliation, and say farewell to the weakness and impotence to which it was destined through no fault of its own. Its first decisive step was to defy its master and disobey his command that every creature should speak its own language. Our mouse chose to speak in the language of humans, in the knowledge that it alone would have to bear the consequences of such a forbidden venture. It was of course an exciting moment, rather like one's first orgasm. It combined the magic of tasting reality with the desire to disappear.

Early that winter morning, the mouse came out of its hole in the kitchen without a care in the world, like a drunk looking for a box of matches. The family was sitting at the breakfast table, lazy and secure.

'Good morning,' said the mouse.

The rules of the fear game changed at just that moment, and the mouse grew to the size of a dinosaur.

Raman visited me in prison and started talking about how decent a person I was and how unlucky I was to see this charitable initiative of mine end in disaster. He clearly had a thousand and one questions in his head about everything that had happened at the bloody dinner. I told him he was the only friend I could trust and talk to candidly about anything. Raman didn't hesitate: he came straight out with the question that was troubling him: 'Did you really rape her?'

'No,' I said.

Raman almost jumped out of his seat. 'Shit. I was sure you hadn't done it,' he said. 'But why did you say you raped her when you were questioned?'

'Listen, Raman,' I said, 'the invitation was a trap set by Katrina and her Nazi boyfriend. Everything was planned from the start. But according to what Katrina told me, the agreement wasn't to kill the guests in cold blood. Katrina had been depressed for ages. She had taken time off work when her mental health had started to deteriorate. Her Nazi boyfriend's aggressive and domineering behaviour made her even more unhappy and depressed. He would abandon her, humiliate her, and often beat her. She said he was addicted to cocaine. Katrina's boyfriend had heard about the dinner initiative that Marko was working on. He called Katrina and set one condition for going back to her. She had to call Marko and invite some refugees to her house. He told her he only wanted to give the refugees a fright, in revenge for the girl they had raped in the forest. He drew up the plan. He told her to pretend she had an allergy to mobile phone vibrations so that she could collect them and hide them in her bedroom, that way we wouldn't be able to call for help. He suggested she wear something provocative, and said he was sure the uncivilised refugees would harass her. Katrina would call him, and the man of the house would arrive and save his beloved from the clutches of the guests who were harassing her. But carried away by drunkenness and anxiety, she took the idea too far and came up with the idea of going into the sauna naked and accusing someone of harassing her. I don't know whether her boyfriend had always planned to open fire. The police say he was under the influence of drugs when he committed his crime. Maybe when he saw Karwan naked, the drugs exacerbated his aggressiveness and the sick hallucinations that he had. I don't know. I still think about what happened. I can't stop going over the details and all the images I still see of those terrible moments.

While I was hiding in the bathroom that night, my mind was working overtime and I felt an amazing strength coursing through me – a mixture of anger, fear and resentment. I looked for anything I could use to defend myself, and then I found a large pair of scissors. I repeated to myself dozens of times the words: 'I'm going to kill him.' I held the scissors with an iron grip and stood on the toilet seat so that I'd be the same height as him, and got ready to pounce on him to defend my life. As soon as he smashed the door lock and broke into the bathroom I jumped on him and stabbed him in the face with the scissors, twice in quick succession. The first stab injured his nose and the second went deep into his left eye. He slipped and fell on the bathroom floor. I grabbed the rifle and fired a bullet into his head.'

'But why did you say you raped Katrina?'

'When the police were interrogating me, and hurling abuse at me constantly, they said that Katrina told them I raped her in the sauna. I didn't believe them at first, but then they showed me a video in which she spoke about the details of this rape. I was very angry that she had lied. The thought of raping her never occurred to me at the time. For a moment I did think of shooting her in the sauna, but I knew I couldn't. I left her sobbing in there and threw the rifle into the courtyard. I don't know how I managed to drive back to Laura's studio.'

'Shit, my god, you're really crazy. Why are you ruining your own life, buddy?'

'Raman, my friend, if the police were really looking for the truth, they could find it. Those miserable people who want to make us their one and only nightmare, let's feed their sick imaginations and their racism with more nightmares, until they vomit up from deep inside them all the selfishness and superiority that has nestled in the caves of their consciousness for centuries. Let the mask fall and let them plunge into the mire of contempt for others and be poisoned with xenophobia until their dying breath.'

'You've changed, my friend. You used to criticise other people for their superficial judgments and generalisations. You yourself reminded me several times that hatred usually stems from misunderstanding and, in many cases, loathsome ignorance.'

'These Northerners, Raman, and those with the skin of white supremacy want to liken us immigrants to locusts. They want to think they're waging war on swarms of locusts pouring in from backward parts of the world, threatening the proceeds from their sacred affluence. In fact, these sons of affluence and selfish consumption are the real locusts, the ones most dangerous to the planet. More than that, they're the most dangerous locusts in the whole history of humanity. Their technology, their factories, their selfish madness won't save the depleted resources of this Earth from the fever of industrialisation and consumption that they've been practising for centuries. Even ten earths wouldn't satisfy the hunger of these white supremacist locusts.'

'Time will heal your injuries. You need some therapy sessions. Have you started any yet? I'm sure you'll get back to the way you were, my friend, a nice, smart guy with a heart full of love.'

'The answer is to keep moving.'

'What do you mean?'

'Forget it. Tell me about your plans.'

Ah, okay. I told you I've quit the fish restaurant. I now have a taxi that I drive at night. I'm planning to take a long holiday from work and have a big adventure, a historic journey on foot. I want to walk from the South to the East, then across the continent all the way back to this happy North.'

'Great, that's a big ambitious project. It would definitely be productive and fun.'

'What about you? How are you spending your time?'

'You know, reading and writing most of the time.'

'What are you reading?'

'About ants and bees and scorpions and spiders. But I know what you really want to ask me; you want to ask what I'm writing. Just jottings, assorted scenarios, ideas and thoughts, and the occasional poem.'

We fell silent, holding what we had to say inside ourselves. Raman took out his phone to look at the time.

'Why don't you read me something you've written? he asked.

I looked him in the eye and read:

A refugee in the white heaven,
You flee from death.
They beat you at the border:
They insult you in the racist papers.

They analyse your child's dead body on television.
They gather and discuss your past and future.
They paint pictures of you drowning.
They put you in their museums and applaud.
They decide to stop beating you and marshal a military force against
*   you.*
The academics get a new grant to study your body and soul.
The politicians drink red wine after an urgent meeting to discuss your
*   fate.*
They study history in search of an answer for your daughter, who's
frozen in the cold of the forest.
The neo-Nazis insult you and burn down your house.
The neo-fascists climb into parliament, standing on your shoulders.
You are the nightmares of people old and new.
They cry crocodile tears over your pain.
They come out in protests against you and build walls.
Green activists put up photos of you in the street.
While others sit on their sofas, commenting languidly on your
Facebook profile, before falling asleep.
They take away your humanity with clever debates as sharp as
*   knives.*
They write you one day and, with the eraser of selfishness, they rub
*   you out the next morning.*
They expect to stumble upon their own humanity while wading
*   through your tragedy.*
They welcome you into their paradise then whip you night and day
*   with their own fear, fear of your eyes, how they radiate*
*   dread and hope.*
The past goes to sleep and wakes up inside you.
The present hems you in.
You produce children for their paradise, grow old,
and then die.

Bulbul

THE SAYYID'S BULBUL

MY NAME IS MUHSIN al-Bulbul and I was born in the 1980s. My mother died while giving birth to my younger sister Zahra, and later, when I was six, my father died as well. He was travelling to Amara for his cousin's funeral when his bus turned over and he was burned to death. As orphans, Zahra and I then went to live in our uncle's house in Section 29 in al-Thawra, an eastern district of Baghdad. I wish I would write in *fusha* Arabic, but it's very hard and I can't. It's true that I completed the third year of middle school, but Arabic grammar was torture for me, and I didn't understand much of it. Besides, why do we learn *fusha* Arabic when we don't speak it and we don't love or dream in it? Anyway, this isn't the right time to talk about that. I want to tell my story, starting with my role in the sayyid's love affairs. Of course, everyone knows the sayyid has millions of fans and followers, but no one ever talks about his female admirers – the ones who adore him and dream about him and stay up all night writing love poetry to him. I know that what I'm going to write might cost me my life, even now I've escaped Iraq. These days I live in Sweden, but *husseiniyas*[1] and Shi'ite rituals have caught up with us even here. I decided to write in order to get my story off my chest before I go crazy. I feel disheartened and depressed and I miss Iraq so much that I want to die. A few days ago, I met a Moroccan friend of mine who lives here in the city of Malmo. Of course, Moroccans really loved Saddam Hussein, but they love Iraqis even more. 'Iraqis are heroes,' he told me. 'Even their dialect has the taste of battle!' He said that when people from most Arab countries leave their homelands they say, 'I fled my country', but Iraqis say '*inhizamit* (I was defeated) *from* Iraq'. What they say, in essence, is true, my Moroccan friend said, if you leave your country you're defeated; you lose everything.

When I was young, before the Americans came into Baghdad, I worked in the Muridi Market. It was hard work. At first, I sold ice cream, and then vegetables and fruit juices from a cart, then shirts and jeans. By the time they tore down the statue of Saddam, I was selling Artane pills. Not long after Iyad Allawi became prime minister, I was arrested, but my uncle Tahir, my father's brother, got me out of jail. He was a prominent leader in the Ahbab Allah Army, the Shi'ite militia that supported the Ahbab Allah movement. The sayyid, the cleric who led the movement, had set up the army to resist the Americans and it still had a presence where I lived in the Thawra district, which had been once known as Saddam City but became Sadr City after the overthrow. Leaders had come and gone, but the area was still in the same pathetic state. My father's family was from Najaf and my mother's from Amara. My father's relatives had always served the sayyids and my uncle Tahir had grown up and lived in the homes of the sayyids as a servant. 24 hours a day he boasted about how the sayyid had grown up under his care. Of course, my uncle was exaggerating, but anyone who heard him would have thought he was the sayyid's spiritual father! My uncle had cleaned, swept the floor and made tea for them. But now he's something else altogether – a big leader, who's bought himself a mansion and taken a second wife. People listen to him and are in awe of him. All my relatives were impressed when

Uncle Tahir got me released from the police station ('Muhsin's a good lad. As if this poor sweet boy who never says a word would be selling Artane! Impossible!').

Of course, the few friends I have nicknamed me *bulbul* after Twitter started spreading in Iraq, because bulbuls are especially vocal birds. My real name is Muhsin Abd al-Zahra and I was one of the first people in Iraq to open a Twitter account. I always loved the internet. I was crazy about YouTube, for example, and when Twitter arrived I tweeted constantly. But I've never been into politics, sports, news or religion. I don't know what's wrong with people — in the past they used to say 'someone's making fun of someone' or 'finding fault with them'. Now they call it cyberbullying. Iraqis live really shitty lives and they never show the slightest humility. They find fault and make fun of each other all the time. I just wanted to write nice things like every morning, I say 'Good morning, all you lovely people', or 'Bon appétit' at noon as I post a picture of my lunch, and at night time, 'Hope you revellers are having fun'. Every day I'd write innocent stuff like that and sometimes I'd post pictures of love birds. After the occupation though, I faced an annoying problem. Everyone who saw me would laugh and say, 'For heaven's sake, man, you look like Saddam Hussein when he was young.' Even the sayyid, when he saw me for the first time, said, 'God protect me from the accursed devil! Grow a beard so that you look a little different, not like that vile son of a bitch.' That day, the sayyid had come to visit al-Thawra and he dropped in on the Ahbab Allah office that my uncle ran and where I had started working, bringing people tea and sandwiches. 'I don't understand it, my friend,' the sayyid said. 'You're very tall, but all your uncles are shorter than me.' He laughed. I didn't know what to say in response. All my life, I've never known how to do small talk. I get flustered. Miss Basma, the English teacher, used to call me the daydreamer, and she was right. I've spent my whole life daydreaming. Sometimes I wonder about this world we live in. They say God made us out of clay, but occasionally I think how nice and funny it would be if God had made us out of plasticine. Don't like your nose? Just squeeze it with your finger and change it anyway you like. Upset that you're bald? Make yourself some hair. Turn yourself into an apple or a bird or a palm tree. We'd be like Barbapapa, the shape-shifting blob and the greatest of magicians. Anyway, I'm not that stupid, but many people do say I have a rather strange personality. I gave up telling people about my daydreams because they just laughed at them. No one tried to understand me. I don't know what other people think about, but I'm sure I also think about ordinary things like them – work, food and drink, marriage and children. But shouldn't we think about other things as well?

After the sayyid visited the office, he asked my uncle to bring me to his house to work alongside him. I thought I was going to do the kind of work my uncle used to do, as the sayyid's house servant. But rather belatedly, I began to understand why the sayyid had chosen me and taken an interest in me from the start. They gave me a tiny room of my own, with a computer, a printer, paper and pens. The first thing the sayyid asked me to do was open a new email account under the name 'Bulbul al-Sayyid', meaning the sayyid's bulbul.

'I'd be honoured to be your bulbul,' I told him.

He waved his hand and said, 'Okay, let's go!'

Then I said, 'But sayyid, can't you write an email address in Arabic?'

'My dear, what did I choose you for? Because you're a donkey? Apparently so. Listen, my dear, there's no Arabic. Write the name in English letters.'

I was kidding, of course, but he didn't get that. I set up an email account and waited, not knowing what to do or what my job would be. The sayyid had told all his advisers, bodyguards, friends and assistants not to talk to me, saying he was the only person who could speak to me. He also said I could interrupt him at any time. I was delighted and suddenly felt very important. But I still didn't know why I was important. After a week, the sayyid brought me someone to teach me Farsi. I was frightened, of course. Anything to do with lessons or education scared me because I thought I was slow to understand and wouldn't learn a thing. Then they brought me an English teacher and finally an Urdu teacher. I had a weekly schedule with language lessons in my room and the sayyid gave me a salary that was more than I'd ever dreamed of. He even bought me a car.

Of course, the sayyid had plenty of assistants to manage his pages on Facebook, Twitter and Instagram. There were also special email addresses to which people sent him questions on matters of religious law, and the assistants published the sayyid's answers on the Ahbab Allah website once a week. The Bulbul al-Sayyid email account, by contrast, was private, apparently meant for use by poor, needy people who wanted the sayyid to help them. The idea was that it would be a secret between me and the sayyid, supposedly because the sayyid didn't want to publicise his charitable work. He wanted it to remain between him and God. Of course, the sayyid was a real son of a bitch and had planned everything from the start. He was looking for a suitable person and there was no one around better than Muhsin al-Bulbul, that poor donkey, that good lad who didn't say much, whose uncles were trustworthy and had a long history of serving the sayyids.

The days slipped by, as they say, and the sayyid finally explained what it was all about. The Bulbul al-Sayyid account was just for his female admirers. If anyone else got word of it, the sayyid would chop me to pieces and turn my flesh into kebabs, to use his words.

Now, I'm sure some of you will be asking: how would his admirers know the email address? Indeed that was my first question. But be patient, I'm going to tell you, and not just about that. I'm going to spill the beans on everything, and damn the consequences. I know lots of people think I'm being unfair on the sayyid and say that none of my stories about him are true. Although, if what I said came from WikiLeaks or the BBC or any foreigner writing about this, people would believe it, of course. But Iraqis are like that, totally schizophrenic. They insult America and Europe 24 hours a day, and at the same time they're obsessed with European football, and American news, leaked information, television channels, clothes, fashion, Netflix serials and so on. Anyway, what's the use in talking? The English, Urdu and Farsi teachers were assigned to me, of course, because the sayyid had admirers all over the world and he wanted to correspond with them. But the sayyid couldn't wait till I'd learnt all these languages, he wanted to get to work in them right away. I thought I'd start with the Iraqis first and then gradually expand my work as I learned more and more foreign words.

Even now, I still occasionally walk along the streets of Malmo and daydream about the sayyid. I remember how much I liked him: I've never known anyone as sensitive as him or who loved people so much. Anyone who knows the sayyid knows how much he laughed. He's also a big-time jokester. People retell stories about him as if they were folk ballads. Once I got an email from an admirer who said, 'Dear Bulbul al-Sayyid, you're a genius. When millions of people take a couple of words someone says randomly, and then repeat them in the street, in parliament, at demonstrations and on television, then that person is clearly one of Iraq's greatest geniuses. Dear Bulbul al-Sayyid, I have just one wish. I'd like to rub my cheek against your hand and kiss it. I wouldn't dare ask to put my hand to your lips, those sources of so much wisdom, poetry and good advice.'

As I said, the sayyid is clever. The expression 'a clever bastard' might be more appropriate, but it might hurt the feelings of people who worship things they consider holy. The sayyid would choose from his female admirers at random to start with. You might say he followed his instincts. How? Of course, he'd get text messages on his phone and he'd meet lots of people personally, people who came to visit him at home with grievances, needs or requests, and who brought female relatives with them. When a girl caught the sayyid's eye, he'd give her the address of the Bulbul al-Sayyid email account and tell her to contact him that way. The sayyid was patient and wouldn't get involved with a woman recklessly. And, for the record, at this stage the sayyid would never exchange messages with a married woman, a widow or a woman with children. He wasn't interested in any of that. Only girls who were still virgins. And of course he wouldn't agree to ever meet them. He just enjoyed exchanging love letters and writing the occasional poem.

Once, he developed a bit of a crush on one particular woman, so much so he considered meeting her, but he grew frightened and hesitant. She was a girl called Fatma and she was pretty. I started communicating with her, or rather the sayyid and I did. All her messages were romantic, full of love and admiration, and her only wish in life was to be alone with the sayyid so that she could kiss his toes. Some background checks were run, at the request of the sayyid. I took the car he'd bought me and went to the area where Fatma lived in the al-Shaab district of Baghdad. I nosed around, asked about Fatma and her family and kept the place under surveillance for two weeks. Her father was an old man and her mother stayed at home to look after her only son's children. Fatma was 22 years old and had three sisters. She had completed secondary school and stayed at home. She wore a hijab and had set up a Facebook page to support the Ahbab Allah Army. After monitoring her, I went back to the sayyid and explained her situation in long, arduous detail.

'Describe her to me,' he ordered.

'She's not tall but not short, a little plump, light-skinned with big breasts and she likes to buy lots of necklaces, rings and beads,' I replied. The sayyid asked me what I thought, whether we should rent a house and meet her. Of course, I didn't have an opinion and I simply found my mind wandering again. 'Do you think you're going to solve all Iraq's problems with your daydreams?' he barked. 'Okay, drop it,' he added.

'Forget all about it. But have her send you some pictures.'

Months passed in this way: love letters and flirtation. My Farsi started to improve and I learnt a little English and some broken Turkish. Then, one day a girl called Zeinab showed up and turned both the sayyid's life and mine upside down. Before Zeinab came along, there was some silly bitch who emailed in a song called 'There's Nothing Wrong with the Sayyid's Cock'. I didn't want the sayyid to hear it but he was insistent that I tell him everything. He roared with laughter when he heard the song, and after that he and I used the phrase 'nothing wrong' as a secret codeword. When the sayyid sent me a text message saying 'Nothing wrong', it meant he wanted me to go and see him about his admirers' emails.

One day, the girl called Zeinab sent me a voice message. She kept communicating in this way, recording her voice and sending it by email. She never wrote. This Zeinab worked as a translator in the Iranian embassy. The ambassador came to visit the sayyid one day and he brought Zeinab with him. As soon as I heard her voice, I felt my heart stop. She spoke colloquial Iraqi but with an Iranian accent. She had a kind of sing-song voice that could make your heart melt. It was so gentle and sexy and to be honest I wanked to her voice several times when she talked about love, passion, longing and the fire of desire, especially when she said, 'I can feel fire breaking out throughout my body when I think of the sayyid's bulbul.' Zeinab had lived and grown up in Iran. Her family had been deported and they came back to Iraq after the fall of Saddam. She was divorced and had a five-year-old daughter. She spoke Iraqi, Farsi, English and French. Immediately I knew the sayyid was very interested in her. She seemed to have a hold over his mind and thoughts. Every hour he'd send me a text saying 'Nothing wrong' and I'd go to see him and he'd ask if Zeinab had sent a new email. In the end, the sayyid lost patience and asked me to come up with a plan for him to meet her.

I rented a house for two weeks on the pretext that I was

visiting from the provinces and that my wife was sick and had to visit a hospital in Baghdad. Of course, the idea was that Zeinab would be my wife. The problem was: how could the sayyid come to the house with his usual large entourage? But the sayyid came up with a plan, and frankly it was risky. He told his family and his advisers that he wanted to go in disguise to the home of some poor people to help them, and he wanted only two people with him for protection, as well as Muhsin al-Bulbil. Naturally, there was a big fuss. The head of the security committee responsible for protecting him rejected the proposal to start with, but the sayyid gave him a talking-to and he kept quiet.

We set off in the car with me driving and the sayyid sitting beside me, and the bodyguards in the back seat. Zeinab was waiting for us at the house I had rented and she'd brought her daughter with her. The bodyguards stayed outside at the door and the sayyid and I went in. We quickly completed the arrangements for a temporary marriage and the sayyid went off to be alone with her. I stayed with Zeinab's daughter in the kitchen. When the sayyid came out of the room, his face was beaming and he had tears in his eyes. You felt he was suddenly humble, like someone on whom the angel of inspiration has descended. He didn't say a word, not to me or to the bodyguards. In fact, he was silent all the way home.

A week later he sent me another message, asking me to rent a house in another area, with the same basic plan. This time the sayyid decided to go in disguise, but he went completely over the top. He put on a big blue hat and clothes that made him look like a rapper, and it almost became a problem. We were stopped at a checkpoint. The sayyid had taken precautions, of course; he had a fake ID card giving his name as Omar Ali Nawzad. The policeman at the checkpoint looked at him and said, 'Amazing, you look just like the sayyid, the leader!' But the other policeman said, 'Come off it, shut up. You're comparing this loser with the sayyid!' They gave back our ID cards and we went on our way.

From the very first time Zeinab saw me, she was really nice to me. On the sayyid's second visit, I left her daughter in the kitchen and went to have a piss. The door to the lovebirds' room was ajar. They were naked and Zeinab was like a goddess, beautiful that is, slim and almost as tall as me and she was licking all of the sayyid's body and he was almost unconscious. Then she mounted him and I got a hard-on just watching. I mumbled a prayer to myself, had a piss and went back to Zeinab's daughter.

We went on like this. I mean we managed to arrange five such sessions over the next several months. The sayyid asked me to study some sexual positions from websites. The sayyid was managing two orgasms per session and he wanted more, but his cock needed more time to get hard again. I bought him some Viagra and he tried it but he didn't like it because it gave him a terrible headache and upset him.

One day I rented a house and drove Zeinab there. She came and sat next to me and said she wanted to speak to me about something very important. As if confessing, she explained that she'd been crazy about me right from the start. She started talking about my height, my calmness and my rough manly voice. She waxed lyrical about the beauty of my body. 'To be honest, Bulbul, I really really love you,' she said. She told me about hearing my voice in the messages to her. The sayyid would write love poems to Zeinab and I recorded them in my own voice and sent Zeinab the audio file. She said that even when she slept with the sayyid, she still had my voice in her head. She brought her lips close to mine. I was sweating and my whole body was trembling and I slipped away. I went to the fridge and drank some cold water. 'I'm a widow,' she said. 'It's true I fancy the sayyid but I don't have a future with him, and this is just a temporary marriage. Bulbul, you're a young man and you're not married, and I swear I'll serve you well if you marry me.'

I couldn't believe what she said. This girl, who was such a stunner, was in love with *me*, Muhsin al-Bulbul, the daydreamer who was as tall as a palm tree and had the mind of a goat! After she said this I often looked at myself in the mirror. It was the first time anyone, woman or man, had told me I was handsome. Then she told me I looked like a film star – so masculine and awesome. Of course, I was worried. If the sayyid found out, he'd skin me alive. Zeinab kept trying with me and didn't give up. She sent me private messages by email, and at one of the sessions, before the sayyid arrived, she tried to point me in the right direction. She hadn't brought her daughter with her. She went into the bathroom, came out undressed and smelling of shampoo, and then came up close to me. 'Muhsin, I love you so much,' she said. She could feel how I felt. She reached out and took hold of my cock, which was hard and ready like the cannon they fire to mark the end of Ramadan fasting. I left her and went out to go and fetch the sayyid. For days, I was dizzy about what happened and gradually I began to fall in love with Zeinab, with her wonderful body, her eyes, her smell and her breasts.

One day the sayyid was in my room, the door closed behind him for privacy. I was explaining a sexual position I'd seen on the internet, where you bend the woman over the end of the sofa and take her from behind while standing. The sayyid was enjoying it and laughing at the way I acted out to him how I would fuck a woman over the arm of a sofa. In fact, he almost died laughing. I was imagining actually putting my hand on Zeinab's ass from behind and pushing with my cock. I was frightened to stand up in case the sayyid noticed my erection.

Two weeks later I was worried and decided to confess everything to the sayyid. He was a wise man who would surely understand the situation and find a reasonable solution to the problem. Like a complete jackass, reckless and messed up, I thought we could talk about anything. For some reason I imagined the sayyid would say, 'No problem, Bulbul. Marry her and I'll leave Zeinab alone.' That was certainly what I wanted him to say and what I fooled myself into thinking he might say, but what a complete idiot I was!

Of course, and I swear by Hussein Abu Abdallah, I didn't want to implicate Zeinab, but my loyalty to the sayyid didn't allow me to keep quiet and hide the truth from him. 'Sayyid,' I told him,' Zeinab likes me and I don't want to hide it from you because, to be honest, she says she loves me.' You can't imagine what came over the sayyid when he heard what I said. The jealousy went straight to his head and turned him crazy. First he asked me to tell him everything that had happened between me and Zeinab. I swore to him, by his grandfather's soul, that nothing at all had happened and I hadn't laid a finger on her. But all the sayyid could hear was the jealousy inside him. 'So you've been sleeping with her all these months, you bastard?' he said. 'I swear by those seventy -two dancing virgins, today will be the end of you.' I swore to him, bent down and kissed his foot, begging him to believe me: 'In the name of Hussein, nothing happened!' I kept swearing oaths and kissing his foot and imploring him. He kept shouting at me and cursing. I took my fill of insults, kicks and punches. 'Wait in the room,' he said. He came back with a red hosepipe in his hand and said, 'Strip as naked as you were born.' I felt he was surprised by the length of my cock and it made him even crazier. He almost killed me with the kicks, beatings and whiplashes he gave me.

When he sent me a message a few days later, he was rather calmer. He asked me to close down the Bulbul email account, give up my work and go back to the office where my uncle Tahir worked. Several times he advised me to forget about everything that had happened. If a single word leaked out about the Bulbul al-Sayyid emails I would see hell with my own eyes.

Before I closed down the email account, Zeinab and I sent each other a few messages. She told me the sayyid had cut off relations with her. 'This is our chance,' she added. 'Now we can get married.' If the sayyid was a bastard, Zeinab was like one of the djinn. The last email she sent me included a picture of her half-naked in bed with an empty space beside her. 'There's room for you. The love bed is warm and waiting.' I finally closed down the account, stopped contacting her and went back to the Ahbab Allah Army office to work beside my uncle.

I spent months dreaming of Zeinab every night, God bless her.

Bulbul's Daydreams

At my wedding, I met Sadiq Hassan, the son of a friend of my uncle Tahir. Sadiq worked for the Ahbab Allah radio station. I wasn't convinced by the idea of getting married. 'Let me do some useful work first, and get married later,' I'd said to my uncle Tahir. At the time, me and my sister Zahra were still living in the home of my other uncle, my mother's brother. But Uncle Tahir said, 'Your uncle's kids have grown up and a day's bound to come when your sister gets married. You have to start a family. Life passes quickly.' Later he added, 'You're a soldier in the Ahbab Allah Army now and there's no work easier than that!' Uncle Tahir helped me rent a small plot of land. Zahra wouldn't agree to move with me to my new house. 'I'm used to living in my uncle's house,' she said. So I left her to herself and said, 'You're welcome to come over any time.' Uncle Tahir himself found me my wife, Karima, a good poor girl from our neighbourhood. She had completed primary school and had six brothers, who were all in the Ahbab Allah Army. If I spent my whole life daydreaming, Karima spent hers sighing. She sighed even when there wasn't a problem. I often wondered if she was prone to sighing because she had some lung condition. Even she didn't know why she sighed 24 hours a day. She sighed when we were eating, she sighed when she was washing in the bathroom, she sighed when we were sleeping together, she sighed when she was happy and she sighed when she was upset. Karima says she might have inherited it from her mother. My work life was troubling me greatly, because it didn't make sense for me just to sit in Uncle Tahir's office without any real work to do. They would give me little jobs now and then, such as: 'Go to so-and-so and tell him we're having a meeting' or 'Go to al-Shuala for so-and-so's funeral, give my condolences to his family and do the necessary' or 'Go and deliver these leaflets to Habibiya' or 'Go to the demonstration and give out water.'

Sadiq Hassan, my new friend, had studied at the faculty of fine arts and worked as a radio producer. One day we were in the coffee shop. He loved to smoke shisha, but I don't smoke and even the smell of cigarettes makes me feel sick. We were playing dominos, which I like very much, along with backgammon, because they make for good daydreams. Sadiq noticed and said, 'You really believe in this game, don't you? You think about each move for so long it's like we were playing chess.'

'I'm not thinking about the game,' I explained. 'Thinking is my hobby, or you could say it's my disability, like something you're born with. My daydreaming has been the problem with my life, ever since I was a little kid.' Sadiq laughed and insisted on knowing what I was daydreaming about. I said, 'Mind you don't call me an atheist like those people in Ahbab. You only have to ask them a question and they give you your fill of insults and accusations of heresy and treason.' Sadiq promised he would listen to me and try to understand. 'God's capable of everything, okay?' I said. 'So why are the Islamic countries in such a ruinous state, with wars, diseases and backwardness? Why doesn't this Lord of the Worlds come and help us? We worship him and love his prophet and respect the prophet's family and weep and flagellate ourselves for them, raise their banners, swear oaths by them, give blessings in their name and yet look at the state we're in. Why doesn't God love us as much as we love him? In Europe, for example, where they are infidels who drink alcohol, eat pork and live together without marrying, doing all sorts of things, why do they have such nice lives? It's like they're living in paradise. I mean, if God improved our situation and showed the infidel countries that Islam is the true religion, then the whole world would be guided to the religion of Muhammad and follow the Prophet's family.'

'God must have a reason, and this is a test,' replied Sadiq.

'You mean he tests the obedient ones who love him and lets those who do all the forbidden things have a nice life?' I said.

'This is a big subject,' Sadiq replied, 'and there are people who are specialists in religious matters. They could certainly give you an answer.'

'Anyway, I'm only asking,' I said, 'and, in the name of Hussein Abu Abdallah, I'm not an atheist.'

A few days later Sadiq got in touch with me and said he had some very important business to discuss. I went to see him. He told me how annoyed and angry he was with the work he was doing at the Ahbab Allah radio station because the programmes, he said, were needlessly earnest, whereas people weren't yet in the mood for serious things. 'These days people have got Facebook and Netflix and YouTube and thousands of other channels. The religious programmes are so old-fashioned, compared to them. Who would listen today to a religious radio station that repeats the same old subjects? It needs a little updating.' Then he had this idea inspired by the daydreams I told him about that day. 'You have a simple and very pleasant way of talking, and you're funny,' he said. His idea was a programme called *Bulbul's Daydreams*. I would be the presenter and he would do all the preparation and production. 'Sadiq,' I said, 'How on earth did I get caught up in this?'

'Don't worry about it,' he said. 'For a start, you have a wonderful radio voice, believe me. And the way you speak, people will love it. There are some simple things about the work, technicalities and stuff like that, but I'll train you and teach you about them.'

'Okay,' I said. 'But give me time to think about it.'

I consulted my wife Karima. She sighed and said, 'Oh God, I don't know. As you wish, Bulbul.'

I called my sister Zahra and asked her. She laughed and said, 'Wow! So you're going to be a radio broadcaster. But how are you going to manage it? You don't tell stories and you've spent your whole life daydreaming.'

'Well thanks a lot,' I said. 'Neither you nor Karima are very encouraging.'

I called Sadiq and said, 'I'm persuaded, but find me someone who can persuade my Uncle Tahir.'

Sadiq said, 'Leave your uncle to me. He'll be proud of you and delighted, once the programme's a hit.'

How right he was. I went to the radio station and Sadiq started teaching me how to speak into the microphone and how I should listen to the person giving me instructions and lots of secondary details. It all made me dizzy the first time. But slowly, with practice, I started learning things. Sadiq and I would sit down and choose the subjects for the programme. He asked me to take notes on all my daydreams, so he could see which of them would suit the programme. Each of the programmes began with one of these musings. I could speak with complete freedom, or so Sadiq said, and then we would open the phone lines for people to call in and give their opinions on the subject and share their own musings and bafflement about this world.

Sadiq recorded several of my ruminations. One of them was about temporary marriages, and another was about the man who couldn't reach the grapes and so said they were sour. In another, I spoke about people who spend their whole lives complaining about their lives, their neighbours and all Iraqis, but who don't do anything themselves about their lives. There was one about Facebook fights and how one battle began with shoes being thrown in parliament and then continued on television after the presenter added a little spice to it, and ended in curses and insults and people blocking each other on Facebook and Twitter.

Anyway, we put our trust in God and the Family of the Prophet and started the first programme:

'Dear listeners, good evening. My name is Muhsin al-Bulbul, the Daydreamer, and this is the first in our series of *Bulbul's Daydreams*. I don't like introductions so I want to get straight to the story. A few days ago I was in the market to buy some fish and some pickles. I bought a good brown fish. I went home and found my wife Karima watching a television programme in which two parties were fighting, each one defending its own sect. 'Karima, what's the story?' I asked.

'I really don't know, Bulbul,' she said. 'I don't understand at all.'

Then she asked me, 'So what difference does it make if you're a Shi'ite Iraqi or a Sunni Iraqi?'

'There are people who live off this story,' I told her. 'I mean, you know how the neighbours make a living by selling lambs in the farmers' market. These people make a living by selling sectarianism.'

She laughed and said, 'Ah, so sectarianism is like lambs.' Karima sat down in the courtyard to wash the fish, and I sat facing her making a salad. I always like to help with preparing the food. When Karima slit open the fish's belly and the guts spilled out, I went into a long daydream. I thought about my own guts and then I started thinking about all the body organs inside me that I obviously can't see. For some reason, I started imagining the liver, the pancreas, the heart and the stomach as being like tame animals living inside me. Then a question popped into my head: why do we so rarely think about what's inside us and only about what we can see on the outside? Why don't we try to understand and love these animals and try to build a relationship with them? They're the closest things to us. You could even say they *are* us. I mean, when we fall ill and the doctor tells us we have a problem in our kidney or our pancreas and explains to us how people's lifestyles can affect their health, we go straight to the internet and look for more information and try to understand the effects of diet, cigarettes, fats and sugar on our health and on the life of these beings. I know maybe the word 'beings' or 'organs' is better than the word 'animals'! But I like the idea of 'a small zoo inside me' – like the title of a TV series or a novel. We ate the fish and drank three cups of tea, and Karima and I slept downstream of the air conditioning unit. From that day on, you could say I started a love affair with these animals inside me. It got to the stage where I started crying when I thought about us humans living and dying without ever seeing the organs in our bodies. In other words, as the intellectuals say on television, there's an irony here. You'd have to fall ill and have a heart transplant, for example, before you ever had the good fortune to open your eyes in the hospital, and see the doctor bringing you your old heart and you can see it and meet it for the first time. I kept trawling the internet and looking for information, and my love and passion for all the things inside me started to grow. For example, I didn't know that the lungs are the only organ in the human body that can float on water. I was amazed, and at night I dreamt of a lung floating on water, while I sat on the bank fishing with a rod and then I caught a spleen. I fell more and more in love with the tame animals inside me and I started to take an interest in what I ate, because it wouldn't be fair if I was cruel to these beautiful, wonderful creatures when I eat, believe me! I had a love affair with myself for many days and abandoned the world around me. Why don't we think or care, every day, about the lives that move us and that keep us alive in this world? I mean, does it make sense that someone should think about politics or sectarianism more than they think about a living organ in their body that keeps them alive?

When I finished talking on the subject and we opened the lines for callers, the lines were jammed with people wanting to speak. The next day, social media was abuzz with all kinds of comments. There were plenty of sarcastic comments and jokes, but also people thanking us for airing these important topics and other people insulting us for being so trivial. I was very upset when I saw people making fun of the idea in my daydream. One person said, 'Ahbab Allah Radio has a presenter who says you have to masturbate on your pancreas,' and someone else wrote, 'How can you have a temporary marriage with your own kidney? #AhbabAllah #SpleenLove.' You can imagine how Iraqis turned it all into a joke.

When I went to the radio station the next day, I was too embarrassed to seek out Sadiq. I thought the managers must surely have told him off and now we were going to be fired. But Sadiq greeted me with a smile and a hug. When I told him about the hostile comments, he said, 'Bulbul, are you serious? How else could it become a hit? These comments are proof that it's a stunning success. It means people will be in suspense waiting for the next programme. We'll have to get a strong programme ready. Didn't I tell you you're a natural talent. Very creative. In the name of Hussein Abu Abdallah, you're an artist, believe me, Bulbul.' To celebrate, we went and ate at a nice grill restaurant and began to prepare a topic for the next programme.

The programme worked well and started to succeed. It was discussed widely on social media and TV. Some programmes started to invite me for interviews. After half a dozen episodes of the show I had become pretty famous. But after the thirteenth, I don't know but I rather felt that the number of listeners had fallen. Maybe the daydreams weren't good any more. But also, to be honest, I felt that Sadiq had become a little ambitious and he wasn't happy with the audiences we were getting. One day, we sat down and talked. 'We have to make a few programmes that are daring and shocking and cause trouble, so that people talk about them more. 'I want to stir things up,' he said. He asked me to think of a daydream that would cause problems between the secularists and the Islamists. 'We'll tell the listeners you're going to take a week's sick leave. That will get people interested and they'll be waiting for you. Go and think about it at your leisure, but I want you, Muhsin the creative artist, sweetest Bulbul, to come up with a really nice and powerful rumination for me.'

They did give me the week's holiday and I went off to think. I've loved walking since I was young. After Friday prayers that week I went for a walk. 'I'll start here and walk till I get tired,' I said to myself, 'then sit down in a coffee shop and have a rest.' I thought about politicians, religious and secularist. Both of them say they love Iraq and seek its best interests, but people have grown tired and fed up with them. People say they're just talk and they're all thieves. The religious ones say, 'So who are these secularists? Wasn't Saddam a secularist? Well, he was a monster', and then the secularists say, 'Saddam was a dictator and a monster but he doesn't represent secularism or civilisation,' finishing their response with their own question: 'And who are these Islamists? They're the same as Daesh, the Taliban, Zarqawi, Saudi Arabia, flogging, sharia and backwardness.' And then the Islamists say, 'Those people don't represent real Islam.' Okay, leave aside their endless arguments. What do they have in common? Of course they're all human beings who want to live happily and bring up their children and live in a decent country with a good health and education system, at least as good as people in neighbouring countries that have oil. Okay, why don't they agree if they both want what's best for Iraq and Iraqis? If only they could both compromise on their religious or secular prejudices and give up stealing and being hypocritical.

I felt that my daydreams had changed after I started working at the radio station. Previously my daydreams hadn't been planned. They were just personal things I thought about freely. But now Sadiq the producer had intruded on my daydreams and they were slightly exaggerated and unnatural. I mean, my daydreams had once been private, but now I'd started to tailor them to public problems. I changed my plan, took a taxi and went to Bab al-Muazzam. I walked down Rashid Street and then turned into the densely crowded Mutanabbi Street. I used to love this street and was in awe of it. At the time I didn't read many books. The street was really nice and looked like a market just for intellectuals. I looked at the titles of the books and the idea for a game popped into my head. I said I would read the titles of the books on the stalls and then daydream about the title I liked, instead of Sadiq's daydream about secularists and religious people. I walked up and down the street reading the titles but there was nothing. Nothing inspired me.

I saw a boy maybe twelve years old carrying a sack full of books. Sometimes he dragged them along the ground, looking for a place he could lay them out. The street was already fairly full of book stalls. I asked him why he didn't display them in Rashid Street, and then people going to Mutanabbi Street would pass by and see his books. 'I don't know,' he said. 'Let me help you,' I said. I picked up the sack and threw it over my shoulder. 'Come on, let's find a spot,' I told him. I found a good place next to a cart that a young boy had brought. He looked like a good kid. We laid out the books, I ordered two teas and sat down with the kid next to the stall. 'Where did you get the books from, kiddo?' I asked him. 'They belong to my father,' he replied. 'And where's your father, habibi?' I asked. 'They killed him a month ago,' he said. He told me some of the story. Some faction had assassinated his father because he was a journalist and once they had invited him to appear on an Iraqi television channel and he had criticised corruption and sectarianism. So now we were supposed to think he was a terrorist who had planted a car bomb or that he'd stolen people's money. My god, it's a disaster, this Iraq! The poor boy's family were living in rented accommodation and he was his mother's only son and he had five sisters. His mother had diabetes and was ill. 'What was your father called, habibi?' I asked him. 'Sami al-Mahdi,' he replied. I wanted to help him so I bought a book from him at random and gave him some extra money too. I went and sat in the Umm Kulthoum coffee shop in Rashid Street and looked up the name Sami al-Mahdi on the internet. Some people said terrorists had killed him and others said it was the militias.

There was one group that said, 'Hey man, it was just an honour crime, something to do with women.' I felt sad about this journalist. I saw the video of an interview with him and he was clearly a good guy, and smart too. When those ruthless people kill someone, they don't think about what's going to happen to the man's family and children. I mean, when you kill someone, you kill his whole family with him. I opened the book I had bought and the title was *The Chimera of Reality*. I read some of it, but didn't understand much. I shut the book and called Sadiq. 'What does *chimera* mean?' I asked him. He laughed and said, 'Now don't tell me your next daydream is going to be about chimeras! So now you're an intellectual?' Sadiq then explained to me and I understood a little. Chimeras roughly means mental illusions or fantasies. A daydream occurred to me and I thought I would call it *Reality is Stranger than Fantasy*:

Dear listeners,

Today I want to talk about a reality that is stranger than fantasy. I know you're going to laugh and say that Muhsin isn't in the habit of spouting philosophy at us and acting intellectual. I want to tell you the story of a boy who carries a sack full of books on his back. I want to tell you how injustice makes life stranger than fantasy. There was a journalist called Sami al-Mahdi who was killed by some group or other. There hasn't been any kind of investigation whatsoever. Iraqi murderers are always unknown. Only the victims are known. You could make a whole new *Thousand and One Nights* out of their stories. Dear listener, just imagine the scene with me again – a boy carrying a sackload of his father's books on his back. In other words, a boy carrying your crime on his back. Or you could say a boy carrying abandoned scholarship and knowledge on his back. So you're going to kill everyone who speaks? You're going to silence everyone? Instead of people saying that in the land of the blind the one-eyed man is king, they'll say that in the land of the mute the man who speaks is king.

Only you'd be speaking in the name of religion and sect and jihad and struggle, while you attack people. For God's sake, think! Surely what's stranger than fantasy is the fact that the backward and ignorant should survive and that everyone who can carries a gun, while the ones who die are those who have worked hard, read books and studied and who wish well for their people and their family? Isn't it strange that thieves live in comfort, while the honest live hungry? Isn't it strange that a country with more oil than any other country in the world has children living in the streets? Isn't it strange that we broke out of the dictator's prison only to be imprisoned again by sectarianism and militias? When I think about it and ask 'Why? What's the real problem here?', I end up asking myself how we could ever understand, now that our problems are stranger than fiction and quite incomprehensible. I mean, it's all a big mess and our life has become a fantasy, sometimes brutal, sometimes enough to make you cry, sometimes enough to make you laugh, and sometimes stranger than fiction.

I rambled on and on in this episode. I felt I was in a trance, as if someone else was speaking inside me. When I finished, the phone lines were jammed. Many people thanked me for what I had said and some insulted me. One man threatened me directly on air! When the programme ended Sadiq had a sour look on his face and was very upset. 'Bulbul, what have you done?' he said. 'You went too far. God help us. Let's see what's going to happen.'

I went back home, slightly worried. I logged onto Facebook and saw that many people were taking my side, that is to say, they agreed with the substance of my daydream, and how strange all the killing and sectarianism was. Some people had recorded the programme and uploaded it onto YouTube. On Facebook someone had written, 'Bulbul is more honest than any member of parliament.' and another said, 'Muhsin al-Bulbil should run for prime minister. He might daydream about Iraq, find us a solution and save us all.' People expressed their views on Bulbul's ponderings through likes, love hearts, crying faces, laughing faces and faces turning red as tomatoes out of anger.

I didn't like to sleep in my clothes. I always got into bed naked and I told Karima to do the same. But she was shy. She finally agreed to sleep in just her underwear. Karima was snoring and I was playing with her left nipple and dreaming about her large breasts. I imagined myself as a tiny human the size of the fictional Swedish boy Nils, sliding around on Karima's breasts. In the morning I would climb onto a goose's back and fly off to another country. I'd see lakes and forests and people and listen to stories that were stranger than fantasy.

The next day al-Haji, the director of Ahbab Allah Radio, sent a message to me and Sadiq. He told us off sharply and said he was in a mind to come and gave us a good kicking. In the end he fired us, saying, 'By Hussein Abu Abdallah, if your families weren't good people, I would have had you skinned, by God. Get out of here, you morons.'

I went back to the Ahbab Allah office and had another rollicking from Uncle Tahir. Three months later, Sadiq called me from Turkey saying he was going to cross the sea to Greece. 'Curse the father of Iraq and his father who loves him,' he said. 'Look after yourself, Bulbul, and beware of the fantasy of Ahbab Allah!' We laughed and I said I wished him a safe journey.

BULBUL'S DRONES

Before operations to liberate Mosul began, I joined the Popular Mobilisation Forces.[2] The Ahbab Allah Army had been divided into different companies. They put me in one of their so-called Pigeon companies, which specialised in operating drones and whose mission was to carry out reconnaissance and monitoring. Along with a group of mujahideen, I spent two months training with 'our birds', as we called them. As a mujahid friend who died in battle, may

God have mercy on his soul, once said to me: 'We are now pigeon fanciers but our pigeons come in the form of these drones.'

The drones we operated came in two kinds: drones with thermal imaging cameras for use at night and those with visible-light cameras. I was given a visible-light one that could fly four kilometres at an altitude of 100 to 120 metres, depending on the conditions.

Poor Karima was pregnant by this point. My sister Zahra came over to our house to be at her side. Karima begged my uncle to let me stay in the office rather than send me to Mosul. To be honest, I was worried too. This was a deadly war, not a game. I was very worried my child would be orphaned and forced to live a life of deprivation, reliving the disastrous experiences my sister and I had been through. But there was no other option, especially after a fatwa by the Ayatollah Sistani, the country's most prominent Shi'ite cleric. And if we didn't come out and defend Iraq, our sect and our honour, then who else was going to stand up to these Daesh people who called us all infidels? May God take revenge on those responsible for bringing Daesh to our country to destroy it. I made new friends in my company. The one I liked best was Ali Aboul Qasim, a nice guy from Nasiriyah who loved a good laugh and had a beautiful voice when he sang folksongs from the south. We had something important in common, and that was daydreaming, which I tried to minimise because we were at war and my work required concentration. But Aboul Qasim's daydreams were poetic and mostly about the beauty of women, and were most often about their breasts. He was crazy about any poetry that mentioned breasts. He had memorised every Nizar Qabbani poem that included the word 'breast'. He liked to read popular poetry and novels. He was the person who told me that my year of birth, 1984, was the title of a famous novel by an English writer called George Orwell and that the idea of a Big Brother who monitors and controls everything came from this book. He told me a little about the novel, about the mysterious leader who knew everything, even the details of people's lives. I remember that Aboul Qasim had memorised many quotes from the novel, such as the one that goes, 'Politicians in the world are like monkeys in the jungle. If they quarrel they damage the plants. If they make peace they eat the crop.' I remember how I once asked Aboul Qasim about standard Arabic, which we call *fusha*. 'Why don't we study and read novels in our own Iraqi Arabic?' I asked. 'Why do we hang on to *fusha*, which is the difficult language they use in old religious serials on television? Doctors, engineers and scientists can't speak it, can they?'

'You're right,' Aboul Qasim said. 'Even writers and journalists make lots of mistakes with it. We've got over the problem in popular poetry. No one holds it against us if we write in Iraqi Arabic. But if a novelist writes in a local *ammiya*, they'll hand him over to the guardians of *fusha*.' He was a mine of information. He told me that if you look closely you'll find there are two groups that want to protect *fusha* – the Arab nationalists and the hard-line Islamists. Look at Daesh. When they cut off someone's head they speak *fusha*.'

At night, with my head on my pillow, I had a long daydream about what Aboul Qasim had said about Arabic. I mean, every nation studies its native language, but when we start studying Arabic in primary school, *fusha* is like a foreign language, not our mother tongue. In our everyday language, we call a lightbulb a *gloob*, but in fusha it's called a *misbaah*. We call a table a *mayz*, but in fusha it's called a *taawala*. So how can *fusha* be our mother tongue? I understood Aboul Qasim when he said that if we wrote books in Iraqi Arabic, the Arabs wouldn't understand each other. Well, who said they understand each other anyway? What, so if people speak their own dialects they're going to hate each other! Even the Arab heads of state can't put two lines together in *fusha*. If the Arabs want to understand each other and call each other brothers, why don't they learn each other's languages and solve the problem that way? I mean, people are willing to learn English, French,

Russian or even Chinese, but they're not prepared to learn Moroccan or Syrian Arabic, which, in the end, are just different versions of Arabic, which, with a little concentration, they can easily learn. I dozed off and a nightmare bombarded me. I was in a hall full of writers, critics and poets and they were all smoking and glaring at each other. The hall was so full of smoke that people could hardly see each other or breathe. In the dream, I had become a writer and I had to read from my new book, which I'd written in Iraqi Arabic. As soon as I finished reading the first line of my novel ('One day someone was sitting on the banks of the Tigris daydreaming about the well-known saying: "Life's bullshit, if you don't die by the sword, you'll die by the shoe".') the first shoe hit me from the front row, and then more shoes came thick and fast like a swarm of locusts. It was chaos and the air was dense with cigarette smoke. I started and sat up in bed, only to find Aboul Qasim next to me with his mouth open, snoring like a suffocating fish.

We took part in several battles and started to disrupt Daesh and destroy its lines of defence. In one of the battles, we captured a Daesh member. We took his radio from him and used it to talk to another Daesh fighter, who was trapped on the roof of a house in a residential area surrounded by Popular Mobilisation Forces. I launched my drone and started looking for him as the guys next to me chatted with him on the radio. 'How long are you going to stay in hiding, you coward?' Abu Haidar asked him.

'We're coming for you. I swear, we'll shave off your moustache,' he added.

'Look, if you're such a hero, drive here like our immersion squads do,' the fighter replied. 'Come on, coward!'

'I don't have any suicide bombers like you, because God bans them and the Imam Ali says...'

The Daesh guy interrupted him. 'Keep at it, mate, keep at it. The Imam Ali and the Imam Hussein aren't like you say they are, you ignoramuses.'

'Now you be polite. Abu Haidar's coming your way, you bastard,' retorted Abu Haidar, 'and I don't want to hear any mention of the Imam Hussein from your filthy tongue.'

I swung my drone to the right and saw the Daesh guy as he spoke on the radio with Abu Haidar. There were three Daesh members with him, hiding behind a water tank on the roof. The guys came and gave the order to deal with him, but just at that moment I saw a little girl playing hopscotch on the roof of a house near the hidden Daesh men. 'Now what's that little girl doing on the roof when the world's on fire?' the guys asked.

Someone in our group said, 'Hard to tell. Maybe her parents are dead or have run off and forgotten her. It's up to Abu Hashim to decide.' They called Abu Hashim and without discussion he ordered an immediate attack on the target. The coordinates were sent, our group fired mortar rounds and the girl disappeared in the smoke from the impact. I turned the drone again and saw her on the roof, lying on the floor and still moving. I was ashamed. I wanted to keep my drone hovering over that roof to see if anyone would come to help the girl, but I received an order to check if there were any car bombs at the entrance to the neighbourhood.

When we took control of the area, we found some Yezidi women in detention – five women, all in their twenties – and they told us what the Daesh people had done to them. I mean, even monsters couldn't have done what they had done to these people. Those dogs. The girl who had been on the roof was found to have bled to death. Her father had been killed by Daesh and her mother was sick in bed and couldn't move. The mother had told her six-year-old son to look after his sister but the boy been busy playing with a water pistol in the bathroom.

We received information from the Yezidi women about a boy called Fahd who was in the neighbourhood. He had been bringing food for Daesh when they were gang-raping the women. There was a fourteen-year-old girl who passed out when they raped her and they went on raping her when she was unconscious. God is greater than this brutality and these crimes. Even Saddam didn't do what they have done. Our groups caught Fahd and interrogated him. He turned out to have trained with Daesh and was their spy in the neighbourhood. I don't know, but he seemed poor and confused and he didn't understand anything. Our group beat him up because they wanted more information from him. They interrogated him and asked him if he had raped any Yezidi women. He swore by the Quran that he hadn't taken part. But one of the Yezidi women said the Daesh people once invited him to go and rape one of the women. There were two horrible men in our group that I didn't like. One was called al-Hassan Abu Ali and the other was Khdeir. They were two of the filthiest men in God's creation and they had no morals. Khdeir had worked as a tattooist for a while and to be honest he did draw well. One day, al-Hassan suggested to his friend Khdeir that they teach a lesson to Fahd, the Daesh boy. That night they pulled down the boy's trousers and tattooed a picture of a penis on his right ass cheek and wrote 'Enduring and Expanding', one of the slogans of Islamic State, on the left cheek. Of course, our commander, Abu Wala. gave them a serious telling-off.

After that we relocated to Tal Afar in a big convoy. It was sunset and the air had turned dusty. Why, O Lord, are we doomed to all these disasters, all this fear and death? Ever since I was born the wars haven't stopped. There was the war with Iran for eight years, then the hunger and humiliation of sanctions, then the invasion and civil war, then after that Daesh. What's after that? Where are we going? What's wrong, O Lord, with us Iraqis? Or are there people in the world who just don't want Iraq to thrive? Fine, how could it thrive when we're still just Sunnis, Shi'ites, Kurds, Turkomans and Christians? If, as our group says, the Sunnis sold us to Daesh, who are the Kurds going to sell us to tomorrow or the day after? And haven't we Shi'ites sold ourselves to Iran? I wanted to tell Aboul Qasim how I felt, but I was worried he might inform on me and reprimand me, because we Shi'ites have been oppressed and we have to assert our rights and protect ourselves from the takfiris, the Sunni extremists who dismiss Shi'ites as infidels.

We arrived on the outskirts of Tal Afar at night, camped there and had rice and green beans for dinner. After that, I sat with Aboul Qasim. We checked our drone and the guys in the group with the heat-sensor drone launched theirs after sunset and monitored the neighbourhood. Our task – Aboul Qasim's and mine – would begin at the first light of dawn.

Aboul Qasim was a very heavy smoker and lit one cigarette after another. He gave me one. I tried it and kept coughing, and he kept laughing. 'I've never been a drinker or a smoker,' I told him.

'I used to drink arak, but I've given up now,' said Aboul Qasim.

I confessed to him that, for a while, I used to take Artane pills when I was selling stuff in the Muridi market. 'Tell me,' he asked, 'what did it feel like?' I tried to find words to describe how it felt. 'I really don't know,' I said. 'I mean, I felt really good, I mean, totally okay and life seemed great. I was there and not there. I mean, how can I explain it? When I worked at Ahbab Allah Radio I learned the word *chimera*. Do you know it?'

Aboul Qasim laughed. 'Of course,' he said, 'It's like fantasy. I read books when I was young, and writing poetry is basically fantasy.'

Then I asked him, 'How can one live beyond one's problems, even if one has problems?'

'What do you mean?' Aboul Qasim replied.

'Like drugs, I mean,' I said. 'Even if you do have a problem, your mind tells you that life's good and going fine and everything's perfect.'

'You need an old Farid al-Atrash song that goes: "Life is good but if only we could understand it." Just find someone who understands it.'

'So if you understand life, then life feels good.'

'Maybe,' said Aboul Qasim. 'Definitely, the more you understand and learn and open your eyes and senses, the more the cares of the world fade away slightly. I mean, you know, for example, when someone gets old people take what they say seriously and listen to them. Of course, not everyone who grows old becomes wise. I mean, the more experience you have, the better you'll understand your own life and other people's lives. And the better you understand, the more patient you are in dealing with problems and the more peaceful your relationships with other people are. Reading books teaches you a lot. I mean, for example, when you read a foreign novel, let's say one set in Brazil, while you're reading it's like you're living there. So reading makes you become an outsider, and by being outsiders people always learn about themselves and about the world. They gain more experience of life. But, even so, few people learn from their experiences, and by their nature people soon forget. This is a blessing and a curse at the same time, because if you don't forget, you'll go mad from thinking too much, and if you do forget you won't be able to take advantage of what you've learnt in life.'

'You're a philosopher, Aboul Qasim. I had no idea!' I said.

He laughed and said, 'Listen, this is another story: When I was young I totally loved nature. The sound of the birds, rivers, and trees!! I always imagined myself as a tree. In my daydream, a pretty girl would come and sit in my branches and talk to me.'

'A girl with nice breasts, of course,' I remarked.

Aboul Qasim laughed again and said, 'When Saddam was overthrown, I was a young man and I was in love with a girl called Salma, and because of her I started writing poetry. She was our neighbour and sometimes, after sunset, I'd jump onto their roof and we'd hide behind the oven. She'd expose her breasts to me and I'd suck on her nipples. We messed around. Salma got married and time passed. Years later, can you imagine, we got in touch again. Text messages and Facebook, but we never met. I'd write to her about the smell of the oven and her breasts and the sunset. Her husband was in business, importing goods from China. Once he went on a long trip for about a month. Salma told me to arrange a place because she wanted to see me. I arranged a flat through a friend. She came with her young kids. She wouldn't let me sleep with her and said she only wanted me to suck her tits, like in the old days on the roof. Her breasts had grown larger and smelled of milk. It wasn't as much fun as it used to be. She was worried and I was uneasy, thinking of her children when she breastfed them. I tried to persuade her to let me fuck her, but she wouldn't and she was frightened. A few days later she sent me a text message, begging me to break off our relationship and not communicate any more. I'm telling you this story for the first time because the poem I read to you before, if you remember, came from this situation.'

'Yes, that's the one where you say your beloved's heavenly breasts have two rivers, one of milk and one of wine. To be honest, it's rather a ridiculous poem,' I said. I felt that Aboul Qasim was a little upset and he changed the subject.

'Tell me about your love life,' he said.

'When I was a teenager, I was in love with the neighbour, but she was an older woman,' I said. Aboul Qasim nearly died laughing. 'You're right to laugh,' I said. 'Later, when I was a little older, I thought that maybe I was in love with her because I wanted to have a mother like her. I don't know.' I wanted to tell him about dear Zeinab, but I was worried I might let slip something about the Bulbul al-Sayyid emails.

There was a photographer called Nassir al-Maliki with us. He was making a documentary about the Popular Mobilisation Forces and the humane way they treated people. Of course, he exaggerated a little and even lied. I mean, when we caught Daesh people, we punched and kicked them and roughed them up, but they deserved it. But he would reenact the scene and show us giving them water and food, treating their wounds, and reminding them to follow real Islamic ethics, treating the prisoners with full respect. Once I had a quarrel with this Nassir. He came and told me he wanted me to launch my drone for him so that he could take some shots for his film. 'Come and shoot when I have an official assignment,' I told him. 'These aren't homing pigeons I can set free just so that you can watch.' But he didn't like what I said. He went to our boss and complained about me. He turned even crazier when my boss sent for me and thanked me in front of him because I had been committed to my job and hadn't disobeyed orders. Of course, I don't bear a grudge against anyone for long. I forgive and forget. I went to Nassir and apologised to him. He turned out to be a good guy, accepted my apology and told me his story. He had been a refugee in Germany, but his asylum application was rejected. He came back with plans to fight for Iraq. Within a few days we became friends and he would join Aboul Qasim and me when we sat around telling stories. One day he said he had a joint. We were surprised, and he said that when he was in Germany he would only smoke marijuana, which he called *weed*, using the English word. We went somewhere secluded and smoked the joint together. Of course, I kept coughing and got a little paranoid, while Nassir and Aboul Qasim kept laughing at me. Then Nassir told us about a famous disco in Germany called the Berghain. Not just anyone could get in, he said. There was a bouncer sitting by the door, and a long line of girls and boys. When you get to the door, the bouncer looks at you. If he likes the look of you, he lets you in. We asked him how he decides. 'It depends on the bouncer's mood and personal experience,' Nassir said. 'From your eyes, he can tell whether you'll able to handle the atmosphere of the place and enjoy yourself without any problems.' He said that inside the disco there were all kinds of drugs available and sexual activities of all types – boys with boys, women with women, a man with several women, alone, in two, in threes. Whatever you want was there! Nassir thought for a while and then continued his story. 'It was the shock of my life,' he said. 'I took some cocaine and started to wander around the place, which was very big and the music was so loud you couldn't hear what the person next to you was saying. There were people fucking each other in the disco and no one cared what anyone else was doing. Suddenly a girl came up to me. I spoke no English and very little German. The girl was really pretty and her tits were spilling out of her dress.' I immediately looked at Aboul Qasim, the breast specialist, and smiled. 'The girl started pressing against my body, rubbing my ass and stroking the hair on my chest. Then I gave her a long kiss and went into a kind of trance. I had an erection and I put my hand between her legs but it turned out there was a cock there, and a hard one at that.'

We laughed in amazement and thought Nassir was lying or exaggerating about the goings-on in the disco. 'So tell us, what happened next?' Aboul Qasim asked him.

'You know, with the cocaine and the world on fire, to be honest I fucked him or fucked her from behind! But I swear, by Hussein Abu Abdallah, everything about him was like a girl - breasts, lips, voice and smell.'

Of course at the time I thought he was exaggerating or lying to us. But after I became a refugee in Sweden, I could confirm what Nassir al-Maliki said. It turned out that there really are discos like that, especially in Germany, and everything he said about the Berghain, the nightclub in Berlin, was true.

Poor Nassir al-Maliki. Later on, just before the liberation of Tal Afar, he found himself taking photos of a cow that had been cut in half by artillery shelling, when a Daesh sniper shot him in the forehead and killed him. And to think: if he had stayed in Germany, smoking hashish and fucking, how much better off would he have been? Aboul Qasim and I often reminisced about Nassir and the joint, and the way he described the vagina that turned out to be a cock, and we'd almost die laughing.

A day before the assault on Tal Afar, we rose at dawn and got ready. We launched our drones and did a reconnaissance of the area. The Daesh fighters started shooting at our drones, so we called them back. Then they sent up their own drones and our people started shooting at them. We had a laugh about it. We sent up drones and they shot at them, then the other way round again. Aboul Qasim said, 'What's all this? Now the Mobilisation Forces and Daesh are fighting like rival pigeon trainers?'

It went on like that until my drone developed a fault. Suddenly it came down on the roof of a building. I tried to get it airborne again, but it was no use. The signal from the drone suddenly disappeared. I couldn't see anything on the screen and got upset. I thought that maybe Daesh had taken control of my drone or shot it down. I tried to reactivate it, but nothing happened. Then ten minutes later, amazingly, the drone came back online and started transmitting pictures. I sighed with relief and said, 'Thank God for that. Let's hope it doesn't happen again.' I launched the drone and brought it back to see what kind of state it was in. I landed it on the ground and as I walked towards it, it exploded.

The next thing I knew I was in hospital with my left leg bandaged up and unable to move. The doctor came and said, 'You're lucky you survived.' He explained that the injury was serious. The muscle was torn and some of the nerves were damaged. He said I would have a limp, at least a slight one, for the rest of my life.

My friends from the Pigeon companies came to visit me en masse, bringing tikka, kebabs and oranges. After a while the lads left and only Aboul Qasim stayed at my side. He asked me what had happened. I told him how my drone had gone down on the roof of a building, how the transmission had been mysteriously cut off and how just as mysteriously it came back to life again. My friend smiled and said, 'Our people looked into it and came to some conclusions. Daesh captured your drone on that roof. Then they covered the camera lens and attached a small bomb to the drone. You brought the drone back and it exploded when you went towards it.'

I went home on indefinite sick leave. Karima kept crying and moping over the state I was in. I was also seriously depressed about my life. I went into long and bitter daydreams. At night, Karima would be asleep and, amazingly, even when the poor woman slept she would sigh every now and then. What a strange woman! I left my hand on her chest so that I could feel her breaths and her sighs. Then I remembered Aboul Qasim and his stories about women's breasts and smiled. I'd forgotten to tell Aboul Qasim that when we were young we had a fantasy rather like his lame poem about milk and wine and 'breast paradise'. When we were children, we would tell each other 'Your mother's got two breasts – one with milk and one with tea', and then we would laugh and josh around about breasts.

Bulbul and the Martyrs

Anyway, at least I survived, thank God. Where I had once been Muhsin al-Bulbul, now they called me Bulbul the Lame. People have no mercy. Even when they're surrounded by filth, destruction and injustice, they have hearts of stone. I swear by Hussein Abu Abdallah!

Mosul was liberated and I had a baby girl I called Hawraa. Praise God, she looked like her mother and all she inherited from me was my long nose. 'Let's see,' I said to Karima, 'either she'll inherit your sighs from you or my daydreaming from me.'

Karima laughed and said, 'As long as she doesn't inherit them both and become a daydreaming sigher.'

Thankfully the Daesh catastrophe was almost over and I was delighted with Hawraa. At last I was a father and I told myself that now I had to think seriously about my life for the sake of my daughter's future. I went to see Uncle Tahir and spoke to him. I asked him for help to buy a taxi so that I could work as a taxi driver. 'Why don't you stay in the Mobilisation

Forces?' he asked. 'The state's going to look after them, and your limp isn't that bad. You could get an office job with them.' He could see I was reluctant. 'Okay,' he said, 'go back to the office now and this time I'll make sure you get an official salary. We'll see about the taxi business later.' So I went back to the Ahbab Allah office, singing that line in the song: 'Why do you have to suffer, if not 'cos the alternatives are worse?' A week later, Uncle Tahir gave me what he called an easy assignment, a job that would supposedly give me great credit with God. My new work would be with the families of the Ahbab Allah martyrs who had fought with the Popular Mobilisation Forces. They would send me to visit the families with an envelope containing a modest amount of money as compensation for their loss, and I would also give them promises about future entitlements that the government was going to provide. In other words, a little money and lots of promises. From the start, I didn't like the work. Why me? There wasn't anyone else to do it, I guess. I swear, Uncle Tahir was going to drive me mad.

At home we had a large mirror and I'd walk back and forth in front of it every day and see how I looked and how my limp was going. I was really in low spirits. I had a daydream when I was looking at myself and told myself I had to stay strong and make sure my daughter Hawraa wasn't in need of anything. This would the last time I looked at myself and thought about my limp, I told myself. Life goes on, as they say in the TV serials. I went into the bathroom and shaved off my beard and moustache. I put on new clothes I'd bought in Karrada and went out to the coffee shop to see my friend who lived nearby, Ali Abdel Hussein. I told him about my time in Mosul and he complained to me about conditions in the school where he taught. The building was old, the teachers were rubbish and the syllabus was retarded. He told me about the problems with education in the country in general. I really liked him and respected his opinions. He was a freethinking and honest man, and frankly he was against the politics of all the Islamist parties, lock, stock and barrel. He always said that, after years of sufferings and wars, Iraq deserved something better than these corrupt and backward parties that hide their dishonesty under the cloak of religion. I was always warning him about what he said, saying he should be careful. There were people who wouldn't understand what he was saying and they would soon betray him. He didn't care. He was a brave guy, and he was always telling me about education and health. He said that if Iraq wanted to make a proper start the first thing it needed to do was put all its resources into improving education and health. And the most important of all was mental health. 'Ali, the psychiatrist for Iraqis!' I said.

'After all these shocks and crises and wars, would you expect Iraqis to be still sane?' he asked. 'Bulbul, my friend, if a society doesn't acknowledge its diseases or criticise itself or get itself treated, you can kiss it goodbye.'

He explained to me what psychological damage people suffer when they're subjected to disasters and shocks. 'Physical wounds heal after a time,' he said, 'but psychological wounds are hard to heal, and any small problem can open them up again.'

'And my wounds, when they're opened, they bleed,' I said.

He laughed and said, 'Yes, Fouad Salim said that in a song: "Come back, come back, don't open the wounds, poor woman, come back."'

Ali asked me about my new job. I told him about visiting the martyrs' families and he said, 'I'm sorry, Bulbul, but with this work you'll be helping them deceive people and benefit from the death of their followers and from the misfortunes of their families. I hope that one day you'll wake up and cut yourself loose from those Ahbab Allah people. In fact, I know what people say about you, Muhsin. They say you're a poor guy and stuff like that, but I know you're savvy and smart and a totally good guy.'

The first family I visited was living in a half-built house in the Husseiniya district, and the house was clearly in a bad way.

The man who had died had left three young daughters and a baby boy who was still breastfeeding. His father met me and the dead man's wife came to say hello. I gave her the envelope with the money in it. The poor woman thanked me, started to cry and went off to her children. I recited the spiel I had learned by heart from Uncle Tahir, about how Ahbab Allah would never forget them, how they would get everything they were entitled to through the martyrs' institute, and how the Ahbab Allah member of parliament was going to put pressure on the government to expedite the process of honouring the martyrs. The dead man's father wore a black dishdasha and kept playing with a long string of black prayer beads. I felt he was upset and unconvinced by what I said. He asked me if I had any children. 'Yes,' I said, 'a little girl called Hawraa.' He told me that all the money in the world couldn't make up for the death of one of your sons or daughters. I bowed my head in embarrassment and sadness. I thought I was going to start crying. I felt uncomfortable and didn't know how to reply.

'I'm sorry, I really have to go,' I said. The man stood up and took me to the door. I put out my hand to shake his but he didn't put out his. 'May God be with you,' he said.

On the way home, I said to myself, 'This job is clearly going to cause me lots of grief and embarrassment.' I started daydreaming again, on many subjects: people living in peace, dying naturally, growing older, living their lives, seeing their children grow up, having fun and feeling sad, seeing their dreams grow with them. But in Iraq, death suddenly descends on your life like a thunderbolt, making no distinction between old and young. There's been so much death in recent years that we no longer have time to remember all the people who have suddenly died and disappeared from our lives. In *fusha* Arabic, they say 'death caught up with him' or 'death took him unawares' as if death was a bunch of assassins, and they say of a patient that 'he's wrestling with death' as if death were a raging bull or a wild beast. Likewise, we Iraqis say 'death came to him'. Okay, but how did it come? Was it walking, running, or flying like Azraeel, the angel of death? And sometimes they say 'death snatched him', as if death were some rogue militia that kidnaps people and locks them up. People also say, 'He moved to the environs of his Lord', but how did he move? I imagined myself dead and shooting up like a rocket to my Lord. I was totally overwhelmed by the injustices in the world, and I felt myself seething, like a kettle on the stove.

In the afternoon I went and met my friend Ali and I told him about my ruminations on death. He laughed at the story of the rocket and wrestling with death and abductions, especially the idea of death abducting people like the militias. Ali told me about people's ideas about death in various religions and philosophy. Scientists understand death as the end of the cell. Cells grow old, fall silent and break down. I said, 'So human beings are like machines that break down.' And he told me about a theory that atheists like, about Darwin and evolution. 'Ali, are you an atheist?' I said.

'Almost,' he said, 'they call people like me agnostics, which means they don't know whether God exists or not. Believers are people who believe in the existence of a divine being and atheists deny the existence of a god. Those who don't know, like me, I mean who are simply unsure, they have doubts and think and look for answers and ideas in this world, which is difficult to understand. Of course, agnosticism is an old philosophy and loads of books have been written about it.'

'So old equivocator Allawi isn't the only one who "doesn't know"!' I joked. 'Is this a complete philosophy that arose and nobody knew anything about it?' We laughed. The last thing I said was, 'Ali, be careful, bro, with these ideas. You know the mentality round here.' I swear by Almighty God, I seemed to feel that something was going to happen. A week later Ali disappeared. His family looked for him in the hospitals and police stations, but there was no news of him. They say that before he disappeared he had written a post making fun of Iran and the Ayatollah Khomeini. I told Uncle Tahir that we had to look for Ali and find out if he had been abducted. He was our neighbour and my friend, and maybe Ahbab Allah could find out through its contacts where he was. But my uncle said, 'Your friend Ali is a troublemaker. Several times people spoke to him and told him to be careful what he wrote on Facebook, but he was as stubborn as a mule.' I was upset and told my uncle that Ali was a good guy but he had strong feelings about the lives of ordinary people.

'You don't see the state the hospitals and schools are in and the filth people have to live in,' I said. 'It only has to rain a little and we drown in sewage water.'

'That's another matter,' he said. 'Talking about things that people hold sacred is something else. Don't even go there.'

He gave me a new envelope and the address of a martyr's family in the Shuala district. I left the Ahbab Allah offices in a bad mood. Maybe it was Ahbab Allah that had abducted Ali. Anything could happen! Ahbab Allah was always blaming rogue militias for activities of this kind and saying that the sayyid didn't approve of such behaviour.

I took a taxi to Shuala. I was really upset about Ali. The martyr from Shuala had been nineteen years old and two of his brothers had been killed during the period of sectarian conflict. The only survivors were his mother, his grandmother, his brothers' children and his father, who was an old man. I did the necessary. His family thanked me and kept praying for the sayyid, whose picture covered the walls all over the house.

On the way home, I bought a toy for Hawraa that worked on batteries. Karima cooked us some excellent dolma. It was July and the weather was scorching and we were sitting in the cool air from the air conditioning unit. After lunch, Hawraa went to sleep. Karima and I lay down together and I had an orgasm, and Karima fell asleep. I went to the kitchen, poured and drank some grape juice. I opened the laptop and searched on Google for anything related to things that people hold sacred. I just wanted to understand what the problem was if someone criticised things like that.

In the afternoon, my uncle called me and I went to the

office. This time he gave me three envelopes full of money. 'These are for three martyrs from the same family in the Nahrawan district, and this is a private letter to the family from the sayyid himself. You can go and visit them tomorrow morning.' I took the money, gave it to Karima to hide away and told her I was in a bad mood and going to Karrada for a while to buy some clothes and then I'd come back. I really liked the atmosphere in Karrada and I always bought my clothes there. If I ever came into money, I told myself, I'd buy a house in Karrada and never leave the district. I asked Karima if she needed anything. She sighed and said, 'No, Bulbul, thank you, I don't need anything.'

'It only sounds nice when you call me Bulbul,' I said. 'With others, I think they're insulting me.'

'Bulbul, do you really love me?' she asked.

'Of course, Karima. You're my love and you mean the world to me.'

She hugged me and kissed my hand, and I kissed her hand and went out.

I bought just some t-shirts and a blue hat. Then I went to Amir's fruit juice shop, sat down and ordered a banana juice. I've been crazy about juices since the days when I used to work on a rickety cart during the sanction years. I bought Karima a nightdress and some panties. I really loved to buy panties and bras for her myself. I bought them in a hurry and left the shop because I was embarrassed. They turned out to be too small. Karima kept laughing and said, 'These are for a little girl. I'll give them to Umm Ali next door for her daughter.' She asked me if I had any news of my friend Ali Abdel Hussein.

'My God, I have been negligent. Today I'll go and ask how his wife is doing.' I went to Ali's house. The poor guy had a daughter and a son, may God preserve them, nice smart kids. His wife was also a teacher at middle school, teaching English. The poor woman cried and I told her there was no news, and she begged me to talk to my Uncle Tahir so that he might help them.

The next morning I went to the Nahrawan area to the home of the three martyrs, whose names were Jasim, Hazim and Basim. I knocked on the door and there didn't seem to be anyone in. It was a two-storey house. I knocked on the neighbours' door. A short, bald man appeared, wearing a white dishdasha. I asked him about the martyrs' family and he said they didn't have any family. They were just three brothers and they had been martyred, may God have mercy on them. I found that hard to believe. 'Their mother? Their father? Their brothers and sisters? Their children?' I asked.

'Come inside,' the man replied, 'and I'll tell you their story.' The man, who was called Abu Mahdi, was very hospitable. He brought me tea and cake and told me the story of the boys. Jasim and Hazim were twins, he said, and Basim was one year older than them. A year after giving birth to the twins, their mother had thrombosis and died, may God have mercy on her! The poor kids had a genetic defect. They were all blind, although their mother could see. They inherited it from their father, who was also blind. One day, their father was crossing the street and a car hit him and he was killed.'

'They were blind and in the Mobilisation Forces?' I asked the man in surprise.

Abu Mahdi sighed and said, 'Some blind people can see better than people with good eyesight, and understand more too. The kids were very intelligent and learned to read and write by that method they call Braille, where they learn the letters by touch.'

I said, 'Oh yes. Is it called Breell or Braille?'

'Anyway,' Abu Mahdi said, 'the kids were very smart and amazingly talented, praise the Lord. They learned languages quickly. When they were teenagers all three of them learned to play the violin and they learned English straight off amazingly well. They were talented, may God have mercy on them. Music and languages were their whole life. When the Americans came in, they were still young and people really liked them, and they played at weddings. But as they got older, they preferred to play that foreigner music they call 'classical'. They worked with some young artists in theatre and television. Once they were filmed in a report that was on TV. Anyway, the boys grew up and started to develop by themselves and learn lots of languages. They knew six or seven languages – English, Russian, French, German, Farsi, even Kurdish. When the troubles began, the boys volunteered to join the Mobilisation Forces. Of course, our people in the Ahbab Allah office were surprised. But they thanked them for volunteering and said they'd get back to them later. When the Mobilisation leaders heard about them, they called them in immediately. It turned out that they really needed them. Daesh had people from Europe and every country in the world. The Mobilisation Forces had a unit that eavesdropped on Daesh communications and the Daesh people often jabbered away in foreign languages so that no one locally would understand. So the kids were very useful with that. Then the awful Americans, those sons of bitches, came and bombed the Mobilisation headquarters and said it was a mistake. The three kids were killed, along with ten other members of Ahbab Allah stationed at the headquarters. If you want to honour the memory of the martyrs, you should honour the man who took care of their education and helped them learn languages. He was like a father and teacher to them. He used to live with us here in the area and his name is Ridwan. The people in the area pestered him because he liked to drink arak. Now he lives alone in Rashid Street in a run-down boarding house.'

I thanked Abu Mahdi, took the man's address and went to Rashid Street. I was curious to hear the story of Ridwan's martyrs and find out what Ridwan was like too. His room in the boarding house was filthy and full of empty arak bottles. Ridwan himself was only just conscious, and he was hungry. I ordered a plate of kebabs from the restaurant next to the boarding house and he told me about Jasim, Hazim and Basim. 'Iraq has plenty of talent,' he said, 'but the instability in the country means the talent goes to waste. Iraq as a whole has gone to waste for that matter.' He downed a shot and ate the onions that came with the kebabs. He told me a little about his life, how he used to live in Bulgaria when Saddam Hussein was in power and had a Bulgarian wife who taught Braille. Ridwan learned everything from her and his wife helped him learn Braille too and he became a teacher to the blind. When Saddam was overthrown, he felt homesick for Iraq. He had two options – either die of grief and homesickness in exile, or leave his Bulgarian wife, who had helped him so much, and go back to Iraq. In the end, he chose the latter. He was shocked at the state the country was in and he felt like a stranger. It wasn't the Iraq he had remembered. He phoned his wife back in Bulgaria and she scolded him and asked him not to call her again. She never wanted to see him back in Bulgaria. Ridwan fell into a state of depression and drank more and more arak. The only thing that saved him at first was meeting the three kids – Hazim, Bassim and Jassim. They became his students and his adopted children. In truth, they became his whole life. He taught them to read and write and monitored their progress, helping them with everything. He was more than a father, a friend and a brother to them. When they were killed, hope died inside Ridwan. He crawled into the arak bottle and when he tried to come up, he couldn't. He was like the genie trapped in the lamp.

I was wary of handing all the money over to Ridwan, in case my uncle told me off for giving it to someone who not only wasn't related to the dead men, but was also a drunk. In the end, I told myself that a small white lie would help this poor man and wouldn't have any effect on the Ahbab Allah budget. I gave him the money and the letter from the sayyid. He poured himself a drink and drank it with one hand as he held the letter with the other, laughing and shaking his hand as he read it. I left him and returned home. I called my uncle and told him the money had been delivered. 'Well done,' he said, 'I've prepared two more martyrs for you. Drop in on the office in the morning.' I asked for the day off, saying I felt ill and wanted to rest for a few days. 'You're right,' he said, 'you need a holiday. Take it easy for a week and then come by. If you need anything, just phone me.'

I saw Uncle Tahir a week later at the funeral of my friend Ali Abdel Muhsin. They had found his body in wasteland. By chance some dogs had dug up his corpse from a shallow grave, and the smell had alerted the locals, who called the police. My uncle wouldn't speak to me or even look in my direction. I went and sat next to him. 'What's up?' I asked. 'When you've paid your condolences, come and see me in the office,' he said.

I went to his office and my uncle asked me about the money for Hazim, Jassim and Bassim. 'Who did you give the money to?' he asked. He had obviously heard something. I told him the whole story from beginning to end and apologised to him. I told him I had given the money to Ridwan, the martyrs' teacher.

My uncle was furious. 'You gave the money for three martyrs to a drunk who isn't even a member of their family!' he said. 'What will I tell people? Where can I hide my face?'

'Just calm down and tell me what you heard,' I said. Then he told me what had happened.

A few days after I had gone to Nahrawan and seen Abu Mahdi, the neighbour of the three martyrs, their aunt had come to clear out the house. Abu Mahdi had told her that the sayyid had sent someone with a letter and loads of money. 'But I told him they didn't have any family, and I suggested he track down Ridwan their teacher,' he added. The woman was furious. She was poor and eked out a living selling vegetables in the market. She went to the Ahbab Allah office in Nahrawan and made a scene, saying that she had been like a mother to the three blind martyrs and she was in dire straits and her husband was a disabled policeman. Anyway, she made a song and dance about every misfortune, disease and hardship that had ever afflicted her, until she had God himself in tears. They contacted my uncle from the Nahrawan office and implored him to make sure the sayyid's gift and letter went to the martyrs' aunt.

My uncle gave me a dressing-down and put me on open-ended vacation. 'Go and sort yourself out,' he said. 'while I fix this. You've embarrassed me and let me down. Seriously, look at yourself, why are you so slovenly and disorganised? Whenever I give you a nice job that might do you some good, you ruin it, let me down and embarrass me in front of everyone.' Then he threw me out. 'God won't help you prosper after this dirty trick. Out, off you go, out,' he said.

I really wished Uncle Tahir would lay off me. I just wanted to break free of the Ahbab Allah office and all their bullshit, hypocrisy and lame excuses. We went to sleep on the roof under a clear night sky and I found myself looking at a particularly bright star. We had a light sheet for covering. Karima put her hand on my cock and I immediately had an erection. We came at the same time, Karima and me, without making a sound. The neighbours certainly didn't notice. Karima sighed and fell asleep, and I sighed and went into a daydream about the sky and the other planets. Now, if there was life on another planet, would there be sayyids and and Shi'ite militias on them too? I closed my eyes and imagined myself living with a gang on Mars, all of them lame like me and blind like the martyrs.

Bulbul's Tuktuk

When anti-corruption protests broke out in Baghdad, Uncle Tahir asked me to go along as an observer. On several occasions I told him I didn't understand why we, as Ahbab Allah, were not taking the side of the young protesters. I put it to him that what they really wanted me to do was spy on them. He beat about the bush, and I couldn't get much sense out of him. But I gathered at least that he wanted me to find out if the uprising had any leaders and if there was any foreign funding for the protests.

Of course, I had to obey my uncle and Ahbab Allah. Would anyone say no to them? They bought me a tuktuk and I drove in among the protesters in Tahrir Square after they had taken over the Turkish restaurant and renamed it Mount Uhud. Ahbab Allah asked me to write a report every week.

The tuktuk revolution represented a new start in my life and changed my way of thinking. It not only helped me to understand new things, but also enabled me to meet and discover Baghdad for the first time in my life. I felt like a stranger when I first saw the protests. In the past, there had seemed to be many Baghdads: Karkh on the west bank of the Tigris, Rasafa on the east bank, the Sunni areas, the Shi'ite areas, migrants from the rural south and the old Baghdadis, rich areas and poor areas, educated people and uneducated. But when I was among the protesters and became one of them I saw only one Baghdad. For the first time in my life, I felt we were all from one city and that we all knew each other. We were strangers before the protests. Everyone was living in their own bubble, trapped with people just like them, waking up and going to sleep with them, to the same concerns and the same narratives.

The tuktuk revolution made it possible for me to see and meet people I had never thought I would ever get to know. It was the first time in my life I had spoken to nice, intelligent, attractive girls from rich neighbourhoods that loved Iraq with all their hearts. I spoke with doctors, engineers, workers and shopkeepers. I saw university students that would make you feel proud, the kind of kids you'd want your sons and daughters to turn out like. It made you sad that it wasn't these talented people who were running the country. I saw Iraqis who lived abroad and who'd left their children, their work, and their idyllic lives in Europe to come and sweep the pavement in Tahrir Square. I saw young men full of enthusiasm, their eyes red from exhaustion and from the tear gas fired by the police.

I saw old women cooking and baking, praying and crying.

I saw artists, singers, journalists and poets. I saw young men from the provinces carrying their shrouds to show they were ready to die for the cause. I saw men, young and old. I saw poor people and rich people. Of course, I saw people who had come to Tahrir Square as tourists to take pictures, and I saw crooks, pickpockets and thieves. I saw people without jobs who had made the square their home. I saw con artists and oddballs who were disrupting the movement. I saw drunks and religious fanatics. I saw good guys and bastards. I saw all kinds of people. But there were far more good things than bad. I saw heroic acts of the kind you see in films, and all the while Tahrir Square pulsated with love, fear, anxiety, anger and hope.

I saw all of Iraq in Tahrir Square. I saw all Baghdad, sitting down in Tahrir Square in the morning for breakfast and saying, 'Good morning, my country. I want you to be a real country.' I felt like I wanted to write poetry, stories, songs. Half my soul was happy and half was sad. Half full of hope and half of fear.

The first problem I faced was with Uncle Tahir, namely the reports I wrote and handed in every Friday afternoon. He was annoyed because all my reports were written in Iraqi *ammiya* and not in *fusha*, standard Arabic. I told him I couldn't write in standard Arabic and anyway, do we speak and live in *fusha* or in the Iraqi *ammiya* you're speaking to me in right now? 'These are official orders, my dear,' he said.

'What does "official" mean?' I asked, 'Even our leader's best known slogans are all in Iraqi *ammiya*, aren't they? And the people who talk on official state television all speak in *ammiya*.'

'That's enough! Don't talk about the sayyid like that,' he replied.

Then Uncle Tahir complained about the content of the reports. 'What's with all these heroics?' he asked. 'You make the protesters sound like action heroes.'

'I swear I don't make this stuff up. I mean, if a twenty-year-old man bares his chest to the riot police and the militias, and is then shot and killed by a cowardly sniper, isn't that heroic? Don't you understand? Only they're different; we don't have film directors like those in Hollywood to capture the reality of this young heroism. We have assholes on television, distorting the image of the protesters and doing them down just to cover up their own criminal corruption.'

My uncle was upset. 'What's come over you? I no longer understand the things you're saying or why you've changed. I mean, now you're up in arms against me?'

'Uncle, just one question, for your father's sake,' I said. 'Aren't we against corruption in Ahbab Allah?'

'Yes, we are.'

'Okay, but the sayyid isn't in favour of the protests?' I asked.

'Of course he's in favour!' said my uncle.

'So why isn't he praising the protesters on Twitter 24 hours a day?'

'Look, don't be snide. Just keep your eyes open. I want a list of every organiser's name and I want a good report, something we can be proud of when we send it to the sayyid's office.'

'Uncle, I've started to no longer understand you,' I said. 'and I don't understand Ahbab Allah or even what the sayyid wants.'

Uncle Tahir got angry and shouted in my face. 'Eat shit and shut the fuck up, you knucklehead,' he said. 'Get back to your work, you jackass! So now the cripple's spouting philosophy at me!'

I looked at him and my blood began to boil. When he said that word *cripple*, Uncle Tahir was dead to me, and I buried him along with everything else I've lost in my life.

My wife Karima said, 'Bulbul, you've changed, I can feel it. Your ruminations have started to last much longer and you're always worried.' I told her about the good young people who were being killed in the protests, cut down in their prime. 'I wish I had some authority,' I confessed. 'Then

I'd put all the political parties in jail for life so that we could be rid of these traitors who kill their own people then go and clown around on television, on the grounds that they're analysing the situation in Iraq. Let them go and analyse their own rotten cock-swallowing arses, those lowlifes who sell their asses to Khamenei and Iran.'

My uncle called and said, 'Next week I want a detailed report on one of the activists or leaders, and if you can't do that, come back to the office, hand over the tuktuk and we'll have some other work for you.'

Later that week, I came back from Tahrir Square with my clothes all stained in the blood of the injured people. Karima was terrified. 'For God's sake, Muhsin,' she begged, 'please give up going to the square.' She threw my clothes in the washing machine, while I went into the bathroom and cleaned myself up. I went and opened my laptop, and on YouTube I watched a sermon by the ayatollah, in which he stated his opinion on the protests and the protestors. My sister Zahra came to visit. So I had Zahra's problems to deal with, as well as the world's. It broke my heart when I thought of the state she was in. 'Zahra, would you like to come to Tahrir with me and have a look?' I asked her.

The poor woman was delighted. 'But I'm worried about the tear gas,' she said.

'Don't worry,' I said, 'I know how to show you around and get you out safe.' I left her with Karima to talk about the price of clothes and gossip about the girls in the neighbourhood, and marriage and divorce and their horoscopes. I went into my room. I had to write the report for Ahbab Allah. In my head, I had a thousand and one stories about Tahrir. I was thinking about all the heroic men and women, part of a generation unprecedented in the history of Iraq. I wished I had the talents of a novelist or short story writer, to tell their stories. Which young hero should I write about, I wondered, and where would I begin? The day must come when there are statues to many of these Tahrir rebels in the streets of Baghdad.

I opened Word and decided to write something specially for Uncle Tahir. I wrote, 'In the name of God the Merciful, the Compassionate...' I thought for a moment and then I deleted 'In the name of God' and started to write:

A Report from Tahrir Square
Activist's name: Diyaa al-Nuwas
Education: Graduate of the College of Fine Arts, design section
Occupation: Unemployed

Diyaa's father was killed in the sectarian conflict. They slit his throat and threw his body on a rubbish heap. He has two sisters and a young brother. They live in a rented house in the Jamila neighbourhood. His father had a small shop selling groceries. In college, Diyaa was clever and did well. Everyone who knew him really liked him and spoke well of his character. They said he was creative and both his teacher and fellow students liked him and expected him to have a great future. When he graduated, there weren't any government jobs, of course. So he worked in a bakery, a hairdresser's and a kebab restaurant and also sold cigarettes in the Shorja market.

Diyaa was handsome, stunningly good-looking in fact. He had a short beard, was very level-headed and had a good singing voice. He wrote poetry and made up the slogans for the protests. Sometimes you'd find him in the first line of defence in the protests and sometimes with the first responders. Sometimes he'd be with the artists, drawing pictures in the tunnel there. I made friends with him and, of course, I was happy that he liked me and always called me when he needed a job done. Somehow I felt that he was my elder, that I was younger than him.

Diyaa had taken part in all the protests before the uprising, from al-Maliki to al-Mahdi. He was imprisoned several times. It's true that he sometimes drank beer, but he wasn't a drunk. He was more honourable than most people who pray and visit shrines and flagellate themselves, stealing money from orphans and profiting from the blood of soldiers, more honourable than those who let the richest country in the world become the plaything of Iran, a mere appendage. A country with no dignity, a country that makes no sense. It's not a protectorate, it's not democratic, it's not Islamic, it's not a dictatorship, it's not secular and it's not a country.

Diyaa wanted a country, but the Islamic parties don't want a country. They want the jobs in government, the ministries and the billions of dollars. Diyaa wanted schools and healthcare and streets and clean neighbourhoods. The parties want to live in the Green Zone and go on pleasure trips abroad and have palaces. Diyaa wanted to live free. They want to live as slaves to Iran, Saudi Arabia and America.[3]

Diyaa's only act of treason was that he sang of his love for his country in the square. His only crime was raising his arm and chanting at a peaceful demonstration. The crimes of the government and of the corrupt parties in the government are too many to count, but one day history will hold them to account and register them for eternity in the annals of shame. Diyaa's only crime was that he studied, worked hard and dreamed of releasing all his creativity, to design streets, gardens, buildings and parks for Iraq. All you have given him, you parties of betrayal and submission to foreign powers, is unemployment and fear. You slaughtered his father with your sectarian war.

In the end, you seized Diyaa from Tahrir Square and killed him. But how many will you have to kill? How many Diyaas in Iraq do you intend to slaughter? You're asleep, up to your waists in corruption. Everyone knows that nations live longer than rulers. If Saddam ended up in a hole in the ground, you're going to end up in the sewers. That's where your life story will come to an end.

The Diyaa that they killed was not just a person of flesh and blood. Diyaa was an idea and a dream. The Diyaa that they shot dead will not die. Diyaa is a child that has just been born, as God created him – a free person. Neither your morbid sectarianism nor your putrid corruption can stand in his way. There are now a thousand and one Diyaas. Like *A Thousand and One Nights*, Diyaa will live forever.

I knew that what I had written wasn't exactly a report. It was more of a letter of resignation from Ahbab Allah. I expected Uncle Tahir would throw me out of the office. In fact, after reading the report he made me hand in the tuktuk and said, 'Go and sort yourself out. As for the crap in your report – mind you don't speak about it to anyone, or else, by Hussein Abu Abdallah, I'll have you cut in half.'

I was so happy to be leaving the office. With all my heart, I hoped they wouldn't send for me again. Even if they wanted me for another assignment, I couldn't possibly go back. No way! They force you to become a soldier in the Ahbab Allah Army, but even a soldier's term of service comes to an end eventually and then he can take it easy. I walked around in the crowds, full of energy and enthusiasm. I went and ate baklava in the market. I bought some bras for Karima, a black one, a red one and a white one. I was anticipating what she would say when she saw them. What she said was: 'Well now, Bulbul, those are the colours of the Iraqi flag,' and she laughed.

'Try them on,' I said, 'nothing suits a pair of breasts better than the colours of the Iraqi flag!'

We were alone in the room. She tried them on one by one and said, 'All they're missing is the words Allahu Akbar.' I kissed her breasts and whenever she changed the colour I shouted 'Allahu Akbar', the slogan inscribed on the Iraqi flag. Then, speaking in *fusha*, I said, 'Your bosom, my love, is the most precious flag waving in my life. Give me more breast, give me more, O sweetest of my bouts of madness.' We laughed and licked and sucked each other and had fun and then fell asleep.

I went back to Tahrir Square as a free man, unattached to Ahbab Allah, and helped with everything – cleaning, cooking, writing slogans and chants, through happy times and sad. I posted on Twitter, with all my posts being designed to serve the tuktuk revolution and the revolutionaries. Later, I had an idea. There was one young activist who was always on the front lines at every gathering and every confrontation – in al-Khilani, in al-Sinak and in Tahrir. The kid, who was called Murad, live-streamed the protests and talked about them online. He was a good, brave guy and he had thousands of followers inside Iraq and abroad. I told him I had a request to make of him. 'I want to film you with my phone and follow you wherever you go. I'll film you when you're live-streaming, when you're taking a break, when you're attacking the riot police and when you're defending. In other words, I'll film your whole daily activities in the protest.'

Murad welcomed the idea unreservedly. 'You'll have to wear a helmet and be careful,' he said.

'But *you* don't seem to care,' I said. 'You've no helmet, no mask, as if you're going out for a picnic.'

'Don't worry about me,' he said. 'I have experience.'

'Were you a regular soldier? Special forces?' I asked him.

'Later. Another time, you'll hear the story.'

Anyway, one day there was trouble in al-Khilani and they killed seven young guys from our side. I filmed Murad as he was retreating. He was devastated and he was talking excitedly about Iran, the militias and the Islamic parties.

The next day a correspondent from al-Arabia Television came to see me and said, 'I hear you were filming at al-Khilani. Could I do an interview with you and could we broadcast your video?'

'Of course,' I said. I wanted the whole world to know

about the crimes being committed by these has-been stooges. They interviewed me live on air and I poured out everything that was in my heart, all my pain. In the next news bulletin they repeated the interview and broadcast the video I had filmed, in which Murad spoke about Iran and the Islamist parties.

When I went home, a car stopped near me and three masked gunmen got out. They forced me into the car and blindfolded me. I expected them to kidnap me and I was prepared for it. Many protesters and activists knew that if they weren't killed they might be kidnapped and tortured. They asked me to take my clothes off and then they gave me a dishdasha. My eyes were still covered. They interrogated me, but there was no beating or torture, just insults, shouts and threats. They asked me how many protesters there were, where the money came from, what America's role was and what the Joker story was all about.[4] Loads of stupid questions had nested in their heads – things their addled imaginations had concocted. They wanted me to tell them about instances of rape or drunkenness in Tahrir Square. I spent four days with them. They gave me food but only questioned me for the first two nights. On the fourth day, two masked men came in and took the blindfold off. 'You're from the Ahbab Allah group!' one of them said. 'Why are you mixed up with these Joker people?'

'And where are you from?' I asked them. I was about to suggest 'some rogue militia' but I was too frightened, and I just wanted to get out and go home to Karima. I really missed my daughter Hawraa.

One of the masked men said, 'The sayyid himself put in a good word for you.' A car came and took me home. Poor Karima was very happy to see me. She cried and made me swear I would stop going to the protests in Tahrir.

The next day a car came from the sayyid's office and they took me with them. I sat waiting in a room on my own for more than an hour, and then the sayyid turned up alone. I stood up. The sayyid sat down and said, 'Sit down, Bulbul. I got in touch with your uncle Tahir and understood from him about your job and the protests and the tuktuk and how you gave up because you're a genuine, incorrigible jackass! Do you think Iraq would survive if it wasn't for the Ahbab Allah Army?' Then he said he wanted me to tell him everything I saw in Tahrir and at the protests, from the first day I went there till the day they kidnapped me. I told him everything quite honestly and the sayyid was moved. Sometimes he smiled and sometimes he shook his head and looked upset. In other words, I didn't find out what he thought or felt about the protests. Before leaving the room, he asked me if I had any news of Zeinab. I swore to him, by Abbas ibn Ali, that I hadn't been in touch with her and hadn't spoken about the subject to anyone ever. 'Zeinab married an Iranian who works at the embassy,' he said. 'Be sensible, Bulbul, go back to your wife and daughter and do what your Uncle Tahir tells you.'

Karima made tea and sat beside me, combing Hawraa's hair. I was watching the news. A report came up on the sayyid's position on the protests, with some of the protesters accusing Ahbab Allah of attacking them. I opened my laptop and started to write and write. I stayed up late alone, sometimes writing and sometimes sighing like Karima. Iraq isn't a place for thinking and daydreams. It's a place for sighs. This is what I wrote:

No, I swear by the Lord of the Dancing Virgins,
The fox has slipped away, the damning evidence tied to his tail.
He's gone!
But you cannot escape, nor will the past be easily forgotten.
The martyrs' blood is like an albatross around your neck, shame upon shame,
You worthless stooge, you creature of every filth.
Yet you beat your chest and slap your face for Hussein, and raise your banners,
Banners that bear the stain of betrayal, the ignominy of compromised clerics.
No, By the Lord of the Dancing Virgins.

Bulbul and the Coronavirus

This time I walked to the Ahbab Allah office and volunteered to work with them. Not because I had forgotten who they were or because I didn't know what they were really like. It was just that the coronavirus had spread and their office had sterilisers and they had set up sterilisation teams in our neighbourhood and elsewhere. This was charity work to help people and save the lives of our families and our poor people, I said to myself, so I went and spoke to Uncle Tahir.

I put on white protective gear with four young men, and on our backs we carried drums of disinfectant. We started going around the backstreets and the market, spraying and sterilising. There were four of us – Saad, Mazin, Safaa and me. One day we were spraying in the market when Saad said we looked like the people in the film *Ghostbusters*. I hadn't seen the film, so I looked it up on the internet and it turned out that we really did look like them. While they hunted ghosts, we imagined we were hunting coronavirus and killing it.

You can live anywhere in the world and eventually you get used to it. I mean, it comes to feel normal and you forget the details that make the place what it is. Our neighbourhood, and the city as a whole, were in quite a state. I mean they had been run-down since the day God created them, like someone with a disease from birth. But when we started going around the backstreets, my thoughts opened wounds old and new. I felt we were fooling ourselves when we sprayed disinfectant on the rubbish and filth in the shabby street markets. Whole trucks of disinfectant wouldn't have been enough, not just to kill the virus but to disinfect all those piles of dirt and rubbish, so teeming with diseases and viruses. First of all, we needed an antidote to corruption. We needed to decontaminate the minds that had taken hold of the country and brought it to its knees. Saddam had already given it its fair share of beatings and punches, with his crazy wars. Iraqi society had poor immunity, and ignorance was the disease. The most dangerous virus was the exploitation of religion. To quote the protesters in Tahrir Square: 'in the name of religion, the thieves have robbed us!' Not only had they robbed us in the name of things people hold sacred, they had taken us backwards a hundred years. In the name of religion and religious sects they made people forget that we are living in the 21st century, with inventions and technologies too far advanced for people to understand. Science? What the hell!

Mazin said the coronavirus was an American conspiracy, and Saad said that because, in the West, guys fucked guys the disease had spread like AIDS, and so they say the medicine for AIDS worked with the coronavirus too. As for Safaa, he said we shouldn't sterilise and spray. We needed to exclude all the gays in the area because there were too many of them in Baghdad and all of Iraq. Mazin asked me what I thought.

'Well, for a start,' I said, 'can any of you tell me what viruses are? For example, how are they different from bacteria?'

'Bulbul, now what are you pretending to understand?' Mazin said. 'Viruses, bacteria, they're all diseases.'

'Okay,' I said, 'another question. People who die of coronavirus get lots of problems with their lungs. Do any of you know what lungs are – what they're made of and how they work?'

'Bulbul my dear,' said Saad, 'that's the doctor's job.'

'Okay, Saad,' I said. 'now be honest, you don't know the difference between viruses and bacteria, and you don't know how the lungs in your body work or what they're made of. But do you take the word of the billions of people who are trying to control this virus and are frightened of it? Of course not! You want someone to teach you a conspiracy theory about sexual perversion and homosexuality. Then you can relax and not bother to do any research or educate yourself.'

'On Twitter,' Safaa added, 'the sayyid posted a prayer that protects you from the disease. You have to recite it seven times a day and then you're immune.'

'So why are we spraying this disinfectant?' I said. 'Why don't we just spray prayers on people?'

I had a feeling they were upset with me, and I concluded that having a debate with feeble-minded people brought up on rustic superstitions wasn't going to lead anywhere. I went back home and Karima said, 'Straight to the bathroom.' She was wearing gloves and cleaning the house. She was terrified of the coronavirus and on high alert, cleaning and washing everything 24 hours a day – the house, the shopping, all the surfaces. I said, 'Karima, with us Iraqis it's either one extreme or the other. There are people who dismiss the virus and laugh at the plague, and then there are people like you who are going to war against it. As you like, my dear!'

'Muhsin,' she said. 'You've given up all kinds of jobs and now you're wandering around the backstreets sterilising. If you get infected, God forbid, Hawraa and I will get infected too, and this disease is a complete mystery.'

'For a start, children have good immunity,' I said, 'and we're still young too. We don't smoke and we eat well. Hopefully nothing will happen.'

Around that time I started staying up very late and I found it hard to sleep. I was anxious. I didn't know what about exactly, but I always felt there was something troubling me. Karima and Hawraa went to sleep and I stayed up with the laptop. I turned it off and went up on the roof. I sat on a chair in the middle of the roof and thought about the state we were in in Iraq. When the Baath Party took power, it drove everyone away. It treated everyone brutally – Arab nationalists, Islamists, communists, they even fucked over other Baathists. Some Shi'ite parties went to Iran and their members grew up there and studied and became soldiers fighting under the banner of Khomeini. In short, they used to kill Iraqi soldiers, but now they're governing Iraqis. Sure, this is the nature of political struggle and jihad. And the communists, they went and lay low in capitalist countries that they had long denounced in their slogans. You could find communist refugees wrapped in capitalist flags. My god, the world laughs, or maybe cries. The Shi'a inside Iraq, us, the ones who were out of favour, we were another story. We stayed in Iraq and we ate shit when we were under international sanctions. And when we rose up against Saddam in 1991 America, or capitalism, allowed the dictator to launch his warplanes and deploy his army until he put down the uprising and buried people in mass graves. In other words, America has, at different times, handed the Shi'ites of Iraq over to Saddam, and handed power to the Iraqi Shi'ites who came back from Iran.[5] The bastards play with the world as they like. Now, I swear, the Islamic parties, with all their slogans and manifestos that claim to be against America the Great Satan, are in fact the same people who came in with the American tanks? Okay, now leave that story aside! What have they achieved between 2003 and today other than the freedom to flagellate themselves, visit shrines and weep? Of course, forget about freedom of expression. One post on Facebook or Twitter and you'll vanish off the face of the earth. But I genuinely wanted to find out what their achievements have been. They worked hand-in-hand with some corrupt Kurds and corrupt Sunni parties, following the American model for democracy in Iraq.

First, they ignited a sectarian civil war that spared no one, big or small. The wounds of that conflict won't heal easily in the memories of Iraqis. Okay, corruption and theft. More than 500 billion dollars have disappeared since the day Baghdad fell, and that's an old statistic from several years ago. And with these people, how can you get good statistics? Then, because of their lousy sectarian policies, they opened the gates for every country in the world to drop in – Iran, Saudi Arabia, the Gulf states and Turkey. And those who came to Iraq fucked the country over, and eventually their sectarianism and corruption led to many of our cities falling into the hands of Islamic State. There were rapes, displacements and brutal crimes, and so far no minister, no security official, big or small, has been held to account for the fall of those cities.

So what were the achievements? Just tell me. Unemployment has reached unspeakable levels. Half the young people in the country are out of work. And, of course, more than three quarters of Iraqi women are out of work because of the traditions and 'morals' of the Islamic parties. The economy is wiped out. Industry is dead. Infrastructure has collapsed. Agriculture is finished – even vegetables are imported. There are countless security problems, gangs and mafias and crimes. It's a lawless state, where clans and tribes and sects have come back into power. The water is polluted, the environment has been destroyed and the land has dried up. Subservience to Iran and neighbouring states is now paramount. A few people have acquired privileges, money, and houses because of their sectarian affiliations, because of the roles they played against the dictator! Members of parliament are now among the richest people in the world, having somehow acquired state property. The Islamic parties have taken control of the embassies, the ministries, state-owned companies and all the finances and affairs of the state. In short, in the modern or ancient history of Iraq, there have never been such despicable people as these sectarian parties, these bastards.

After two weeks working with the sterilisation team, I had a very slight cough and felt a little tired. I was definitely anxious, but I didn't want to freak Karima out any more. It's just the dust and the dirt in this part of town, I said. But sometimes people are stubborn and overconfident, and they deceive themselves so much that they fall into a hole and even God can't get them out of it. A few days, later Karima had a very high fever and her terror that she might have Covid quickly sapped all her strength. Her whole body was trembling. I called my sister Zahra and she came and sat next to Hawraa. I took Karima to hospital in a taxi. They did some tests, the results came back confirming she had Covid. They said they'd put her in quarantine. The doctor asked us who at home had had contact with Karima. I said there's just my daughter Hawraa. He asked if I or Hawraa had shown any symptoms. I said I didn't think so, there was nothing. 'As a precaution,' he said, 'bring your daughter tomorrow and we'll check her, just to be sure.'

I was shocked. I felt like someone had hit me over the head with a cosh. I went home and told my sister Zahra that she should go back to her uncle's house because Hawraa and I might have coronavirus too. 'Even if you do have the coronavirus, how on earth could I leave you alone when Karima's in hospital?' she said.

'Sis,' I said, 'I can look after Hawraa, so please go back to uncle's house and look after yourself.'

That evening I spoke to Karima by phone and I didn't know what to say. We ended the call in tears. The next day I went to the hospital and we were tested and the results come out. Hawraa and I both had the virus but we had no symptoms. 'It's normal,' the doctor said. 'Lots of people don't show symptoms and hopefully you'll soon get over the disease, you and your daughter. But you'll have to quarantine yourselves at home. If you feel you've taken a turn for the worse, you must come to hospital.'

Nothing at all happened to me or Hawraa. We didn't feel any symptoms. I just had a slight cough. Three days later Karima became very ill and they put her on a ventilator. I called the doctor and spoke to him. 'Karima had a problem with her lungs in the first place,' he said, 'a disease related to shortness of breath.' I told him about Karima's sighing, and he said, 'It's not just sighing. She had shortness of breath and she should have been examined a long time ago.'

'I might have infected her with the virus,' I said. I told him how I'd been going around the backstreets and the markets sterilising.

'Anything's possible,' the doctor said.

I stayed at home with Hawraa. Zahra called me every day and Uncle Tahir called me too, as well as friends and other relatives. Karima could no longer speak on the phone. I felt guilty and frightened and everything around me looked bleak. How stupid I was, how thoughtless and cowardly. I felt like a criminal who had stabbed Karima in the back. She was apprehensive and fearful, while I was horrible and inadequate. I kept crying and praying to my Lord to save Karima from her ordeal.

On the tenth day of quarantine, while Hawraa and I were at home, they called us at night. Karima had died. They said I shouldn't come out of quarantine and they were going to arrange for Karima to be buried with three old women who had also died of Covid. Of course, I rejected their plan and couldn't stop shouting at them. They warned me not to leave the house and the doctor tried to explain to me the importance of burying someone who has died from the virus as soon as possible. I went crazy and started talking to everyone I knew by phone, relentlessly. I wanted someone to say, 'Muhsin, this is fate and you're not to blame!' Uncle Tahir called me and said, 'You and your daughter are in quarantine now, but does that mean we have to let strangers bury our daughter? Karima's brothers and I are going to bury her. You stay with your daughter and look after her.'

Karima was dead, and the world was dead all around me. I felt like I wanted to disappear, not just from the city but from all of Iraq. When Hawraa and I recovered from the virus, we held a little funeral at home, just for close friends. Uncle Tahir spoke to me and said, 'If you go on like this and you don't eat, you'll die and your daughter will be an orphan.' I hated him for saying the word 'orphan' even more than I hated him and Ahbab Allah already. He had never been interested in us: it was my mother's brother who had taken care of bringing up me and Zahra. Uncle Tahir had been too busy kissing the hands of the sayyids. I wanted to strangle him and be done with him. But I kept quiet and patient. He said, 'Do you need anything before I go?

'I want to get out of Iraq!' I said.

'Okay, that's easy,' he said.

'How?'

'The Iraqi ambassador in Sweden is from Ahbab Allah. I'll arrange for you to get a job there in the embassy in Stockholm. You can take it easy for a year and then come back,' he said.

Of course, I would be crazy to go back! Anyway, Ahbab Allah arranged for me to work as cultural attaché in the Swedish embassy. I went there by plane, saddened by Karima's death. But I told myself that at least my daughter would be safe and I would ensure her future and she could breathe some clean air and not go through the nightmares I had lived through in Iraq. I worked out a complete plan in my head. I stayed with them in the embassy. They rented a flat for me and I received a really good salary. I spent my time sitting in the embassy in front of a computer screen, pretending to be working on long-term cultural projects. But I was really doing research and collecting documents that revealed all of Ahbab Allah's secrets. I got in touch with acquaintances and friends and dug up dirt on the Ahbab Allah leaders one by one.

I was planning to seek asylum, but I had to come up with a plan. I had to have a strong case so that my request would be accepted, because I had come to Sweden as an official, at the embassy, not under any other pretence. When I had gathered lots of information and documents about Ahbab Allah from the days of sectarianism, I went and made my asylum request. I told them everything – about the role of Ahbab Allah in the sectarian war, the killings and the abductions, areas where weapons were stored in Baghdad, Ahbab Allah's ties with the other militias, its corruption, and all the ministers, directors and grifters who played a role in monitoring the protest movement and attacking the demonstrators. Throughout my questioning in the immigration department I felt they wanted to check the information I was giving them. Of course, by this point I had left the flat the embassy had rented for me and moved into a small flat in Malmo. No one knew where it was. Then I waited for the results of my asylum application.

Six months later they accepted my application and a new phase in my life began. There was a wooded area close to my flat and I would take Hawraa there for walks. I chose a nice, strange tree, a little apart from the other trees, and decided that the tree would be Karima's spirit, a symbolic grave, a secret candle of love that Hawraa and I would come and visit.

I had plenty of time and I began to daydream more than necessary about all the things that had happened in my life. I became seriously depressed and started neglecting myself and Hawraa. I was worried I couldn't look after Hawraa, so I decided to go to a psychiatrist. It wasn't as easy as I expected to find a psychiatrist in Sweden. Eventually, I spoke to my nurse, and she helped me book an appointment with one. The psychiatrist then gave me a prescription for some antidepressants and started giving me advice on how to overcome my depression. He asked me if I had any hobbies. 'I don't have any hobbies,' I said, 'but I often daydream and sometimes I feel that I want to write.'

'That's the best form of psychotherapy,' he said. 'Write down everything. Empty out everything that's inside you. Make writing your closest friend. Write without worrying or hesitating or feeling guilty.'

Bulbul the Writer

Hawraa grew older and started going to kindergarten. I was very pleased and I wished Karima could have seen her and how she had blossomed, as she walked to kindergarten with me, taking her first step with into her future.

My life seem to calm down a little. I really enjoyed life in Sweden. There were two things that were most important to me – the clean air and the freedom. There were people of all kinds and all colours and everyone did what they wanted without anyone else interfering in their lives. If someone wants to go to a nightclub, there's a nightclub. If someone wants to pray, there's a church and a mosque. If someone wants to have a drink, there's a bar. If someone wants to eat halal food, Sweden is full of halal restaurants. Eat, drink, speak, pray, dance, sleep, sit down and think as you like. You're free and this is a sacred right. It's not easy for someone to come and deprive you of that right or deny it. The law is above everyone, as they say. When I thought about Swedes, most of whom have nothing to do with religion and never speak about it, I wondered what form God took in Sweden, for example? Then it dawned on me that the law was god in Sweden. Most Europeans and Swedes worship the law. Our Allah is law too, but the difference is that Allah's laws were written down in the seventh century and they haven't changed since then and no one can go near them or change them, because His laws are sacred. But Sweden's god, by which I mean the law, is man-made and they can change it and develop it after getting together and thinking about how to update it. But one thing has not changed: their respect and love for, and their commitment to, the law, the thing they hold most sacred.

The days passed, simply and without storms or surprises. I met a really lovely, pretty Swedish girl called Emily, who worked in a cafeteria. She really loved Hawraa, and my daughter also took to her, and as they gabbled away in Swedish I often failed to understand what they were saying. My Swedish was pathetic, but I started to improve my English, which I had learned in the days of Bulbul al-Sayyid. Emily started coming to stay the night at our place and sometimes we went to visit her in her flat. Our friendship quickly developed and one day she told me she'd like to be like a mother to Hawraa. I was really delighted and I told her I had never seen such tenderness, honesty and compassion. Emily started to take an interest in and ask after Hawraa, and look after her father too, of course. One day I suggested we go on a trip to Agadir in Morocco. We stayed there a week and they were the most beautiful seven days of my entire life.

The Moroccan food was amazingly good. I loved the fish, of which they have many kinds, and the sun and the sea, and Hawraa adored the sea. I enjoyed Emily's love and her gorgeous body. We played and laughed and had fun and took loads of pictures.

When we came back to Sweden, Emily returned to work and Hawraa went back to kindergarten, while I stayed at home. That was the hardest thing about my life in Sweden: how to get work. It was the one consistent theme of my life, the difficulty of settling down to a job. I mean, how do you find work that you liked and you can also live on? Also Sweden is a 'professional country', as they say, and I don't have any qualifications – no trade, no university degree, no experience. What's my experience in life, for example? An expert in Ahbab Allah bullshit?

One day, I had a particularly good daydream and decided to fulfil a wish I'd had inside me for a while – to write my daydreams down, especially as my psychiatrist had encouraged me to write. But first, before writing, I had to read and understand writing and literature. I started downloading dozens of books from the internet. World literature, Arabic literature and Iraqi literature. Difficult philosophy books that I didn't understand properly. Sociology and psychology, very interesting books – there's always more to be read on any subject. But I found myself in short stories and novels. Poetry I didn't like at all. You could say that, for me, reading was like a ship that took me to a different island every time. I became a traveller like Sindbad. I felt full of wonder and joy, sad and enthusiastic, as I moved from story to story and world to world. I also started to understand the discourse current in Arab literary circles and learn about the role of publishers, corruption, piracy and censorship. I saw interviews with, and documentaries about, writers from everywhere in the world and I gained a modest knowledge of literary matters. After a few months, I felt like a new person. I felt I had shed an old, obsolete skin and grown a new, young one. But when I felt I was ready to write, the same old problem arose. The question that bugged me was, of course: why don't we write novels and short stories in our local, modern tongues?

In Sweden, I closed down my Twitter account and opened a Facebook one. Recently, I've started making friends on Facebook with writers and people interested in literature, art and ideas. Facebook was the best way to understand what educated people think on the subject of writing a novel in colloquial Iraqi. I wrote a post: 'What do you think about the idea of writing a novel in Iraqi *ammiya*?' Lots of people made comments: some people said it wouldn't work because Iraqi Arabic is coarse and not sufficiently expressive. 'So Iraqi *ammiya*,' I responded, 'which people have used for hundreds of years when they're in love and courting, in all forms of communication, isn't expressive?' It's such a strange position to take. Okay, so how do we communicate and express ourselves and love and hate in this Iraqi *ammiya*, which is the only one we have? Apparently some writers had tried before, for example in *The Palm Tree* and *The Neighbours* by Gha'ib Toama Firman and Fouad al-Takrali, two writers who included some Iraqi *ammiya*. Some people produced long lists of Iraqi novelists, new and old, who had tried it. I replied to them, saying, 'Yes, I know. But they didn't write their novels wholly in *ammiya*, only the dialogue parts. Many Arab writers write the dialogue in their own colloquial forms of Arabic. Egyptians have even written whole novels in Egyptian *ammiya*, but in Iraq there isn't a single writer who's written a whole novel that's in Iraqi ammiya from cover to cover. I mean not just the dialogue but also the narrative.'

Of course, I heard the old familiar tune: 'The other Arabs won't understand'. And there were people who got completely carried away and said all kinds of things, while others didn't know what we were talking about in the first place and just wanted to have their say. The only thing that mattered, they assumed, was taking part and sticking their oar in.

The last comment, which led to one of my daydreams,

was this: 'Colloquial Iraqi won't be able to reflect the real world.' I wrote a reply to that one: 'So it's *fusha* that can reflect the real world? Is that so? To me, any sentence in *fusha* sounds like one of those melodramatic actors in those historical TV serials. When you read a line of *fusha* you hear a very particular kind of voice and tone, one that jars severely with our daily lives. Imagine someone opening a story in *fusha* like this: 'The vehicular explosive contraption fulminated while I was partaking of my matitudinal repast.' Does a sentence like that reflect the real world better and more truthfully than if I were to say, 'As I was having breakfast, the car bomb blew up'? Colloquial language is sensual, warm and honest. You feel it coming from your heart. It is significantly, amazingly succinct.

Anyway, I started writing and I found out roughly where the most difficult problem lies in writing in *ammiya*. If you want to write a novel in colloquial Iraqi, there aren't any books you can refer to for useful guidance on orthography – how to spell words that are not often written. In colloquial poetry it's much easier. There are major poets who have written whole collections of poetry in Iraqi *ammiya*, and you can learn from their experiments. But with novels, apart from the direct speech, there are very few books in Iraqi dialect that you can use as reference points to learn from. So the thought occurred to me that perhaps Iraqi writers should try writing fiction in *ammiya*, exclusively, for a set period, before being allowed to return to *fusha*. Let them try, for example, to write for ten years. Then we would have hundreds of novels and collections of short stories, and then let's see what the experiment has produced. In other words, why is there all this fear, this trepidation? Of course, the people who most objected to writing fiction in *ammiya* were the writers themselves. They dismiss the idea with ominous talk, and you get the feeling what they are really saying is, 'You want to shake the *fusha* throne we sit on!'

I don't know. It's an old topic and the debate on it never

ends. The thing that really worried me and kept me up at night was the Ahbab Allah movement. But I assured myself that they wouldn't sink so low as to harm my poor sister Zahra. And anyway, I was sure no Iraqi or Arab publisher would publish my book. Instead I decided to publish it on the internet. I tried to set up my own website, despite having no experience in such things. But designing a website requires a little money, it seems, not to mention the technical work I didn't understand. So I forgot about the website and just kept writing and writing until I finished the book and called it simply *Bulbul*. Of course, I changed the names of the characters and the names of some of the organisations. In the end, the book, like any book in the world, even an autobiography, was a work of imagination. Isn't that what the critics say?

I spoke to my friend Emily about the project. She's more than a friend now, she's my partner and we're thinking of moving in together. I just adore the smell of her body – she really takes an interest in her cleanliness – and I adore even more her eyes, which radiate goodness and real love: a kind of serene, angelic look. Anyway, Emily was delighted when she heard about the book. She said it might one day be translated into Swedish. 'I don't think so,' I said. 'It's a first try and maybe only Iraqis will understand it. It's a simple book.' Then I told her about the struggle between *ammiya* and *fusha* among the Arabs, who have spent their whole lives in conflicts and schisms, from the time God created them till now. Then I told her about the idea of a website. Emily said there was an Iraqi kid she knew before I came to Sweden who had experience in web design. She called him straight away and made an appointment for him to meet me. The guy's name was Fadil Ali.

I met Fadil a week later and we had a chat. I learned he was from the Rafha group, former Iraqi refugees who were held in a camp in Saudi Arabia from 1991 and then resettled in other countries.[6] He and his family arrived at a camp in Rafha when he was just six months only, and a few years later Sweden took them in as refugees. He didn't know anything about the 1991 uprising back in Iraq and he didn't remember the camp. He said he just heard heroic stories from his family. I was a little wary of him because many Iraqis in Europe are living as refugees, but a few are actually not. Most leave because of hardship, sectarianism, the militias and the general misery of life in Iraq. But a few are here, still receiving money and salaries from Iraq and are just taking advantage of the freedoms here. And when you bring up anything about religion with them, or about the Mobilisation Forces, or the members of the Badr Organisation or followers of Ayatollah Muhammad Baqir al-Hakim,[7] they turn against you like ogres. Anyway, Fadil Ali seemed to be a good guy, and he drank beer. I was fairly confident that he wasn't very Islamist. But of course you can't guess what people are really like. You find someone drinking beer and smoking hashish here in Sweden and living with a girlfriend without being married to her, but then the first time you discuss sensitive topics with them they turn out to be as sectarian as your average mullah.

Anyway, Fadil promised to set up a website for me and we continued to meet from time to time. He was always apologising for being late because he was so busy. And I didn't object because, in the end, he was doing the work for free and out of generosity. I began to trust him and I told him about my novel, about Ahbab Allah, my Uncle Tahir being a leader in the organisation and lots of other details of my life. He also told me about his life in Sweden.

In one of Sweden's political parties there was a well-known Iraqi called Hussein Aboul Heel, who was also from the Rafha group. He often lied to the Swedes on TV and blamed all of Iraq's problems on Islamic State and Saudi Arabia, never mentioning Iran or the militias. One day, by chance, I was sitting in the park reading a book when a Swedish TV crew turned up saying they wanted to ask Iraqi refugees what they thought of Hussein Aboul Heel. I said I knew the man and I did a TV interview with them. I talked a little about how opposition politicians in Iraq began as victims of Saddam Hussein and later became major sources of corruption and sectarianism. 'People like this politician Aboul Heel, for example,' I said, 'he gets a salary here in Sweden and from Iraq, a salary for life as compensation, and lots of secondary material privileges, while in Iraq there are people living in tents as displaced people.' I talked about how Aboul Heel was biased and didn't mention the role of Iran in controlling Iraq and supporting the criminal militias.

A few days later, the TV channel aired the interview in what turned out to be a full-length documentary, not just random vox pops, featuring refugees speaking about Iran and its support for the sectarian militias. It mentioned the Rafha salaries in relation to Aboul Heel and aired some old dirt on him before he joined the party and went into politics: on Facebook, he had posted racist comments of all kinds, against Somalis, Kurds, Saudis and Jews. Maybe this Hussein Aboul Heel had got it into his head that Sweden was like Iraq? You can be racist on state television in Iraq, and it's no problem!

A few days later I met Fadil Ali and, with rather noticeable sarcasm, he said, 'So you're famous now, giving TV interviews and making statements?'

'You weren't upset, were you, Fadil,' I asked, 'when I spoke about the Rafha group and their politician?'

'No, to hell with Aboul Heel,' he said. 'I hate his hypocrisy too and even Iraqi refugees hate him. They say he's never helped them.' Fadil began to explain how his family had a hard time in Rafha and how Saddam had persecuted them in the years before that.

'Fadil, my dear,' I said. 'We all ate shit in Saddam's time. Is there anyone who didn't suffer? All the oil money should be given to the Iraqis as compensation, if we want to be fair, especially those who stayed in Iraq and continued to suffer hardship.' Fadil didn't look upset at the time and he tried to finish the work he was doing with me, designing the website.

I didn't know whether this Fadil was a dirty rat like the

other brainless Iraqi rats in Europe, not all of them, of course. Some of them are good guys, but many of them are two-faced and sneaky. Of course, when Fadil was working on the website for me, he would keep asking for information – how many email accounts did I have, my exact date of birth, and lots of other questions. I felt it was totally normal, and he said that, in order to buy a domain name for my website, he needed this kind of basic information. Once it was up I would be able to manage the website myself. I put my trust in Fadil, and to be honest, when I came to Sweden and found out how people live here, I forgot about lying and cheating because Sweden is a society based on trust and honesty and it's hard to find anyone who wants to trick you or lie to you. It's like, if our Allah came across the Swedes, he'd let them into heaven straight away, without any questions.

But one morning I sat down and found my Facebook account had been hacked. A hacker had accessed my page and written a post there: 'Bulbul's page has been hacked and we will soon publish his most personal material.' Of course, I was frantic. I didn't know what to do in such cases. A while later I received an email from the hacker. 'So, bastard, you're talking about the Iraqi mujahideen, are you? Wait till I expose you!' Of course, I was shocked. I wrote to the hacker, asking him what he wanted. He said, 'I'm going to embarrass you by publishing all your photos and your pathetic stories.' Of course, I didn't have personal things or pathetic stories on my computer. All I had was some light-hearted messages to and from my friends and it didn't matter much if people saw them. They were just normal – all Iraqis curse and make jokes. 'What photos?' I asked him in a message. The hacker was silent for a while, then he wrote, 'They're pictures of the sea, you and that pretty naked woman.' I thought about it and checked the pictures of Emily and me. I understood what he meant. In Morocco, we were sitting by the sea and I took pictures of us in swimming costumes. One day, I sent Emily the photos through Messenger and wrote, 'I miss you!' Emily called and I told her about the hacker. She drove home straight away and was very upset. It occurred to me that the hackers might publish the photos. 'Calm down, Muhsin,' she said. 'I have a friend who's a hacker and now he'll help us and restore your account. Why are you so anxious? Do you have any dark secrets?'

'No, I don't,' I said, 'but I'm upset because I put you in an embarrassing situation.'

Emily laughed and said, 'How so? Embarrassing because of a photo of me on the beach? If you want, let's take a picture of us two naked and put it on Facebook. The only problem is that Facebook doesn't allow pictures like that.'

If the hacker posted the picture of her she'd be delighted and give it a like, she said.

I wrote a message to the hacker to say I would soon report him to the police and they would find him if he was in Sweden. In the end, Emily's hacker friend helped me restore my page. I reported it to the police, closed down the old page and opened a new page. The hacker disappeared and never wrote to me again.

I kept thinking about the hacking incident and eventually I started to have suspicions about Fadil Ali. I went to his page to check his pictures and his friends. Finally I found his old pictures, including lots of pictures of him with Hussein Aboul Heel the politician. I started reading the comments he had made and then I understood. They were part of a Facebook group and had friends and acquaintances in common. After the incident, I got in touch with Fadil and tried to get him to say something. But he just dismissed the threat from hackers. 'If you'd called me, I would have solved the problem in one minute,' he said. Of course, he let slip other details that made me even more suspicious of him. But I didn't have any real evidence and maybe it was someone else who had hacked my account. Iraqis everywhere are in a chaotic, stressful and unknowable situation. I gave up on Fadil, along with Aboul Heel, the Islamists, the Baathists and all those schizoid Iraqis. I said to Fadil, 'I'm going to break off relations with the Iraqis in Sweden and, thank you, I don't need help with the website.' I'm sure he felt I was a little suspicious of him.

I was really upset, not with the hacker but about the ordeals Iraqis have to go through, generally, because of their situation. The viciousness, the corruption, the battles between clans and sects, and the attempts to silence people reach us even here, in Europe. We are carrying around our diseases, our complexes and our hatreds, and taking them on our travels everywhere in the world. It's sad that a country such as Iraq, with its great history, should end up offering such people to our world. Backward, corrupt nonentities, all viciousness and selfishness.

I set up a free website and uploaded this book, called simply *Bulbul*. I didn't provide any space for comments because I knew that only chaos would ensue. Many people downloaded the book and I received plenty of threats by email. I told the police of course, but after the hacking incident my concern wasn't the book, which didn't mean so much to me at that stage. It was just a beginning, joking with the thieves who robbed us in the name of religion. I did more thinking about the wider, bitter truth. In the name of religion the thieves didn't just rob us. In the name of God, hundreds of years ago, our society started to go backwards and became riddled with superstitions and ignorance. In the name of religion, our society grew weak, became an adolescent society. One idea would take it in one direction, another idea in the opposite direction. It was a society that wasn't mature because it wasn't free. Only someone wearing a turban or holding the microphone for the Friday sermon had the right to think, not Iraqis generally. I collected books about the history of Iraq and religion, from when they slaughtered Hussein at Karbala to the massacres by Islamic State and the militias. The Abbasids and the Ottomans, the British and American occupation, Hulagu Khan's sacking of Baghdad, the revolutions, the Baathists, the Shi'a and the Sunnis and the Arab nationalists. I dug up the history of Iraq, and started to take notes and make cuttings and, little by little the idea for a new book started to take shape in my mind. But this time, the book's going to be in three parts. This time my subject isn't one particular group or militia or sect, or my life. My aim, this time, is a book that will be like a history of ignorance and backwardness.

It was the first time Hawraa had slept the night away from home. I was a little anxious. She went to stay the night with her friend Annika. Emily came to my place and brought a bottle of red wine with her. When she saw I was anxious about Hawraa, she said, 'You have to be calm and open-minded. We're in Sweden. One day she'll get to the stage when she's a teenager and goes to parties, and so you have to prepare yourself for when Hawraa doesn't answer her phone and you don't know where she is.'

I had made some mezzes and a fruit salad, which Emily loves. We took the plates and the wine and went to the balcony. Before my account was hacked, I had started drinking a little. Only red wine and I didn't like to get very drunk, I mean just a little tipsy. It was summer and the weather was stunning. The balcony of my flat looked out on lots of trees and plants and flowers. The smell of the plants and the effects of the wine made us dizzy. Emily stood up and leant over the edge of the balcony. She was wearing a light green skirt. She turned to me and smiled. Of course, she knew I was shy. She turned again and this time she put her hand on her arse, then she laughed at my extreme shyness and turned away towards the trees. I knelt down behind her, stuck my head inside her skirt, bit the end of her panties with my teeth and pulled them down. Then I stood up, kissed her back, lifted up her skirt and casually entered her. Emily still smelled strongly of plants, as I pressed in and out at my pleasure, calmly and slowly. I wanted the moment to last forever and never end. But pleasures are momentary. All the great pleasures in this world soon disappear, like dreams. We came and Emily turned around, kissed me and went to the bathroom. I went after her and we had a shower together. After that, Emily went and stretched out naked on the bed and relaxed, listening to a Swedish song. I put my pants on, took the laptop and went back to the balcony. For some reason an old Iraqi song popped into my head. Then Karima's spectral image came to mind. There was a tear in my eye but it didn't fall. The song played with my head:

> *Throw aside the cloak of sadness,*
> *Till when will you be sad?*
> *Isn't it unfair that life*
> *Should end in a silence?*

Then my tear fell.

I drank another glass of wine and had a strong sense of love for life. I opened a blank webpage and typed out the title of my new book: *To Hell with God, the bastard.*

Notes

1. Gathering places where Shi'ite muslims meet for social and community purposes.

2. The Popular Mobilisation Forces were set up in 2014 in response to the emergence of the Islamic State organisation in northern Iraq. It incorporated various large Shi'ite militia groups, along with smaller militias from minority groups such as Christians, Turkomans and Yezidis. Although nominally under government control, the Shi'ite groups continued to receive some finance, weaponry, training and ideological guidance from Iran.

3. After the US invasion of Iraq in 2003, the country become the main theatre on which international and regional powers played out their rivalries, especially the United States, Iran and Saudi Arabia. Directly and indirectly, these governments channelled money to political parties and militia groups to promote their interests. Through its historic ties with Iraq's Shi'ite majority and because its stake in the outcome was especially significant, Iran probably gained most in this competition.

4. The Joker, as portrayed in the 2019 Joaquin Phoenix film, entered Iraqi political discourse when a graphic designer released images of the character taking part in these protests. Supporters of the protests welcomed the Joker's participation, but opponents soon took advantage of the images to portray the protesters as frivolous and inspired by malign foreign forces.

5, Many Iraqi Shi'ites came back from exile in Iran after the overthrow of Saddam, won elections and took powerful positions in government. Their links with the Iranian government continued.

6. These were some of the thousands of Iraqi Shi'ites who fled to Saudi Arabia as refugees after the collapse of an uprising against Saddam Hussein in southern Iraq in 1991. The rebels had hoped to take advantage of the Iraqi army's humiliating expulsion from Kuwait by US and allied forces, but Saddam's forces soon suppressed the rebellion.

7. The Badr Brigades or Badr Organisation was an armed force founded in Iran in the 1980s by Iraqi Shi'ites in exile. It fought on Iran's side in the Iran-Iraq war of 1980-8 and returned to Iraq after the fall of Saddam. The influential Iraqi Shi'ite cleric Ayatollah Muhammad Baqir al-Hakim was one of the founders.

Translator's Note to Bulbul

ALONE AMONG THE WORLD'S most prominent languages, the Arabic language as it appears in written form, such as in newspapers, textbooks, academic papers and official documents, as well as in almost all literature, is not the first language of any living person. Some Arabs, if they are very well-educated and work in a field that requires skill with words, can speak unprepared in a way that approximates what linguists call Modern Standard Arabic or *fusha*, but it is often a struggle and they will soon blend in elements from their national or regional vernacular language, their *ammiya*, the language they speak at home and with their friends. Not surprisingly, this extraordinary fact has serious implications for writers who want to address their audience in a way that touches their lives as directly as possible and that gives authenticity priority over literary norms.

There have been earlier attempts to write prose in vernacular forms of Arabic, especially in Egypt, but the academic, political and religious elites in the Arabic-speaking world have opposed and belittled such experiments, on the grounds that only standard Arabic, *fusha*, is a worthy medium for serious literature and discourse. Most of their arguments stem from religious conservatism (standard Arabic is the language of the Qur'an and other core texts of Islam) or from Arab nationalism (standard Arabic supposedly unites Arabs and enables them to communicate across the barrier of vernaculars).

Hassan Blasim, who began his career as a film-maker and whose work was first published in the early 2000s, is one of the few contemporary writers in Arabic who has dared to make the leap into the dark and write a lengthy narrative, *Bulbul*, in what he considers to be his native language. As the main translator of Blasim's work into English for the past fifteen years, I have long been aware of his frustration with the literary elite in the Arabic world, who often pay more attention to whether a work complies with the norms of standard Arabic than to the content of the work and the interest of the story it tells. Coincidentally the first major work I translated for publication, *Taxi* by Egyptian writer Khaled al-Khamissi, was written in Egyptian *ammiya*. Khamissi's work, a collection of encounters with talkative Cairo taxi drivers, was similarly dismissed by the critics as unworthy of serious consideration, simply because of the language he used. For the same reason and because of the politically sensitive nature of the subject matter, Hassan Blasim could not find a conventional publisher for his novella, so he ended up publishing it only online

So *Bulbul* is an innovative work in its Iraqi Arabic form and possibly a landmark in the literary history of his country. However, because of the sociolinguistic differences between Arabic and English, its pioneering qualities are perhaps difficult to detect in the English text. The original text is written in the ordinary daily language of educated Baghdadis, and a translation into English can offer only the equivalent in the target language. It would not have made sense to translate the text into some exotic regional variety of English.

In his fictional memoir, Bulbul the narrator talks about the difficulties he faced developing a narrative style without having any models to follow in Iraqi Arabic. Naturally this reflects Hassan's own dilemma at the time of writing. Under the surface, however, the ground is shifting. The sudden development of social media, blogging and online self-publishing is giving aspiring writers in Iraqi and other varieties of Arabic ample space to offer their experimental work to the world. I wish them all success.

The story that Bulbul tells in this novella is a distinctly Iraqi one. The sayyid whom Bulbul serves is a politician, religious leader and militia commander, all in one – an unusual feature that emerged in Iraq's Shi'ite Muslim community in the political and security chaos that followed the US invasion of 2003. It is a tale of patronage, corruption and sectarianism. Bulbul, having served the fictional Ahbab Allah movement in diverse roles and having observed its leader at close quarters, can look back with some objectivity from his refuge in Sweden and describe what he has lived through.

Jonathan Wright January 2025

About the Author

HASSAN BLASIM IS AN Iraqi-born film director and writer. He settled in Finland in 2004 after years of travelling through Europe as a refugee. His debut collection *The Madman of Freedom Square* was published by Comma in 2009 and was longlisted for the Independent Foreign Fiction Prize in 2010. His second collection, *The Iraqi Christ*, won the 2014 Independent Foreign Fiction Prize, the first Arabic title and the first short story collection ever to win the award. His third book, *God 99: a novel* was published by Comma in 2020. (All English editions of his work to date have been translated by Jonathan Wright). His writing has won the Tampere City Literature Prize 2014, the WSOY Literary Foundation Prize 2015, and the Finland Prize 2015. The US edition of his short stories, *The Corpse Exhibition* was picked as one of *Publishers' Weekly's* Books of the Year 2015. Hassan's fiction has been translated into over 25 languages. He is also a playwright and author of *The Digital Hats Game* (Telakka Theatre, Tampere, 2016). His documentary films include *Blank Mud* (1997), *Wounded Camera* (2000), *Sleepless* (2006) and *Credible* (2007). A stage adaptation of his short story 'The Nightmare of Carlos Fuentes' was brought to the Arcola Theatre, London, in 2014, by director Nick Kent and playwright Rashid Razaq, and starring Nabil Elouahabi.